SEIZURES

SEIZURES

MARK ASHLEY

Matador
5 Weir Road
Kibworth Beauchamp
Leicester LE8 0LQ, UK
Tel: (+44) 116 279 2299
Fax: (+44) 116 279 2277
Email: books@troubador.co.uk
Web: www.troubador.co.uk/matador

ISBN 9781 848766 457

British Library Cataloguing in Publication Data.
A catalogue record for this book is available from the British Library.

Typeset in 11pt Palatino by Troubador Publishing Ltd, Leicester, UK
Printed and bound in the UK by TJ International, Padstow, Cornwall

Matador is an imprint of Troubador Publishing Ltd

*For my mother, Pat, whose eternal optimism
and encouragement motivated this story's
completion through troubled times.*

Chapter One

The tarnished needle seemed to slip in easier now. The small fissured wound, hidden snugly between the toes of his left foot, had grown accustomed to its ingress. The softer tissue beneath offered no resistance to the sharp point as it passed deep into the flesh to seek its regular target. Oblivion arrived, expected yet unannounced. With barely enough time to remove the syringe, he sank back onto the discarded pile of clothing, his last recollection being the acrid odour of the urine soaked duvet he otherwise knew as *bed*.

***

As she arched backwards, the warmth of her soft inner thighs pressed gently into his groin. Only his firm grip on her petite pelvis prevented her from falling away completely. She leaned forward, her long black hair copiously unfurling about his face. Kissing his forehead, she guided her slender fingers between them and unclasped the buckle of his belt. A shudder of excited anticipation rose through his body, compelling his hands to move up from her hips and glide beneath the soft cashmere of her midriff-baring halter-neck. Her taut, enticing abdomen seduced his fingertips across the warm undulations of her body, ever upward to meet the acute change in contour that signalled the pleasing fullness of her breasts. Parting his hands, he spread his fingers wide and raked the inquisitive digits across her swollen nipples. A gentle gasp escaped her pincushion lips and she stared intently into his eyes in a way that could mean only one thing. She wanted more. Her hand, now fully within his splayed trousers, wrapped firmly around his … *beep, beep, beep.*

1

David awoke to another day. "Shite," he cursed to himself at the interruption to yet another fantasy dream. The alarm clock at his bedside, although so familiar, had never come to be regarded as a friend. He rolled toward it in a heady stupor and collapsed his left hand down upon its off switch. He knew another eight hours of dull data filing and answering pointless enquiries lay ahead of him. *'Still,'* he thought, *'it paid the bills.'* He stared at the ceiling for a moment. Same crack in the plaster. Same cobweb in the corner. An uncomfortable moment's silence reminded him of his solitude. Was this the life he had foreseen for himself?

He swung his legs out from beneath the duvet and stumbled with his aching feet for his slippers. The floor was cold to the touch and he looked down at his feet to hasten their locating the errant footwear. His body took him through the same clockwork routine of washing and shaving and, whilst still half asleep, he found himself munching the same tasteless cereal and reading the same tedious tabloid. A bared chest, reminiscent of his dream, momentarily peaked his interest but, then again, he had been on his own now for several months since Lucy had found out about his *hobby* and had decided he was not the man for her.

His mind wandered back to the decisions made, mistakes even, which had led to their relationship breaking down. She was all he'd ever wanted: gorgeous, funny and sexy as hell. There was no wonder she was still the core element in his nocturnal fantasies. He finished the milk-sodden cereal and briefly rinsed the dish before leaving it to spiral to a clattering stop on the steel draining board and returning to his bedroom to dress.

As he crossed the street to the bus stop, David noticed an elderly, silver-haired woman shuffling from the opposite direction toward the same destination. She was seventy, if a day, and waddled along as well as her hunched-over body would allow. She was wearing a dark woollen beret, a long tweed coat and thick black socks beneath her calf length skirt. Dragging a two-wheeled, tartan shopping trolley, she was the epitome of *old* and David chuckled to himself at the stereotype.

She traversed the final kerb to the bus stop, her trolley's wheels defiantly locking themselves into the gutter. Unaware of their stubbornness, the old lady almost span in her velour slip-ons as her arm was snapped back by the trolley's change of speed. He may have been bored with his stagnated life but David had not sunken so deeply into despair that he had forgotten *all* the manners his mother had taught him. He reached down to the tiny woman's side and lifted the trolley onto the pavement.

"Thank you dear," she said in reply to the kind gesture.

David found his mouth curling upwards at the corners in recognition of the gratitude but couldn't help thinking that if she had trouble handling the empty trolley *now* she had no hope *after* her impending shopping trip. The old lady lifted her free hand toward David's and steadied herself as she slowly manoeuvred her frail frame into a position to regain some control over the wayward kart. The shiny, almost transparent skin of her arthritically tortured fingers painfully wrapped itself around the flesh of David's young hand and he could feel how cold her decrepit circulation had left the liver-spotted limb.

Suddenly, David felt a bolt of pain down his left side. A shattering torpedo of agony struck hard into his hip and he found himself sharply sucking the cold morning air through his teeth as his body twisted around to allow his left hand to grip the offending area in some vain attempt to subdue the sudden angst. However, as soon as he had reached his side the pain had gone.

"Are you alright dear?" she said, confused by the sudden change in David's features.

"I'm fine," he replied, in as much confusion as the old lady.

David clenched his buttocks repeatedly in an effort to recount the reason for the pain. Worryingly, there was no repetition of the agony that would indicate the favoured diagnosis of a simple muscle spasm.

As he considered less favourable alternatives, the bus arrived and David soon put the moment out of his mind. He fumbled for the loose change he had left in his jacket the night before, after his visit to the off-licence. Once again he found himself lifting the trolley, now onto the bus's loading deck which had failed to pneumatically lower itself quite far enough for the pensioner to manage. He helpfully supported her elbow as she grabbed the bus's entrance rail and painfully rocked her body up onto the platform.

A quiet exhalation of air exhibited her discomfort in the action. She smiled as she half turned her stiff neck back toward him in response to the assistance and then began the tortuous task of locating her bus pass from the large handbag that hung around her neck and across her tweed coat. Suddenly, David felt an awkward disdain for the old lady. He wished he had gotten onto the bus first so that he wouldn't have had to wait behind the dawdling old dear. He could have been sat down by now but, as suddenly as it had occurred, he dismissed the thought and wondered from where the sudden nastiness had arisen. He considered himself pretty laid back, a casual type of guy that held no-one at any particular level of regard.

He recalled the hip-jolt and thought, 'That was it; I just wanted to be off my feet.' But the pain was gone now, so he forgot the moment and allowed himself a wry smile at the pointlessness of his own philosophical argument. Off she shuffled, away to her seat, occasionally looking back at the trolley and mumbling to herself as she drew it behind her as if chastising some badly behaved pet.

"Town Centre please," David offered to the driver as he released the various coins into the payment dish. With barely a glance of recognition, the driver made the relevant selection on his ticket dispenser and the required voucher spat out in David's direction. He gripped it, tearing it away from its perforated retention in the device, and casually discarded it into the pocket of his jacket to join the others left there from the previous week's journeys.

The bus rumbled away from the kerb and, as the journey began, David withdrew his bored mind into the pointless daily task of aimless people-watching: the same bus, the same routine. The same vegetable shop owner stocking the plastic-grass coated trestle-tables outside his store, the same blonde cashier waiting to be let into the bank.

The journey wound its way around the town as surely as the hands of a clock around its face until, eventually, David arrived at the terminus and, yawning widely, rose to get off the bus and continue his day's repetitious work.

***

Finally fully awake, he wandered out into the street. Hands in pockets, he shrugged his head down into his upturned collar and made his way toward the Job Centre. That foot was beginning to bother him. He'd have to start *using* somewhere else or an infection would begin to set into the open scar tissue. Worse still the dreaded gangrene might take a hold and he would lose the adjacent toes altogether. Then again, he could stand to lose a toe or two. After all, that's why he began to inject there in the first place. After Mike had lost a leg to septicaemia and had fallen, brown dazed, into a hot running bath, he would have boiled himself to death if his girlfriend, Clare, hadn't found him.

He dismissed these negative thoughts and convinced himself that the quality of *his* gear meant that *his* veins wouldn't get as clogged as Mike's with the crap the dealers used to bulk up their wares. He even chuckled to himself with the name Mike had been awarded by their friends as a result of his near miss - *The Lobster*.

Thoughts of his next score entered his mind. In fact they were never far away at all. They simply resurfaced, like the rise and fall of the sun - only faster. And there she was, today's easy target; an old lady. God, how obvious could she have been. She should have had 'victim' painted on that old tartan trolley of hers. Still, the way she was hunched over it, it was obvious to him that she wouldn't put up much of a struggle.

He wandered after her, breaking into slow-time to maintain an inconspicuous distance until she left the busier area of the High Street. He steadied his adrenalin filled legs and closed in as the old lady approached an alleyway which he knew led through to Selby Street and the industrial estates beyond. Then he was upon her. He sprinted alongside her frail frame and grasped at the large bag that hung over her shoulder.

Tugging the bag from her side, he felt the slight but sudden weight of the old lady as the handle strained against his efforts. *'Shit,'* he thought. *'It's round her bloody neck.'* She lurched forward as their respective inertias momentarily fought and then succumbed to inevitable momentum in his favour. The trolley, now between them, snagged on a protruding paving slab and wrenched itself from her pathetic grip. It twisted away and fell, rattling to the ground ahead of the toppling old woman. He continued to pull at the bag and the old lady span out of the strap as she fell over the upturned trolley. The worn leather suddenly gave and he was free.

Barely even noticing the glancing collision of his head with the wall, he regained the sprint which had been temporarily faltered by the bag's loyalty and ducked into the alley. The old lady, spiralling out of control, landed heavily across the felled trolley. Her left hip struck the ground, a shattering torpedo of agony striking deep into the joint which in turn exploded into the surrounding flesh. A sharp intake of breath, sucked through her withered lips, was all she could manage before she passed into unconsciousness.

He ran on, ignorant of his victim's plight, along Selby Street and into the underpass leading to The Link Industrial Estate. He'd often hidden here before and knew that, if he could reach the abandoned factory without attracting the attention of any of the regular police patrols, he'd be home free. He almost considered it home. After all, he'd spent many a night here in a heroin induced stupor. He slowed to a fast walk. A guy running with a handbag was bound to attract attention; what was he thinking? This way was safer. Yes. This way he could hide the bag under his jacket without dropping it. And just in time too.

Exiting the underpass, he entered the first estate roadway, Link One. He immediately noticed a patrol car approaching him from the very place he was headed. His lungs burned with the pace of his escape and he desperately tried to calm his breathing as the car passed by. He glanced over in the most nonchalant way he could manage. The driver was looking into the estate and the passenger was deep in concentration over some papers he was holding above his lap. He had been around plenty of filth in his time and now he knew exactly what they meant when they'd said the paperwork stopped them from catching the bad guys. There he was, seconds from mugging some old mawd and these guys were passing him by like any other Joe Public. Perhaps his bad luck with the snagged bag was changing?

He entered the disused factory and climbed the whitewashed concrete stairwell to the first floor. He noticed a new footprint in the industrially thick grime of the dank, draughty corridor. He'd seen this tread before but it wasn't his. *'A copper's boot.'* The patrol had actually been here and he'd managed to miss a direct confrontation with the duo by minutes. *'Lucky bastard,'* he smugly thought to himself. *'Still, better not push it.'* He ducked into the first side office and quickly rifled through the bag for the old lady's purse. Plucking it from a side pocket, he dropped the larger bag to the floor and turned his avaricious attentions to the contents.

'Jackpot,' he silently exulted. He tugged the two hundred and thirty pounds from the cloth folds and tossed the purse to the floor to rejoin the discarded bag. His mind raced. *'This'll keep me in gear for days. And I won't have to dip into the pathetic hand out I get from the Job Centre.'* He rolled the notes into a tight bundle and shoved them down the front of his underpants. If he was going to get stopped by two coppers that's the last place they were likely to grope in any street search. He descended the stairwell and carefully checked outside for the patrol car before walking, now calmly, from the building.

The Job Centre was back near to the bus station but he had to be there for nine o'clock. He picked up the pace a little and headed for another underpass leading to the town centre, one that wouldn't bring him out into what was by now, no doubt, a crowd of do-gooders clammering around his latest benefactor. The idea of the money in his pants began to fill his mind, pushing aside the thought of a tedious morning at the Job Centre offices. *'Sod it,'* he thought to himself.

A quick phone call later and he found himself stepping into the rear passenger seat of an understated blue hatchback. A short drive and a discreet shuffling of hands were all that stood between him and his next score. The rendezvous was as brief as he expected. He had been careful to only buy a couple of brown. He knew that being seen to be flash was dangerous in the company he generally kept, especially as he intended to be in no fit state to deter any crotch grabbing associates within a matter of minutes.

The transaction was completed without incident or superfluous conversation and he was all set. All he needed now was a place to *stick* himself in relative safety. The factory, he felt, was too hot to flop for a couple of hours so he opted for his second hideaway, the bus station. He knew of a quiet dark hole he could crawl into to sleep off the effects of his impending two-bag right under the raised concourse of the dark and dingy terminal. Perfect - provided it wasn't already in-use.

Chapter Two

"Mr Lewis. Can you hear me Mr Lewis?"

David drifted back to a dark semi-consciousness and could hear the gentle voice as if it were somewhere far away.

"David, can you hear me? Doctor Reynolds he seems to be coming round."

David opened his eyes to a painfully bright light. He went to raise his arm to shade his face but found himself unable to move at the expected speed. His arms felt heavy as if he'd been drugged and, as he went to speak, a dull groan passed his lips instead of the intended dialogue.

"Mr Lewis. I'm Doctor Reynolds. You're in Hopefield General Hospital. Can you hear me?"

David nodded a small but heavy nod and rolled his head to one side toward the doctor's voice. Still unable to speak, he numbly accepted that listening would have to do for now.

"Mr Lewis, David isn't it? You were brought in from the bus station. Do you remember?"

David slowly shook his head from side to side. What the hell was he doing here?

"David, you were brought in after a bus driver found you collapsed by the station concourse. We've been doing some preliminary tests. Your blood sugar levels appear normal. Have you ever had an episode of collapsing before? You seem a little under nourished. Have you been eating okay?"

Again, David shook his head but something caused him to doubt his own response. A vague recollection crossed his mind of a draughty office and a damp mattress.

"Well, it's early days but it may be the case that you've suffered some sort of seizure. We'll have to run some more tests but they can wait until you're feeling a little livelier.

Nurse, would you please arrange for a full blood works and an MRI and let me have the results as soon as they arrive? Thank you."

David rolled his head to his right and saw a fresh-faced nurse reaching over him to adjust his sheets.

"Don't worry David. I'll look after you. I'm nurse Mills. We'll get to the bottom of this before you know it." With that, she scuttled away to the nursing station to comply with the doctor's instructions.

David's eyes became heavy again and he submitted to the tunnelling darkness of unconsciousness.

***

"Christ, I hate this place. It reminds me of my time on section with all the bloody sudden deaths and blubbering relatives."

Detective Sergeant Steve Backhouse pushed back the doors to the surgical recovery ward and approached the nursing station. His subordinate, Detective Constable Jem Barnes, nodded in dutiful recognition of his boss's quip and recalled his own earlier uniformed service before his recent posting to the pro-active robbery squad.

"Hello," said Backhouse, casually flipping his warrant card wallet open in the general direction of the first nurse to have caught his glance.

"I'm Detective Sergeant Backhouse. This is DC Barnes. We're here to see Mrs Nugent, the victim of Tuesday's mugging. We're told she's awake after surgery on her hip and would like to have a word if that's possible."

The nurse glanced down at her computer terminal and tapped a few buttons on the keyboard.

"I'll have to clear it with her consultant, Mr Chivers, but she's awake so it shouldn't be a problem. Take a seat. I'll page him if you are happy to wait."

"Thanks," Backhouse replied, scanning round for a seat to occupy.

"So what do you reckon Sarge? One of the regulars?"

"No doubt, but we'll see what the old dear has to say. We don't even fully know what the little shit took yet. One of the witnesses said she saw a lad running off with the old dear's bag so I imagine it'll be drug related as usual. You never know; if the wrinkley's a bit sporty we might finally get the headline BAGHEAD GETS 'HEAD' BAG. Get it?" Backhouse chortled.

"Hmm," Barnes responded to the latest in Backhouse's seemingly unending attempts at humour with a suitably sarcastic grunt. Jollying the job along was one thing but this particular *wrinkly*, as the distinctly old-school DS described her, had been seriously injured and the rising trend of street robberies in the new-town of Hopefield was rapidly reaching epidemic proportions. DC Barnes was fairly young in service, where political incorrectness went hand-in-hand with disciplinary action. Backhouse, on the other hand, was within months of retirement and, basically, didn't seem to care anymore. Well, at least not to Barnes anyway.

"Sergeant," the nurse called over. "Mr Chivers is just completing his rounds in the next ward. He'll be here in a couple of minutes."

"Thanks," Backhouse replied before turning his attention to the printout of the robbery incident he'd brought along. He scanned through it for the informant's first description of the offender.

"So what do you reckon to that nurse, eh? Good rack," Backhouse commented.

Barnes was already all too familiar with his new supervisor's lack of tact but still found himself looking across to the nursing station to corroborate the older detective's observations. She was indeed well endowed but Barnes was not about to qualify Backhouse's trite remark with any form of confirmatory response. The nurse caught him glancing and smiled sweetly in return. Barnes was not unattractive but sadly this fuelled the Sergeant's vicarious lustfulness.

"Hey-hey," he taunted, digging a suggestive elbow into the young man's ribs. "She wants a piece of you."

Barnes was certainly not averse to the idea of offering a

piece but dismissed his superior's lecherous suggestion by returning his attentions to the robbery paperwork in his lap. Backhouse gave up the taunt and the pair fell into silence.

The mismatched duo waited the predicted few minutes before the consultant entered the ward. The doors flung open like the entrance to some old western saloon and Doctor Chivers swept in like a hardened Marshall with his entourage of junior doctors swarming around him like a blood-thirsty posse.

"Ah, Sergeant …?

"Backhouse," the old detective completed the hung sentence while reaching out a hand in an intended greeting of mutual respect.

The doctor looked down at the outstretched offering and loftily said, "Excuse me if I don't. You know, germs and all."

"Of course," Backhouse replied, slowly lowering the hand and turning to Barnes to raise a contemptuous eyebrow. Without need of further explanation, Barnes immediately understood what sort of man Backhouse had instantly evaluated the good doctor to be.

"I believe you're here to interview Mrs Nugent. That's fine with me as long as you don't keep her too long. As for her hip, well it was totally shattered by the fall. To be expected really at her age. We've pinned it for now but I doubt she'll be walking again. Shame really. I believe she was quite the *potterer* before this mugging."

Barnes considered the doctor's aloof attitude and drew his own conclusion as to the doctor's character. The difference between nurse and consultant reminded him of the difference between solicitor and barrister. The former may have been too busy to appear helpful whereas the latter was too far up their own arse to care whether you thought them helpful or not. *'I wonder,'* he thought to himself, *'what would the diversity trainers at Headquarters think of that snap generalism?'* Despite his newly formed opinion of the man, he convincingly nodded in agreement with the surgeon's woeful prognosis of their victim's condition.

They left the consultant to continue talking down to his

subordinate doctors and entered the side ward that housed Mrs Nugent. The raised bed sheets failed to conceal the shape of the surgical frame that now encompassed the old lady's left leg and thigh. Barnes shuddered at the thought of the various steel pins and brackets that must have been entering the tissue-like flesh of the pensioner's hip in some vain attempt to secure the shattered bones which lay, barely healing, beneath.

Mr. Chivers had, sadly, been right. At her age Mrs Nugent's prospects appeared dire indeed. Barnes felt his resolve in capturing her attacker well up inside him and he stepped ahead of his superior to greet the pensioner in a manner he felt would be far more amiable than he expected she would receive from the senior officer.

"Hello. Mrs Nugent?" he said in a softened voice. "I'm DC Barnes and this is Sergeant Backhouse." The sergeant nodded as the old lady glanced past Barnes in his direction. He was happy with Barnes taking the lead. It wouldn't have been long before he'd have directed it anyway; paperwork was looming.

"Hello, dear," the pensioner replied, vainly attempting to raise herself up from her reclined position in the bed. Barnes respected her staunch attempt at good manners but easily saw that the move was unwise in her present condition.

"No, no," he interrupted the movement. "Don't disturb yourself on our account. We're here to talk about the robbery, the man who took your bag on Tuesday. That's if you're feeling up to it?"

"Of course dear. I was in the Air Force you know. It'll take more than that young ruffian to shoot me down." She smiled and Barnes returned the expression. However, he couldn't help glancing at the mass of framework supporting the bed sheets and considering the stark reality of her situation.

"Now, what do you need to know?"

Barnes began the usual interview technique of recollection and confirmation and Mrs Nugent smiled through the gentle barrage of questions, describing her attacker and the contents of her bag.

After an hour or so, the detectives, her first account in

hand, left Mrs Nugent to her sleep and returned to the police station to consider the information they had gleaned from the defiant pensioner.

***

"Good morning David. How are you feeling today?"

Nurse Mills drew back the dividing curtain from around David's bed.

"Much better, thanks," he replied. "Sorry about yesterday. I was a bit out of it. Did I hear the doctor say I had a seizure? Is that a fit, like epilepsy or something?" he enquired.

Mills busied herself with changing David's water from a trolley of jugs she had wheeled into the ward. She had seen his notes. She knew full well that a *fit* was exactly what David had suffered, a Grand Mal in fact, a full blown epileptic seizure. She knew the ramifications of this news for David Lewis, his career, his driving licence, his employability.

"I can't really say," she feigned. "Doctor Reynolds will be doing his rounds in an hour or so. You can ask him anything you need to know then."

David was perturbed by the well intended dodge of the facts but chose not to embarrass the young nurse by pressing the matter. Instead he acknowledged the smiling glance of the approaching news-trolley lady and beckoned her over to make a purchase. Out of habit he chose his usual tabloid rag and began to peruse the pages.

"Here you go sweetheart," the middle-aged news seller announced. "Here's a local freebie that I had left over from yesterday. I saw you weren't up to it then so I saved it for you."

"What day is it?" he asked, whilst simultaneously checking for the date on the paper he already had on his lap.

"It's Friday dear," she answered. "You've been here since your fit on Tuesday. But I'm afraid you've missed the last three days altogether". David was a little shocked. Not only because he'd been unconscious for three days but by the fact that the hospital's news lady seemed far more forthcoming about his condition than the nurse. He concluded that she was less tied by medical etiquette and, from this, that the information the nurse was reluctant to divulge was far worse than he had imagined.

"Thanks", he said. He took the larger local paper and unfolded the sheets to show the front page. The main headline read "MUGGER STRIKES AGAIN". He read the sub-text to discover that an old lady had been knocked down, robbed, and seriously injured in the area of the High Street that Tuesday morning. It described how her handbag had been taken by a young white male but didn't elaborate on the bag's contents or the male's description.

David read the lengthy article, intrigued by the nature of the crime, and suddenly the figure of two hundred and thirty pounds leapt into his mind. The article went on to name the officers in the case and appealed for witnesses to come forward.

David allowed the paper to fold down onto his lap and stared out of the opposite window. The bright, sunshine lit aperture was fairly high up on the wall and, with only sky beyond, was devoid of external detail. David concluded he was on an upper floor of the building and within this blank canvass David's mind wandered. He began to see images of an old lady falling over a two-wheeled shopping trolley, an underpass, a factory and an abandoned, dank office. As he allowed the thought to evolve, the images became more coherent until suddenly, and unwittingly, he cried out "Jesus. It was me." As the other patients and staff turned in stunned silence toward his outcry, he caught himself and considered the revelation in silence. *'The old lady from the bus, Christ, what have I done?'*

Could it be true? Could he be the mugger who had been haunting the town for months? He wrestled with the reality of what he was recounting. He remembered who he was, where he lived. He remembered Lucy, his time at the Job Centre. But he couldn't recall mugging old ladies. It couldn't be him, but what about the images? They were so vivid yet, somehow, disjointed like a dream. It was like he was there but, inexplicably, not there. He felt confused, scared... guilty.

15

"Mr Lewis?" Doctor Reynold's voice shattered the brightly framed daydream and suddenly David was back in the room.

"Good morning. Nurse Mills tells me your head's full of questions."

'He didn't know the half of it,' David thought to himself. "Yes," he glibly replied.

"There's a great deal to discuss, and I'm afraid it's not very good news."

The young doctor reached around as he spoke and pulled up a standard bleak hospital chair to sit down.

'Not good indeed,' David thought as he saw the fact that the doctor was sitting as an indication of how long he intended to take out of his busy day to explain the bad news to him.

"Well David," he began, "the good news is that the cut on your forehead only needed a couple of stitches. I'll whip those out for you in a week or so. I imagine you hit your head on the bus station concourse when you collapsed. The bad news, I'm afraid, is as we suspected. It would appear that you have suffered an epileptic seizure, what we call a Grand Mal, the most serious type. I'm also concerned about the length of time it left you unconscious. The fact is you were borderline comatose."

The doctor paused for the expected reaction but David's face remained blank. His earlier suspicions at the severity of his condition had simply been confirmed. It had not come as the shocking news the young doctor had thought it might. The pause became increasingly pregnant until David broke the silence in a beckoning tone.

"And ... ?" he invited.

The young doctor sprang back into conversation like an old vinyl record which, stuck in a scratch, had been jolted back to life by a knowing thump.

"Well, I notice that you've no history of epilepsy in your medical file, which itself appears pretty incomplete. Have you moved into the area recently? Anyway, no matter," he interrupted himself, dismissing the irrelevant question. "Besides the obvious medical ones, there are a number of fairly serious implications for your future lifestyle."

He went on to describe the medication and methods of reducing the likelihood of a repetition of the seizure which had left David unconscious for three days. He discussed the legal ramifications with regards to driving and employment disclosure and handed David a small forest of informative leaflets casually retrieved from the pocket of his crisp, white ward coat, as if they hadn't *really* been placed there just minutes before his arrival. This young man was obviously uneasy with passing on bad news to patients and David found his mind glossing over the plethora of long medical terminology that spewed from the inexperienced doctor's lips.

David waited for another pause in the seemingly endless list of possible treatments and their respective side effects. He then stabbed into the conversation and asked "Can this epilepsy thing affect your memory?"

He wanted to hear that it could not, that his recollection of the disjointed but incriminating images were just an imaginative extension of his intrigue over the local news story.

"Well," Doctor Reynolds replied thoughtfully, "to varying degrees, yes. With the length of time you were left unconscious by the seizure such a problem shouldn't be ruled out. Are you having problems with your memory?"

"No," David guiltily retorted. "No, no problems." He was reluctant to discuss the images. Why associate himself to a crime he wasn't even sure he had committed? The young doctor looked perplexed. Why ask the question if it wasn't an issue for the patient?

David recognised the confused expression and offered "No, I'm just thinking about the long term effects. You know, whether it will affect me in the future."

The doctor's expression changed to a more supportive one.

"Well, let's deal with the current situation. As I said, we can't rule out such problems, but let's not look too much on the dark side of things. We'll have to see how your condition presents itself in the coming weeks and we'll be in a better position to give a more informed prognosis. Epilepsy is a condition of the brain and, as you no doubt know, it's a very complicated organ. It's difficult to foresee all the possibilities so I feel it would be best to treat the condition *as is* and take it from there. I'd like to keep you in for the weekend until we're happy there are no significant changes under the new medication, okay?"

"Whatever you say doctor." David's tone was agreeable but hid the greater concern that epilepsy was the least of his problems... for the moment.

Chapter Three

"Okay everyone. Settle down now. It might be Friday but we're still a long way off *'Crackerjack'*."

DS Backhouse brought the office to order and the twelve pro-active robbery officers finished rattling their coffee spoons and found their seats in the cramped room of the new, hurriedly formed squad.

"Now you're all aware why we've been brought together and that's to identify, find and take out the low-life that has set up house somewhere around The Link Industrial Estate. To date, we've got six muggings in the area around High Street and Selby Street on the south side of the Midland Road by-pass and three more on the north side of the Link Estate around Viscount Road and Trojan Way. The few that we have anything resembling a description for have been committed by a single, young, white male in dark, casual clothing but, as you know, up until yesterday this arsehole has been targeting old dears which, as you might guess, have been totally useless at describing their attackers. Now, we've had two handbags and a purse recovered in varying locations centring on the Selby Street Park and the subway that connects Selby Street to Link One on the industrial estate. They've all been checked by CSI* and, you guessed it, so far we've got squat in forensics."

A muffled groan went around the assembled officers and interrupted Backhouse's briefing.

"Okay, fair enough. We know the new CSI officers aren't performing as we might have hoped but if the forensics aren't there, they aren't there. It's believed the offender may have been wearing gloves and, because of the vague accounts from all the wrinkleys, we haven't even got definite crime scenes for CSI to check."

"Are we so sure they've all been committed by the same guy?" DC Murray chipped in. The young female officer was relentlessly open-minded when it came to criminal possibilities and it was her ability to think laterally which had won her a place on this elite squad of hand-picked detectives.

Backhouse, although a diversity-nightmare for the divisional command team, had been deemed 'the man to get the job done quickly' and, with the rising pressure from Headquarters to get this series of robberies solved within the month, the divisional Superintendent, Chris Shaw, had given Backhouse's boss, Detective Inspector Pete Priest, cart blanche to draw on any staff available in the Force to form a squad. And he had done just that.

Backhouse had six detectives from the Major Crime Unit, four 'hard hitters' (as he liked to consider them) from the Crime Car Unit, a computer specialist from Headquarters and, of course, Barnes, who had just qualified as the nationally highest scored detective from the recent round of SIU* recruitment. Backhouse wasn't keen on new blood under his supervision. As far as he was concerned Barnes was an unknown quantity.

After his test of Barnes' integrity at the hospital the previous day, Backhouse had concluded that Barnes was a definite black and white type of guy. No laughs, no gaffs. Whether the Superintendent had insisted on Barnes' inclusion in the squad as a gauge of his abilities or not, Backhouse didn't trust him and knew he'd be one to watch. As for the rest, Backhouse had trained half of them himself and had worked, in one capacity or another, with the rest. Only Atticker, the computer guy, was another new face. However, the old bobby, only a little shorter in service than the Sergeant himself, would be securely tied to the desk so Backhouse felt he gave him less cause for concern.

"You're quite right Lizzy," Backhouse continued. "That's why you're here, to keep an open mind and stop me from getting tunnel vision if we hit a particular line of enquiry. That said, time is fairly tight and the descriptions we do have seem to point at the same offender. The rest of us will concentrate on one lead at a time while you, Lizzy, and you, Atticker, research any other information that comes in so that, should one line of enquiry peter out, we'll have something already developed to quickly move onto. Okay?"

"Sarge," "Yes, Sarge," came the replies. Murray and Atticker passed each other an acknowledging nod. It was obvious the mismatched duo would be spending some time together over a hot computer terminal.

"You said *until yesterday* Sarge. What's happened to change things?" asked DC Warren Holliwell. A short wiry character, Holliwell had come from the Major Crime Unit. Renowned for his interview skills, he had a spooky knack of recalling the tiniest detail of a conversation and interjecting with poignant questions at just the right moment to trip an unwary 'bull-shitter' right on their arse.

"Quite right Wazzer." Holliwell was one of Backhouse's protégé's and, despite the fact that his longstanding nickname gave outsiders cause to believe he may have been a bit of a pratt, he was held in high regard by Backhouse and just about everyone else who knew him.

"On Tuesday our shit hit on an old dear called Mrs Margaret Nugent." He turned his torso as he said the name and casually pointed up at the picture of a smiling pensioner on the intelligence board behind him. The board contained the pictures of eight other elderly ladies, some with facial injuries and others with wide-eyed, rabbit-in-the-headlights expressions.

"Now, what Timmy-toe-rag didn't realise on Tuesday was that he was targeting ex-Squadron Leader Nugent of her Majesty's Royal Air Force Covert Intelligence Unit, a Cold War specialist from the late fifties, apparently. And believe me, she might be seventy six but this old dear is still as sharp as a tack. Caroline from the e-fit* office is with her now and she is more than confident she could pick our shit from a line up of identical septuplets if necessary. It's our first real break so we're going to run with it. We've got a witness putting the Nugent crime scene at an alleyway cutting off High Street and CSI are there now. We've had marked patrols doing building sweeps of the industrial estate for the last week and they've turned up a number of locations that appear to be flops for the local bag-heads. I don't want to burn the Squadron Leader as a witness so we're avoiding mug-books. What I plan to do is set up covert obs on the industrial estate at the locations found by section. Atticker, get a RIPA up and running straight away for the surveillance and get the Compliance Unit to stick a rocket up the Super's arse to get it authorised today. Your Op name is Cassandra"

"Roger that Sarge," Atticker replied, understanding the Sergeant's need for urgency. Without further ado he swung around to face his computer terminal and began clicking away with the attached mouse in order to initiate the convoluted surveillance application.

"Okay. The rest of you, I want you to scan the industrial estate and surrounding housing developments for potential O.P's* on each of the seven buildings identified as flops by section. Get back to me on my mobile for any R-v-Johnsons*. Lizzy, Sergeant Blacon on D Block has the full list. They're on earlies today so pop down to the TPT* office now and get it off him before he goes out, would you?"

Murray bolted up from her chair and made for the door.

"I know you've probably figured it out already but, before you go Lizzy, the basic plan is to get the e-fit from Mrs Nugent and obs the seven locations until we fall across our man. Once he's in the bin, we'll get him Viper'd* and get the Squadron Leader to pick him out. Easy, eh?"

A chuckle rose amongst the assembled officers and Backhouse allowed himself a smile too. There was no definitive evidence to point to an itinerant drug-user and they all knew that the decision to carry out observations on this group of individuals was all 'hunch' on the part of their new DS. They also all knew how difficult covert surveillance was, especially at night. All in all, with seven sites to watch between twelve officers, it was going to be a long month. However, not one of them doubted the Sergeant's resolve and his reputation for pulling a hard lead out of a crock-of-shit-situation far preceded him.

"In our favour we've got a switched-on witness and the

fact I've managed to snaffle four NPU* bobbies for each night, to bring our street cover to seven pairs, helps as well. That leaves you, Atticker, on comms and you, Lizzy, on days to continue researching any new leads. I want to start tomorrow night so fill your boots this evening everyone because we're going to start with a seven stretch. We'll review it next Friday but I'm hoping we'll have the little turd in the bin by then. Okay everyone, snap to it."

The squad began to stir, searching for radios, kit harnesses and car keys.

Murray nodded her understanding and left to see Sergeant Blacon but as she left the room she shook her head and muttered "shit" under her breath. She had hoped for a spot on the surveillance teams. She knew it would be long tedious hours but she also knew that when the acquisition took place the following hunt and strike would be the adrenalin thrill she longed for. She had been on the Major Crime Unit for two years now having applied for the job as an obvious stepping stone to the Regional Crime Squad and, beyond that, the Serious Organised Crime Agency. However, she found the Major Crime Unit, dealing with local murders and rapes, was a real bore. She looked on those often protracted enquiries as paper and data shuffles. She'd been overjoyed to have been picked for this temporary squad as she knew DS Backhouse had a reputation for action. She consoled herself with the thought that each member of such a small team had an important role to play and, for now, she'd play the researcher until she could work her way into a surveillance pairing, or even the arrest team. Settling for her lot, she continued to the TPT Sergeant's office to retrieve the flop list.

Backhouse left the briefing and wandered the short walk down the first floor corridor to the DI's office.

"How's it going Steve?" asked the Inspector. "All settled in? What have we got so far? Anything positive, any leads?"

"It's a big dog, boss. We've got jack-shit, bar a potential witness that thinks she's Biggles and a bucket full of nothing in the forensics cupboard."

"That good, eh? Prospects?" the Inspector queried hopefully.

"Cinch, boss. I'll have him in the bin by Friday."

The Inspector allowed himself an assured chuckle at the Sergeant's semi-sarcastic remark.

"Nice one, Steve. I knew you were the right man for the job."

With that Backhouse turned to leave and glibly called back, "And I know that you're the right man when it comes to signing up overtime forms. Get your pen ready, boss."

He wandered back to his intelligence board and perused the links between the crimes. He stood motionless, deep in thought. The phone rang, barely breaking his concentration, and he nonchalantly reached round to answer the call.

The remainder of that Friday passed quietly enough for Backhouse. As expected the news on O.P.'s wasn't good. He knew it would have been a tall order to get decent observation positions on an industrial estate at the weekend. Most of the companies had no weekend security cover so few were happy to leave their alarm systems off just so some hairy-arsed bobby could wander in after dark, help himself to all the tea and biscuits from their canteen and stare aimlessly out of the top floor window from the Director's leather recliner.

Fewer still, curiously enough, wanted to leave keys and alarms codes with the police. He recalled how *helpful* he'd found Hopefield's Captains of Industry in his earlier service and smiled to himself as he recounted the dressing down he'd once gotten from the divisional Superintendent. As a young police sergeant, he'd been asked to actually leave a crime prevention meeting with local retailers, mid-way through, after severely criticising them for complaining to the police but not trumping up the finances to help tackle the commercial burglary problem at the time. It was this outspoken nature, he had always thought, which had prevented his further promotion beyond Sergeant. When it came down to it though, did he care?

"Bollocks", he defiantly announced out loud.

"Sorry Sarge?"

Backhouse span round from the Intel board as Barnes returned to the office.

24

"Hey? Oh, nothing," Backhouse said, realising his daydreams had overflowed into the real world.

"Where's Thomo?"

"He's down at the TSU* getting some night-sights for tomorrow."

"Nice one, good idea."

"It looks like we're going to have to use vehicle O.P.'s. There are no fixed sights for six of the seven locations that uniform scouted," Barnes explained.

"And the seventh?" Backhouse asked.

"Well, there's a disused factory just off Link One. It's about two hundred yards from the Midland Road underpass. You know, the one off Selby Street."

"Yeah, what of it?"

"Well, the by-pass has traffic-management cameras every half mile and I noticed one about three hundred yards east of the underpass. I've been downstairs to the control room and the picture's pretty good. It's got pan & zoom but no night vision because, as you know, the by-pass is always lit. Anyway, the first hundred yards or so into the estate is pretty visible as a result. It may be worth considering for a heads up call," Barnes explained.

"Nice work. Sort it so that the operator has a spare handheld on our back-to-back channel and make sure he gets a copy of Caroline's e-fit from the Squadron Leader. I want you to brief him yourself in case he's a tosser and cocks up the whole thing with a duff call that blows our cover."

"Or her…?"

"What?"

"It might be female operator, you said brief *him*."

"For Christ's sake, you'd better make it a bloody good briefing then, with pictures."

Barnes despairingly shook his head, on the inside. Did Backhouse really just say that or was his sarcastic supervisor deliberately being a sexist bigot, just to deride his comment?

"Will do, Sarge," he replied before leaving the room, to let the dinosaur have more roaming space.

'*Cock,*' Backhouse thought.

Chapter Four

The weekend passed without incident. No robberies. No sightings. Mrs Nugent's e-fit of her attacker was detailed enough, right down to the cut she said he would probably have from accidentally head-butting the wall as he pulled her over. However, as with most surveillance operations based on an area rather than a specific target, it was more of a fishing-trip than a fox-hunt.

Backhouse suspected the rumour around the station that an operation targeting druggies had been set up had caught the interest of the young keen-to-impress section officers who had then begun a concerted operation of their own to stop and search every known drug user in the town. Despite Backhouse's objections, and the fact he had issued strict instructions for the uniformed officers to stay off The Link Estate, the e-fit had been on the daily bulletin since its compilation and he knew that *everyone* wanted to be the hero that caught the serial criminal.

It wasn't the first time surveillance had gone sour because of this particular problem. The circles of pond-scum, as he liked to refer to the criminal element, soon smelt a rat if the rate of turn-over searches went through the roof and they'd simply go to ground for a week or so until the police had moved on. It was early Monday morning. They had been monitoring seven sites. So far they had three itinerants, a milkman and twelve sightings of marked patrol cars to show for their twenty seven hours of observations. Backhouse was most definitely *not amused*. He depressed the push-to-talk button on his radio and addressed his team.

"Okay lads, stand down, stand down. I'll see you all back at the office for debriefing. I don't imagine it'll take long.

Atticker, how many pages tonight?" he asked, referring to the log Atticker had been keeping of the team's efforts.

"Not even one, Sarge," Atticker's voice replied over the back-to-back channel which he had reserved away from that of the busy main-section patrols.

"Okay, you get off then. See you tonight."

"Cheers, Sarge. See you later."

Backhouse waved a 'Home Jeeves' hand at the young NPU officer with whom he had double-crewed himself.

"Let's go," he added and the young, fresh-faced probationer started the car, no doubt wondering why the hell he had eagerly volunteered for this particular duty.

***

"Morning David. All dressed and ready I see."

"Yeah, I feel I've wasted enough of your time Doctor."

"No, not at all. Like I said, the brain is an unpredictable organ. Better safe than sorry. Make sure you maintain the regime of medication we've settled with and I'll see you in outpatients in a week."

"Will do, Doctor. Thanks again."

There had been no change in his condition since Friday and David was feeling a bit of a fraud. Worse still, he couldn't take his mind off the strange belief that he had committed the series of robberies he had read about in the local paper. He only recalled details of the latest attack but whilst laid up in a boring hospital bed he had managed to convince himself that, if he was responsible for that, he must have been the attacker all along.

With no-one to visit him at the hospital, David had very little to pack. No cards or soft toys like those that adorned the other beds within his side-ward. He slurped the last mouthful of cola from the can he had bought off the news lady before Doctor Reynolds had finished his rounds. Then he discarded the magazines and papers he had been reading over the previous two days. All he kept was the carefully folded article about the robberies, particularly the names of the officers involved. He was convinced that, if he was the mugger, his near death events of the last few days were some sort of sign that meant it was time to turn over a new leaf.

He had decided to hand himself in.

He waved a thankful goodbye to the nurses at the ward station and walked out into the corridor. He suddenly realised he had not been conscious on the way in and, having never been a patient or visitor here he had no clue of the way out. He looked up to the ceiling, scanning for overhead direction boards. He found the required 'MAIN ENTRANCE' sign and began the surprisingly long walk to the exit. He finally walked past the reception and security stations and between the exit doors, which obediently slid apart upon his approach.

A community ambulance was parked outside the entrance and its elderly driver was helping an even older patient in a wheelchair from the vehicle's rear hydraulic-lift ramp. A sudden wave of guilt washed over him and he purposefully turned away from the pair and headed off toward the main road. He had no clue where the nearest bus stop was but was not keen on returning to the hospital to ask for directions, not past that old lady.

He wandered up the road, instinctively toward the taller buildings of the town centre, until he suddenly got his bearings. He was now confronted with a choice. The bus home, or one to the town centre and the police station? A logical clarity took over the decision. *'They're going to be locking me up. I'd better go home first and get a shower and a change of clothes. Might be the last chance I get for a while.'* With that he headed for the nearest stop and caught the 106 out of town.

***

"Morning Lizzy," Backhouse greeted his subordinate, mid yawn.

"Morning Sarge. What's keeping you here? Have we locked up?"

"Fat chance. No, in fact it's just the opposite. I've stayed on to have a word with the Intell Unit DI. I'm sick of seeing uniformed bobbies crawling all over the patch when I've asked they stay clear of it."

"Quiet night, then?"

"And some! Can you contact the press office this morning to check if there have been any new leads. You know what it's like. By the time it goes through the system it's days old and this operation needs a swift kick in the arse, today, if you get my meaning."

"No problem Sarge. I'll get on to it as soon as they're in at nine."

"Cheers Lizzy. Leave me an e-mail if you get anything even close to solid, okay? I'm going to get straight off after I've been upstairs so I'll see you whenever. Take care."

"No problem. See you."

Backhouse pushed down on the office table and grunted his tired bones to a stand. He grabbed his tatty old jacket and left Murray to start her daily trawl of the intelligence systems.

***

David's mind was in a daze of guilty contemplation as he continued to mull over the disjointed memories of the robbery. It was definitely the old lady he had seen at the bus stop the previous Tuesday. He could almost see her face, but it was the recollection of the dark woollen beret, long tweed coat and tartan trolley that had stayed with him. The whole incident was anchored firmly in his memory by the outrageous pain he had felt after helping the old woman. What was that all about?

His thoughts raced for a logical explanation, desperately hoping that the answer would dissuade him from his intended course of action by proving that he was innocent of the crimes. He played and re-played the events but his self-torturing struggle was in vain. However he looked at it he always came to the same conclusion, that he *was* the mugger.

The bus slowed as another passenger pressed the stop-request button. The short bell-ring drew David's attention long enough for him to notice that this was also his stop. The bus was already swinging into the lay-by and he hurriedly rose and walked toward the front of the vehicle. The passenger alighting ahead of him was particularly over-jolly and engaged the driver in an enthusiastic farewell. David, desperate to be alone with his guilt, pushed past the woman catching his thigh on one of her many shopping bags. In a joyous refrain she actually apologised.

"Oh, sorry dear," she said.

He mumbled an embarrassing "sorry" himself, keeping his face away from the pair, and quickly hopped down from the bus. With barely a glance, he crossed the fortunately empty road behind the vehicle and it revved its engine to lumber away from the stop. He fumbled in his pocket for his keys and climbed the short flight of concrete stairs to the front door of the building. Letting himself in, he glanced over at the row of pigeon holes the resident landlady had installed to separate the various occupants' mail and, finding no post, quickly jumped up the stairwell taking on two steps at a time.

He opened the door to his singularly dull bedsit and fell backward against the panel as it closed behind him. He sighed but the usual silence of his solitude seemed less invasive than normal. His heartbeat, quickened by the effort of leaping up the stairs, pounded within his chest and the thoughts, too, had returned. They shouted at him now, like a crowd of angry hecklers and he swiftly stripped off his clothes before drowning out their cries in a powerfully hot shower.

The steaming water reddened his skin and as he ducked his head beneath the needle-like jets he felt the sting of the liquid as it pierced between the butterfly stitches to stab at the small gash on his forehead. He sucked in a retort of warm air, heated by the rushing hot water, and sharply repositioned his head to avoid further pain.

'Probably no less than I deserve,' he thought to himself but dismissed the self-pity as woefully underachieving when compared to the shattered hip of the old lady he had read about in the local newspaper. The comparison drove his resolve and he quickly washed before dressing. He grabbed a cold sausage-roll from the fridge before collecting up his jacket and exiting the small flat, letting the door slam shut behind him as he started down the stairs.

***

Exiting the bus station, he wandered the town centre streets for a while, breathing in great gulps of air to clear his head. It had been almost a week since he had been here but the familiarity lay heavy on his mind. The old lady that he'd robbed had given him the funds to keep his head down for days. He'd thought it safe enough to return to his place but with all the police activity he hadn't stayed there for long. He decided to re-trace his steps from the previous week, to see if there was still any attention being paid to the scene of the attack.

He walked along High Street and, on reaching the alley leading through to Selby Street, noticed the remains of some blue and white police cordon tape wrapped around the lamp post that lit the exit of the alley each night. They'd been here alright. He wondered what evidence, if any, they had recovered. Did they already have his identity? He glanced nonchalantly into the alley and, seeing no further police presence, walked down the muddy, hedge-lined cutting through to the street beyond.

As he continued along the pavement, he noticed a man and woman in suits exit the last house at the far end of the road. They were carrying clipboards and made their way to a plain blue hatchback car parked at the roadside. His suspicions, that they were police, were confirmed by the woman who, waiting by the passenger door for her partner to unlock the car, brought a hand held radio to her mouth before beginning some conversation, intelligible from this distance. Should he speak with them? Learn what they already knew? His decision was made for him by the vehicle starting and driving away before he was even close enough to attract their attention.

He carried on, Selby Park to his right and the Midland Road by-pass ahead of him. At the end of the road, the underpass left the town centre area, passing beneath the busy dual-carriageway and leading to the industrial estate beyond. He exited the foul smelling tunnel and, turning right, started along a pathway worn through the tall grass. It cut across an open area that lead toward a large multi-floor factory standing apart from the main row of saw-tooth topped buildings.

The route was all too familiar. There was no sign of police activity so his only decision now was how long he was going to stay here before heading back to the town centre.

***

"Good morning Sir, can I help you?"

"Err, yes. I'm here to see DS Backhouse or DC Barnes on the robbery squad."

"Take a seat, Sir. I'll give the office a call. Your name please?"

"Lewis, David Lewis."

David reversed himself to the row of fixed plastic chairs in the reception of the Hopefield Police Station and sat down. His mind was torn.

'Crap, what am I doing here?' he suddenly thought to himself. The adrenalin was welling up inside him. Watching the reception staff busy themselves behind the glass screen, he began to sense a metallic taste in his mouth. Then, perplexingly, they seemed to slow down.

'This is wrong,' he thought. *'I know this.'* A curious sense of déjà vu came across him and David began to feel light-headed. As the world about him slowed to a crawl, David's mind raced ahead. He felt nauseous. The entrance doors began to twist over to the left and David had a sudden urge to run through them before their distorting shape made it impossible.

"Mr Lewis?"

David's head snapped sharply to face the inner wall of the reception area. The room clicked back into shape and the world resumed its regular pace.

"Mm?" the confused David meekly offered the young woman addressing him.

"Mr Lewis. I'm DC Murray."

David could only offer a dazed, almost child-like expression.

"From the robbery squad." Murray thought she had a right nutter here.

"Oh, yes. I'm here to see…" Murray cut him short, instantly dismissive of the mild-mannered moron in front of her.

"…DS Backhouse, I know. I'm afraid he's on nights at the moment. Can I help?"

The 'auto-assist' line spat out of her mouth before she realised what she was saying. *'Shit'*, she thought, *'I'll be tied up with this pratt for hours now.'*

"Actually, yes," David said. "It's about the muggings."

Murray's interest teetered on the narrowest of arêtes.

"Yes?" she asked.

"It was me."

"Sorry?" The embarrassingly high-pitched reply almost choked Murray.

"I did it. I'm here to hand myself in."

Murray's mind ran the fastest gauntlet of pillock-v-protocol she had ever experienced.

"Err…okay. Come through." She stepped backward through the door she had been holding open and directed David down the corridor to the reception area's interview rooms. She had decided she was not going to be arresting this guy on the strength of *that* confession. In addition, she was definitely not going to even think of waking her sergeant who, she thought checking her watch, could only have been in bed for a maximum of two hours. No, she would let the guy pour his heart out and make a more informed decision then.

Murray opened the door to the interview room and reached in to turn on the light. The fluorescent tube flickered to life and Murray held the door back with one arm while guiding David through the opening with the other.

"Take a seat," she directed. As David passed close to the young DC, she encouraged him by briefly touching his left elbow with her guiding hand. David had removed his jacket and the skin-to-skin contact sent him into a buckling convulsion. He folded like a Chinese lantern and the air from his lungs expelled in a loud groan as if he'd been thumped heavily in the stomach.

"Jesus!" Murray jolted instinctively away from the collapsing man and she quickly checked the corridor for alarm pads and section staff to help her.

"Jamie," she frantically beckoned to an approaching TPT officer. He was already on his way to her and reached down to the foetal-curled David to control what he believed to be a violent suspect.

"I'm sorry... sorry," David wheezed. He struggled to a stand and continued into the room to take his seat.

"Are you okay?" Murray asked.

"I don't know," he genuinely replied.

"Wait there, I'll get you some water." Murray nodded to Jamie who obliged and stepped through to the adjacent office.

Murray stayed at the open door and waited for the uniformed officer to return with the plastic cup of water.

"Jamie, are you free for half an hour or so?"

The tall officer hesitated.

"Err..."

Murray understood exactly what he meant. Section officers were never 'free', certainly not for half an hour. Murray let the door close to within a few inches of the frame. Quietly she whispered to the officer.

"I think this guy's a sandwich short of a picnic but he wants to cough the robbery series and after that little performance I'd rather not be on my own, okay?"

She had won the young probationer over with the word 'robbery'. He was one of those keen-to-impress types which Backhouse had spoken to the Intell Unit DI about that very morning.

"I'll just let the control room know." He stepped away and keenly informed the deployment centre of his immediate unavailability.

"Cheers," Murray acknowledged his assistance and the pair let the interview room door close behind them. Murray drew back a chair opposite the pained face of the curious visitor and, as she sat, pushed the plastic cup of water across the table in his direction. The uniformed Jamie stood by the door, easily within arm's reach of the alarm pad on the adjoining wall.

"Thank you," David acknowledged, picking up the cup and taking a short sip.

"Okay, Mr Lewis. Tell me about these robberies."

Murray already doubted this guy's integrity and thought she'd give him free reign to bury himself in a web of lies before divulging any specifics herself.

A calmer David leaned forward placing his hands onto the table that separated them. He took on a more serious tone.

"I know you don't believe me, but I did it. The old lady on the High Street, her bag, I took it."

Murray was unimpressed and maintained a reaction free expression. These simple details were all public knowledge following the previous week's press release.

"Please, go on," she beckoned, barely able to conceal her sarcasm.

David recognised her tone for what it was worth. He lowered and shook his head in despair. Without recovering her gaze, he leaned his elbows onto the table and steepled his fingers toward his forehead. It had taken all his resolve to get him to the station and there he was, being considered a total liar. He thought for a moment.

"Two hundred and thirty pounds," he mumbled at the table.

Murray's attention was instantly peaked. This information had not been released. In fact, it had been intentionally retained along with details of the other incidents so that the interviewing officers could gauge the accuracy of interviewees and be able to disregard any uninvited confessionals, such as she had *initially* thought *this* was. She paused for a moment and then asked, "What was that?"

David raised his face to look directly at her and repeated, "Two hundred and thirty pounds; that's what you're looking for, isn't it?"

His hands were now at his chin and Murray, now fixated with the sudden seriousness of the man, carefully studied his body language for a clue of further sincerity. Concentrating on every feature she noticed his wrists begin to redden. Slowly at first, a single, red ring of deepening intensity began to rise on each wrist. Then, before her very eyes, they erupted into bracelets of bubbling sores.

At first, David didn't feel the metamorphosis but, as the first blisters swelled and burst, he parted his hands and watched in disbelief. Then the pain caught up with the visible transformation.

Across the corridor, the reception staff simultaneously fell silent and turned toward the noise as the scream rose and rose.

Chapter Five

"Jesus Sarge, you've got to get down here. You're not going got belie…"

"Whoa, whoa, Lizzy, slow down," Backhouse interrupted Murray's phone call while rubbing his face with his free hand.

"Has someone died or something?"

"No. Why?" Murray sincerely quizzed, unprepared for her sergeants fatigued sarcasm.

"Because with door salesmen and the bin-men I've had about twenty minutes sleep. So, unless this is very good within the next ten seconds be prepared for me to tear you a new arsehole!"

"No, Sarge, it's good. Well, more bizarre really."

"Five seconds."

"A guy handed himself for the robberies and..."

"Okay, stand easy. Who is it?"

"That's just it. He's no-one. No record, no intel, nothing. And get this; he's the Police Liaison Officer at the Benefit Office!"

"Really?"

"And that's not all. We've had to get an ambulance for him. He was just sitting there, right in front of me, and his wrists just … well… boiled."

"Boiled?"

"Yeah, just blistered up and burst into loads of sores. It was awful."

"I'll be right down."

Backhouse was too tired to take on any more revelations over the phone. He dragged himself out of bed and walked to the bathroom. He splashed his face and, leaning two-handed on the sink sides, looked up into the mirror and recounted out loud,

"Boiled?"

***

Backhouse swung his car into the police yard. He still didn't really know what to expect but, boils aside, this guy was offering himself as a quick result to a serious problem. Good or bad, Backhouse wanted answers but he was seasoned enough to recognise a Trojan gift horse when he saw it. With his reservations securely centred in his mind, he made the short walk to the reception doors of the station. He had seen the ambulance parked there on his approach to the building and wanted to enter via that route rather than through the normal staff entrance at the rear.

As he approached the doors, they slid open and he paused as the two paramedics exited the station and walked, patient-less, toward their vehicle. One had a medical kit-box in his left hand while the other had a folding stretcher-chair under her right arm. They were shaking their heads and chatting about what seemed to be a wasted journey. His curiosity was heightened but Backhouse wasn't about to add to their apparent contempt by asking any daft questions about 'boiling sores'. Instead, he strode up to the doors which halted their closure and jolted open again to greet him.

He entered the reception foyer to be met by Murray holding the internal mag-lock door to the staff corridor open with one hand. She had her empty hand held out, palm uppermost, her wide-eyed, brow-raised expression and shrugged shoulders telling Backhouse that the paramedics were leaving with the proverbial wild-goose. He lifted a single, questioning eyebrow at Murray and swept silently past her into the corridor. The door to the public area closed slowly behind them and as it clicked shut Backhouse began.

"Well?" he said solemnly. "Impress me."

"Sarge, it's just too bizarre. This guy walks in off the street claiming to be 'The Link Estate robber' but he's got a weird demeanour, all dazed as if he's out of it. I was there, thinking he's just another attention-seeking nutter. So, not wanting to wake you for a decision, I thought I'd verbal him up to see if his account held any water."

"And did it?"

"I didn't really get that far. First, he does a dying fly routine as if he's been punched in the guts and then, suddenly, he's fine. I *was* set to kick him out but he mentioned the two hundred and thirty pounds from Mrs Nugent's bag. Then he became all serious and then, get this, his wrists went red and blistered-up right in front of me."

Backhouse raised a doubtful eyebrow.

"Seriously Sarge, no messing. I wouldn't have believed it either if I hadn't seen it. Even PC Peterson was in the room, and I don't think it was a gag either. The bloke seemed as surprised as us. He screamed the place down."

"Well, where is he now? I saw the paramedics leaving alone."

"Well…" Murray seemed reluctant to try and explain what happened next. "He's still here. We got the first aid box and dressed his wrists. Then we called the ambulance and just tried to keep him calm. And here's where it got really freaky. He calmed down and I thought he was just being brave. The ambulance guys were here in minutes. They must have practically been on the doorstep. They came in and removed the dressing and it was gone."

"Gone?" Backhouse shifted his weight in a manner that clearly told Murray he was fast losing his patience.

"Yeah, just gone. I was watching them as well, so I know they didn't even apply any cream or anything. His wrists weren't even red. It was as if it had never happened."

Backhouse had heard enough. He had no idea what the weird stomach cramps and magic wrists were all about but he was more interested in the confession and, more specifically, the guy's knowledge of the contents of Mrs Nugent's bag.

"What's his name?"

"David Lewis."

"In here?" he asked, impatiently pointing at the interview room door.

Murray nodded and Backhouse pushed the door open, walking in past the young detective. She knew this simple manoeuvre of putting her behind him was a reflection of his dissatisfaction and she meekly followed him inside, accepting his reaction as understandable.

"Mr Lewis. I'm DS Backhouse. How are your wrists?" he asked sarcastically.

David raised the unmarked limbs and paused for a moment searching, partly out of his own curiosity, for a reasonable explanation.

"I don't know. They seem fine. I can't explain what happened. It's been a tough week."

"Oh?"

David was reluctant to discuss his stay in hospital. He already knew the female officer didn't believe him and he suspected that the fact he'd been unconscious for three days would hardly add credence to his story.

"Let's say some odd things have been happening."

Backhouse wasn't in the mood for a better explanation so cut straight to the point.

"Well, I believe you have some information for us regarding the recent robbery in the High Street?"

"Yes. As I told your colleague I think it was me?"

"You *think*? DC Murray seemed to think you were pretty certain before your *wrist* episode."

Backhouse looked disapprovingly at Murray. Had she really got him out of bed for this?

"What about the two hundred and thirty pounds you mentioned? What do you know about that?"

"I'm not really very sure anymore. I remember the amount was in the bag but I can't remember how I know."

That was enough for Backhouse. He looked at Murray, nodded at the door and turned to follow her out into the corridor. As he passed through the doorway, he dismissively remarked to David,

"We'll be right back." He knew full well that 'we' would *not* be including him.

"What the hell is going on Lizzy? You got me in here for a confession which turns out to be a lucky guess and a freak show that would hardly win a place with PT Barnum."

"Sarge, seriously, he came across as the real deal. I just

can't explain the wrist thing. He does resemble the e-fit, sort of, and what about the cut on his head? That fits." Backhouse raised an eyebrow and pursed his lips in response to Murray's grasp at a comeback. "Sorry Sarge," she ended.

"Right, well I'm going back to bed. Check out his details and get his full version of events in your pocket book. After that, cut him loose and don't call me again unless you get something *real*. Understood?"

"Completely," she replied. She knew this *incident* had dropped her around a thousand percent in his estimations and, as a result, her prospects of getting out of the office were now slim-to-none, that's if she would be allowed to stay on the team at all. She wanted desperately to change that. She returned to the interview room to finalise this sorry episode so she could ditch 'Mr Lewis' and return to investigating other more viable leads. In fact *any* other leads.

*****

David wandered confused and bitter from the police station. Dr Reynolds had contacted the Job Centre from the hospital while David had been unconscious the previous week. That's how the staff had identified the anonymous male, from his government staff identity card. As such, there was no need for David to concern himself with returning there. Janet Seymour, his supervisor, had booked him off for a fortnight pending a medical review board over his suitability to continue working. It wasn't, however, the prospect of being unemployed that concerned David. It was the extreme self-doubt that now played on his mind.

The female detective had completely thrown the convictions he had formed, whilst lying inactive in hospital, totally off kilter. He was no longer sure of his involvement. She had been right about his recollection of the crime. His memories of the old lady could easily have been from him meeting her at the bus stop. Furthermore, the factory and the route he believed he had taken there were quite possibly an imaginative guess. After all, the location of the attack at the alleyway had been in the paper. As had the direction the offender ran off, up Selby Street. That much had been seen by the witness passing in her car, the woman who had stopped to tend to the fallen old lady and who had called the police.

What he didn't understand was why the young officer had dismissed his knowledge of the amount of money taken. It was as though she was treating it as a lucky guess but he *knew* he'd been right about it. He could tell by the reaction she'd shown in the interview room, right before his wrists had flared up.

Strangely, he had almost already forgotten about it but his mind suddenly recounted the agony he had felt. It was as if it had been a dream, as if he'd seen it third hand or on a film. What was going on in his life at the moment?

He scoured his deepest thoughts for clues. Sure, he'd seen movies about paranormal powers. He'd seen programmes about people with the willpower to move stuff about or set things on fire. But that was all fiction, wasn't it? He'd even seen documentaries about people suffering physical symptoms brought about by the power-of-the-mind. The doctor had said the mind was complicated, even unpredictable, but this? This was something else.

Could he really have caused the blisters to rise and burst by pure thought alone? That said, even if he could, why his wrists? He hadn't been thinking about anything painful happening. Maybe it was an allergic reaction to that uniformed officer? His aftershave, hand-cream, anything! He had helped him up by the wrist, but only one. Even then, how on earth had the marks disappeared so quickly? Those bandages the detective had used were just that, bandages. There had been nothing special about them.

David's mind raced as he plodded toward the bus stop for home. He couldn't help sensing something bad was about to happen. What concerned him, though, was the thought that it didn't feel like it was going to happen to him.

He stepped up the lowered platform onto the bus.

"Viscount Road please," he requested, showering various coins from his pocket into the driver's payment dish.

The driver let out a derisory wheeze and sorted through the coins leaving the change for the annoying young daydreamer to collect for himself. David scooped up the remaining money and took his seat. His head began to ache again and he knew he had to take *something* for the pain and get his head down. The bus trundled away and David was on his way home.

Chapter Six

Murray released the door and let the sprung return arm take it back to its frame. As she stepped out into the police yard, she barely noticed it rattle to a close behind her. She'd been through this particular entrance so many times now that it had become one of life's oblivious noises. Besides, her thoughts were clearly fixed on reclaiming some credibility with her sergeant. She felt childishly embarrassed by the incident with David *bloody* Lewis and, with the scraps of information he had divulged to her, she was determined to recoup some ground on the truth by padding out the images he had described with matching facts from the crime scene.

She wanted Backhouse to see she hadn't been remiss in believing that Lewis and his performing wrists were, in fact, involved in some way. At the same time, she was definitely not going to be waking him until she had the *real* evidence he'd referred to in their parting conversation. No, she'd show him she was a decent detective and present that night's shift with something concrete to look at.

She stepped into the standard plain hatchback SIU car and manoeuvred out of the over-crowded parking area. The barrier drew back at its usual, slow pace and she pulled away in the direction of the High Street. A short drive later and she arrived at the scene of Mrs Nugent's robbery. The CSI forensic tent was long gone and children were coming out of the primary school across the park from the alleyway which led to Selby Street.

It was no wonder that the crime scene staff had failed to find anything the previous Friday. Even with Mrs Nugent's accurate description of the location, with all the parents and pre-school toddlers that were meeting their darling siblings from the school, there must have been a thousand sets of muddy shoes and inquisitive little hands passing over this site twice a day. To add to the forensic carnage, it had been three days after the attack before CSI had even been tasked with setting up shop there at all.

The first thing that Lewis had recounted was banging his head on the wall. Unfortunately, he hadn't recalled exactly where and Murray knew that, with this particular rough brick wall being at least fifty yards long, there was no way that CSI would even entertain checking its entire length, or even the alleyway portion of it, for DNA.

Entering the alleyway, she tore the remains of the blue and white crime scene tape from the lamp post next to the entrance and imagined the tired section officer being finally relieved from guarding the scene and hastily tearing down the makeshift barrier to get back to the station for a hot cup of tea. She slipped the overlooked litter into her coat pocket and moved on up the narrow access.

Dozens of different footprint marks were squashed into the mud, decades' worth of decomposed leaves mulched there after falling from the overarching trees. Finally, the route was overridden by dozens of school bicycle tracks and littered with the wrappers of a thousand chocolate bars and she suddenly felt a twinge of guilt for deriding the efforts of the CSI staff. New or not, they had very little chance of picking anything evidential out of this mess.

After the alley, she continued on into Selby Street. She knew that Backhouse had already had the local NPU plain clothes staff out canvassing the entire area with house-to-house enquiries since his visit to the hospital the previous Thursday. With this in mind, she briskly walked on toward the underpass and the industrial estate beyond. The stale smell of urine filled her nostrils as she entered the fifty or so meter tunnel.

The coving-style lighting stretched the entire length of the dank tube but less than half of the bulbs still worked and the remainder flickered uneasily, like catwalk paparazzi flashes, as she passed them by. The tunnel bellied out at its centre and a puddle, an inch or so deep, had pooled almost three quarters of the way across the dingy thoroughfare. The surface was speckled with flecks of dirt and she declined to imagine of what the stagnant liquid might consist. In any event she carefully walked around the foul pond and continued on toward the exit.

Bearing right as she left the tunnel, as Lewis had described, she walked onto an area of rough wasteland. Beyond she could see a number of industrial buildings in varying states of repair.

Although Hopefield was classed as a new town, it had, in fact, been rebuilt as a commercial 'super-estate' on the old industrial suburb of Atherton. That eyesore had been here since the early sixties and had almost become a ghost town, synonymous with failure, after the North East's steel industry had all but collapsed in the early eighties.

After millions invested in transport infrastructure and link-ways, the town had been renamed in the 'hope' of turning this particular 'field' into a computer-industry boom town. All that remained of the old town were a few of the taller, historically more pleasing town centre buildings, a few churches and these dated factories.

Murray scanned down the row of saw-toothed roofs for the factory described by Lewis as the dumping spot for Mrs Nugent's bag. There, right at the far end of Link One, she settled on a single, detached building. It had the correct tall chimney, topped with a black ring and the row of lorry-sized, roller-shutter doors at the right hand end of the facing wall.

She crossed the rough ground of thigh-high weeds and grasses. There was a distinct pathway through the undergrowth, suggesting the cut-through was regularly travelled. However, either side of it she could hardly see the ground for the thick coverage of weeds and tall, unkempt grass. She thought this area could easily conceal a thousand handbags and made a mental note to improve her standing with Backhouse by cleverly suggesting that they had it thoroughly checked later by the divisional search team. That said, she knew the bag she was looking for was not here and she continued on toward the lone factory

She exited the waste ground and crossed the access road that served the desolate building she had now finally reached. She walked over to the roller doors and, seeing no obvious external locks, gave one a tug to see if it had any movement in it. It clattered loudly and the echo told the young detective the place was well and truly devoid of any worthwhile activity. It failed to respond to her weak efforts to lift it so she began to circumnavigate the building to try and find a more amenable entrance.

Round to the right side of the building, out of sight of the roadway of Link One, she found a double-door entrance. She concluded it must have been the round-on-the-right access which Lewis had described to her after Backhouse had left her with him to get his version of the offence. The entrance was recessed a metre or so into the building and the roller door, flush to the outer wall of the factory, was three quarters of the way open. Its awkward angle told Murray it had, at some distant point in the past, been forced and had seized in this jaunty position.

The twin-panel doors had been boarded up, 'repeatedly', she thought by the differing materials apparently used to do so. The lower left panel was dislodged and the broken, wired glass beyond gave easy access to the building's main corridor. She crouched down and peered into the dank factory. The ammonia smell of pigeon excrement was overpowering and loud resonating drips from somewhere inside told her that either the roof had been open to the elements for some time or there had been a recent water burst which was still finding its way to the ground floor.

She briefly considered whether she had come far enough, or whether she should return later with some back-up. Then she recalled Backhouse's face as he'd said 'something real' and she decided that a generic factory and a broken door would fail to impress.

She contorted her small body through the opening and crunchily stood up amongst the pieces of shattered glass. To her right she saw a narrow staircase leading up and round, out of sight, to the first floor. It was whitewashed as Lewis had described and, with her confidence growing that she was on to something, she tentatively began to climb, unsure of what she might find at the top.

***

A sudden clattering woke him from the dreamless void of his latest score. He had no idea how long his last bag had knocked him out for. All he knew was that he'd needed it. His headache was gone, for now at least. The last week had been really difficult so he had decided to wipe it away with an hour or so of chemically induced oblivion. Now, however, he was suddenly awake, confused at first but then instantly lucid. He was not alone.

He instinctively checked for the cash he had left over from the job on the old dear last week. It was still there. He could hear crunching on the glass, which he knew was by the entrance downstairs, and concluded that, whoever it was, they were on their way in, rather than out, after having helped themselves to *his* cash. He scrambled to his feet but, hearing the echo of his bedding scraping across the floor, he paused and then began to move more deliberately. He briskly, yet silently, moved to the side office overlooking the access road to the factory.

Roughly scrubbing a small circle in the dirt-encrusted window with the cuff of his sleeve, he looked outside. He couldn't see any cop cars. In fact, he couldn't see any cars at all. The person slowly moving around beneath him was here for something other than him and he had no intention of letting them have it. He returned to the main open plan office and recovered a baseball bat from beneath his duvet. He always kept it close when he knew he was going to be out-of-it for any length of time.

He positioned himself at the top of the narrow stairwell. The intruder was not yet past the turn in the stairs and he could hear the slow, deliberate steps. Quiet yet distinctive, each step scraped and twisted in the dirt as its owner carefully lifted and placed each foot. He tried to slow and shallow his breathing which he felt, under the drive of adrenalin rushing through his veins, would surely give him away.

48

As his senses counted the last few paces of the intruder, he raised the bat to his side, away from the opening to the stairwell, and held his breath completely. He was pressed back hard against the wall, a meter or so from the opening, and there he waited until he saw the leg of the intruder pass into the room.

He swung down hard, roaring loudly with the effort he imparted into the swing. He struck the intruder cleanly and massively across the stomach. The form crumpled to the floor in front of him and it was only as the second blow came raining down upon her upper back that he realised it was a woman that now lay unconscious and face down in the dust before him. He flung the bat aside, shocked at his own ferociousness. Then, he noticed an identification badge lay next to her which had been snapped from a lanyard around her neck by the force of his first strike. He bent down to see a small picture of the woman and read the name.

"Shit," he quietly exclaimed to no-one but himself. "DC Murray."

He'd just laid out a copper. His mind accelerated instantly from naught-to-panic, his thoughts floundering back and forth.

'What the hell is she doing here? Where are her mates? She knows about the mugging. Did she see my face?'

The unanswered questions filled his mind and overflowed until, hands frantically clasped on top of his head, he cried out loud,

"Shit, fucking shit."

He couldn't decide what to do. He checked her pulse. She was alive. If he just left her and ran would her colleagues find her here and know who he was, who she'd been looking for? She'd tell them that much, surely? He needed time to think but she might not be out for long. He couldn't risk hitting her again to keep her unconscious so he decided, in his illogical panic, that tying her up for now would be the best thing to do.

He ran around the factory, like the proverbial headless chicken, scouring every office for rope or tape. He'd almost reached the last office when he skidded to a halt outside the old, ground floor boiler room. Out of the corner of his eye, he noticed a cupboard, barely ajar, tucked away behind the huge tanks that once supplied the factory with hot water. He ran in, rounded the tank and flung the door open. Inside he found an old toolbox, left behind when the factory was abandoned. He quickly rummaged through the unfolding compartments and with a triumphant "Yes!" he pulled out an old roll of masking tape and a small, rusted drum of steel wire.

Bolting back up the stairwell, he found Murray still prostrate on the floor of the dusty workroom. To begin with, he covered her mouth so that, should his subsequent binding efforts awaken the subdued woman, she wouldn't be able to call out to any mates who might still be nearby. He tugged the detective's arms behind her and wrapped them in tape. However, the paper binding was old and tore too easily to be trusted as a secure way to restrain the woman. Instead, he opened up the drum of rusted wire.

The strands were beginning to oxidise together and he had to peel lengths from the drum in order to use them on the prone officer. He bent and re-bent the strands to break them from the reel and, once free, wrapped them around and around the pale slender wrists of the unconscious woman. The corroded wire immediately began to raise wheals on the constrained flesh and, before he had even moved on to binding her legs in a similar fashion, the first signs of blood began to ooze between the red/brown strands.

With her wrists tightly bound behind her back, he moved on to her legs and repeated the method of peel, bend and break to give him sufficient wire to ensnare her around both the ankles and knees. He was happier now that she would remain subdued for as long as he wanted her that way. Finally, he taped over her eyes and sat back to consider his options.

Now he had time to think straight, that is about as straight as his drug-damaged mind could manage under the circumstances. He tried to make some sense of her arrival. He checked the window again, still no cars. She was alone but it was miles from the police station. She must have had a car somewhere. He quickly searched the trussed officer's pockets and found her car keys, along with her phone and note book.

Strangely though, she had no radio. What the hell was she up to? Why had she followed him in here, alone and out of touch with her mates?

His curiosity alone found him flicking through the note book as he thought of what to do next. He didn't actually expect to find an answer in there. Then, on the last written page, he noticed the word 'factory'. He looked more intently into the later entries and, realising the pages were dated, he turned to the start of that day and read the notes in full.

***

Murray began to sense the world around her. An ache across her back soon faded against the sudden panic that she could not see anything and that her breathing was restricted by something in her mouth. Letting out an increasingly pitched squeal, she realised, with horror, that she had been gagged and blindfolded. She suddenly jerked to reach up to her face to release the gag but she found herself immobilised. As her senses fully returned she began to feel a trickle of liquid running from her right wrist into her left palm.

She began to violently squirm but soon found that she could only achieve an increase in the level of pain in her tied wrists. It suddenly dawned on her that whoever had done this could be standing mere feet away from her writhing body, watching sadistically as she panicked like a caged animal. She instantly made her body fall silently still and centred all her concentration on straining to hear for the slightest clue of her assailant. The room around her was quiet. She needed to get her bearings. For her continued sanity, she wanted to know where she was. She decided to play it safe, as much as someone gagged and blindfolded could, that is, and assumed she was still on an upper floor of the factory to which she had come searching for *something real*. The current irony of that goal's insignificance harshly struck home and she suddenly felt very stupid.

There was no time for self-analysis now though. She refocused her mind back on the *now*. Was she still at the factory? The smell was certainly the same. If she could manage to stand she would have to be aware of the stairs and open balconies. That point considered, her argument was mute if she couldn't get to her feet. She rolled over onto her backside. The wrapping around her wrist cut into the flesh making her wince but she knew she must persevere if she was going to get out of this.

She couldn't feel her mobile phone in her back pocket and the thought that her attacker had searched her sent a shudder through her body as she considered what else they may have done while she'd been unconscious. She heard a loud clatter and returned to being attentively silent. She recognised the noise as that of the roller-shutter doors downstairs in the factory. At least she now knew, or could at least confidently guess, where she was.

This time, however, the clattering was extended, repeatedly faster and then slower. Someone was opening the door with a chain-driven crank. Should she call out when the clattering stopped? Was it her attacker? She concluded that, because she'd heard no reactive noise in the upstairs room at the start of the ruckus below, her attacker was not with her. But was this him, or her, downstairs?

She waited for the clattering to stop and hopefully listened for the sound of chatter that one might expect between co-workers, innocent employees who would help her. However, the relieving banter did not come. Instead, she heard the rising and then echoing tone of a vehicle's engine as it slowly drove into the ground floor warehouse area beneath her.

The engine stopped and she heard the door open and casually close. Still, the welcome noise of friendly chatter did not come. No unloading of boxes, no dragging of cargo. Instead, she listened as the clattering shutter was closed behind the vehicle and the unnerving footfalls of her captor came up the whitewashed stairwell. She waited silently and prepared herself for the worst.

Chapter Seven

Backhouse woke late into the evening. It was already dark and, as he pulled back the duvet, his body clock sent confused muscle-messages shuddering throughout his fatigued body. After several double-takes at the clock, his mind finally caught up with reality and he realised the time was 8pm, not 8am.

'God,' he thought. He had to be back in the office in less than an hour. *'Not even time to make a decent meal; another chippy takeaway for breakfast then?'*

He stumbled through to the bathroom and prepared himself for the prospect of another boring, fruitless night. He dressed as quickly as his aching bones would allow and drove the five, or so, bleary-eyed miles to the station. He pushed open the door to the office and was greeted by fourteen, annoyingly fresh looking, youngsters.

'Was I ever that young?' he thought.

"Okay people. What have we got? Anything new from Lizzy?"

The assembled officers shrugged and mumbled in unison.

"Right, there was, well, *an incident* earlier today whereby some barn-pot handed himself in as our mugger."

Everyone's full attention was instantly snared. Some out of genuine interest in solving the case, others because they knew it would mean an early end to a very slow set of nights.

"I'll not bore you with the full details but basically he claimed to be the mugger. Then he crumpled like a boxer with a glass jaw; then recovered as if nothing had happened; then, somehow guessed the figure stolen from the Squadron Leader's purse. Finally, and you'll like this one, he somehow made his wrists burst with a load of blisters."

Everyone sat, silently staring at the Sergeant for a forthcoming explanation.

"This is all according to Lizzy, anyway. By the time she woke me and got me down here, the guy was fine, not a mark, and doubtful, at best, about his knowledge of the offence. I told her to get a full account and get back to me if there turned out to be anything solid. I assume, by the lack of anything here, that she decided to agree with me that he was just a plonker and got rid of him. I'll go and see if she left any e-mails but I'm afraid it looks like another long night."

With that, the team began to break up into their respective pairings and prepared their kit for the night ahead.

"Has anyone seen the keys for HGN?" Thomo asked, referring to the errant fob by the associated vehicle's registration suffix.

"Try Lizzy's desk," responded Wazzer. "I had that car last night and I noticed her collar number in the log book for the daytime before me. She might have used it today as well."

"Cheers," Thomo replied, and he walked over to her desk. "Hey, look. Lizzy's left her computer locked out. Not like her. She always logs out when she goes home. Wazzer, have you got her mobile? The keys aren't here and her desk drawer is locked."

"Try her coat. It's the one hanging on her chair."

Thomo looked perplexed.

"Why's that here then?"

"Who am I, her mother?" Wazzer exclaimed "She probably forgot it. It was quite warm today. I got shag all sleep and have a stomping headache to prove it. Her number's on the board over there."

Thomo glanced over and, recalling the digits in groups of threes and fours, dialled the number and waited for his forgetful colleague to answer. The phone rang out and eventually switched automatically to Lizzy's answer phone service.

Backhouse strode back into the room. "Has anyone spoken to Lizzy this evening? There's nothing from her in my e-mails."

Again, all Backhouse got was a shrug of negativity.

"Tracey, give her a call will you. Her mobile's on the board."

"I've just tried her mobile to find out where she left the keys for HGN. She's not answering," Thomo interrupted.

"Try her home number, Trace. I want to know what she's been up to today. It's on the computer directory."

"Sarge, her computer's still logged on and her coat's here too," Thomo added.

"Okay." Backhouse dismissed this as coincidental forgetfulness on Lizzy's part. After all, she'd had quite a day with Mr Lewis.

If only he knew the whole story.

***

"So, you're awake then?"

Lizzy was unsure at this point whether to let out a muffled response of indignation or to 'play-possum' and hope the man would leave again to give her more time to attempt an escape. Then, of course, he knew she was now conscious because she had been moving around, squirming like a maggot on a hook. Only, unlike that blissfully unaware bait, *she* had a distinctly grim preconception of her fate.

She had now concluded that her attacker was male by the depth of his voice but it seemed muffled and gruff somehow. Was this his real voice or was the gag tape, which was also covering her ears, causing the distortion? Alternatively, was her assailant intentionally altering his voice to avoid recognition? If the latter was the truth, was it because he already knew her or that he simply didn't want to be recognised later? Could this mean she *might* be getting out of this intact at some point?

She was fully in defensive-thinking mode again and her detective mind was playing through her usual barrage of lateral questioning in fast forward. She needed to hear more of the man's voice to construct a better mental picture of his intentions. She let out a stream of pointless groans and squeals, pretending, by their cadence and varying tones, to be constructing a distraught question of some kind.

"Settle down. You're not going to be here for much longer."

This double-edged response was not the answer she really wanted to hear. Did he mean he intended to release her, maybe move her or was his intention to present her with an altogether less attractive form of *departure*?

She shouted and squirmed in objection to the latter. The ties around her wrists bit into the flesh and she let out a genuine whimper of agony. Her adrenalin was rising again and she began to choke on the gag the man had stuffed into her mouth and taped so tightly around her face.

"Shut the fuck up," the man said and Murray heard a short shuffle which was followed by a sudden blow to the stomach as he kicked her to quieten her objections.

She tried to muffle her cries but her choking began to get out of hand and she wheezed desperately to catch what little breath the gag would allow her to suck in between coughs. The man seemed to realise she was getting into serious trouble and she felt his hands suddenly close around her face. At first, she feared he may be trying to end her outcries for good but then she winced as he tore the sticky tape from her neck and then from across her jaw. She tasted his oily fingers as he pushed them into the side of her mouth to pluck out the cloth gag and she spat out a relieved breath in order to draw in a full lungful of un-gagged air.

"There, now shut up."

Murray, now free of the tape covering her ears, had a very slightly improved sense of the man's voice. In addition, the sudden turn of events brought about by her choking had altered his voice to a lighter, less rehearsed, tone.

"David?" she quizzed, "Is that you?"

She was unsure but the stunted silence and inactivity that followed the question led her to conclude she must have been right.

'My God,' she thought. *'He led me right here, into a trap, and I fell for it. You stupid bitch,'* she chastised herself.

Now she was really concerned. If her assumption was

correct, he had planned this all along. Handing himself in, the show he had put on in the interview room to divert her from conducting a proper interview. All carefully played out to lure her into some perverted trap, for God knows what purpose. Her thoughts suddenly centred on that show. The doubling-over and the wrist-blistering, could he have staged all that as some sick, visual prediction of what he had in store for her?

Then again, it was so real, so painful looking. Could special effects make-up do something like that, totally fabricate an animated blistering so convincingly? The chances were that the name and the address which he had given her, which PC Peterson had also overheard in the interview room, were complete fabrications as well. She hadn't even written in the office journal as to where she was going.

She was alone, *dead* alone. There was a heavily pregnant pause.

"So what are you going to do with me?" she defiantly asked her, now quiet, *assassin*. She was beginning to think of him on that level now and feared the very worst. At least this way she could know the truth of his intentions. She could fathom if there was any kink in his plan that she could exploit to attempt an escape from what she now foresaw to be a distinctly shrinking life span. However, this was no egomaniacal spy-thriller villain. He wasn't about to divulge his intentions to his prey and laugh theatrically over her bound and trussed body. His silence sent a cold shiver down Murray's spine as she contemplated the fateful accuracy of her own conclusions.

Minutes passed in an uncomfortable silence. Murray, although curious of her fate, had decided that she did not want to antagonize her captor into a premature finalization of his extravagant scheme and that quiet capitulation was the best way of extending her existence long enough for the formulation of an escape plan.

The lack of a sudden response to her question, as had occurred with her earlier outcry, gave her cause for hope that it was not his intention to do away with her there and then. She lay quiet, stretching out into the blackness with every sense she had left at her disposal for any clue as to what was likely to happen next.

***

"No answer on her landline, Sarge," Tracey called across the office.

"Okay. She's probably out drowning her sorrows after her performance this morning. Is there an answer phone?"

"No. It's just ringing out."

"There's one on her mobile Sarge," Thomo interjected.

"Right, leave her a message to get in touch as soon as she can. I want to know what she got from the call to the press office I told her to make."

"Will do," Thomo replied while simultaneously pressing the redial button on Lizzy's desk phone. The automated message responded to tell the caller that the phone was switched off and Thomo called back across the office to catch Backhouse as he was opening the door to leave.

"It's turned off now, Sarge. She mustn't want to talk to you after today," he quipped.

'What the bloody hell is she playing at?' thought Backhouse.

"Okay, cheers. I'll catch her in the morning again."

With that, he strode out of the main office and back toward his own to finish reading an e-mail he'd opened from DI Priest.

Steve. Just a quick line to update you re: the Command Team & Intel meetings this morning. First I've made it clear with DI Taylor that ALL section staff are to be made fully aware that the Link Estate is 'off limits' for general patrol.

They are to be told only to enter the area if a job comes in. He mentioned your visit this morning and wasn't too happy about you blaming the intel unit for circulating the fact an operation was on in that area. He suggested that if the section were unaware they wouldn't be able to submit any useful intelligence that his unit could link to CASSANDRA's grouping. But I think I won him over with the truth that twelve patrols were seen by yourselves and not one piece of intel was submitted. He couldn't really argue with that!

Anyway, while he understands your frustrations the Super' isn't wholly pleased with our progress. I explained it was early days and that, with the fact there have been no further robberies since last Tuesday, we've had precious little new information to go on. He is of a mind to pull your staff in off nights and use them to extend the house to house enquiries on the previous jobs to see if we can dig up anything fresh. He's getting pressure from headquarters and he's finding it increasingly difficult to continue backing your 'hunch' tactic that the offender is an itinerant drug-user.

I've every confidence in you and our staff but you know what it's like. If it's quiet tonight I want you to knock off around 4 and stagger the shift back to 8/4 days over the next couple of shifts.

Cheers, Pete.

PS. Did anything come of DC Murray's trip out today? I saw her leaving the station around 3pm and she said she had something to follow up that might prove important.

Backhouse re-read the *PS* and grew concerned over the lack of contact from Lizzy. He strode briskly back to the office.

"Wazzer, Thomo, get round to Lizzy's house and see where she is. If she's not in leave a note to contact me on my mobile ASAP."

"What's up Sarge, something wrong?" Wazzer quizzed, curious at Backhouse's change of tone regarding the forgetful Lizzy.

'Can't be this bothered about some car keys?' he thought to himself.

"Not sure. Just something the boss e-mailed me about that doesn't ring true. Go straight there and join us on plot when you're finished."

"Will do." Wazzer grabbed his jacket from the back of his chair and Thomo stood up to follow him. They sensed an urgent nervousness in their Sergeant's voice which they both found uncomfortable and uncharacteristic for the seasoned supervisor.

***

Twenty minutes later Wazzer and Thomo pulled up outside Lizzy's house in the satellite village of Little Dunsford. They immediately noticed that the driveway was empty and the house was in darkness. Wazzer commented on the lack of a vehicle and asked Thomo,

"What car does Lizzy drive anyway?"

"D'know," the heavy built officer replied. He had no cause to know anything about Lizzy's private life. She was Major Crime Unit and he was Crime Car Unit. Prior to the forming of the Robbery Team he had never even met the detective.

"Let's ask around. See if any neighbours have seen her this evening."

"Okay," Thomo replied, opening the car door and reaching with his right hand for the windscreen upright to twist and lever his broad shoulders from the passenger seat.

Wazzer knocked on at Lizzy's adjoining neighbour while Thomo crossed the road to the opposing homes.

"Hello," he said, lifting his Warrant Card identification into the line of sight of the old lady that answered the door to him.

"I'm DC Warren Holliwell. I'm sorry about the late hour but I'm a colleague of DC Murray, your neighbour." The lady looked momentarily confused.

"Oh, you mean Elizabeth. Yes, but I'm afraid she's not home."

"We know," Wazzer confirmed. "We're trying to get in touch with her."

The old lady seemed perplexed and worried by the news that Lizzy was out of touch, much as Wazzer himself was becoming. He saw her concern and, careful not to alarm her further, added,

"Everything is fine. It's just that she has some important information that we need for an operation we're running tonight."

The old lady's face relaxed and she explained further,

"Is she not working with you then? She hasn't been back all day since she left for work this morning."

Wazzer became increasingly concerned.

"Are you sure?" he asked.

"Quite sure, dear. She always calls in here after work to check on me since I had that nasty driveway man round last month. She's a lovely girl, isn't she?"

"She is, yes," Wazzer unknowingly replied, glibly smiling to settle the old lady's mind.

"Thanks very much. Goodnight". With that, he turned to leave. Then he thought on. He span back around as the door was about to finish closing.

"I'm sorry," he said, halting the door's closure. "Do you know what sort of car Elizabeth drives?"

"I'm sorry dear, no. I've never been very good with cars and the like. I know it's a big blue one."

"No worries. Thanks anyway."

Wazzer felt that this development called for more than just leaving a note. He shouted over to Thomo and recalled him to the car.

"Something's not right here," he said. "She hasn't been seen here all day."

He briefly relayed what the old neighbour had said.

"What now then?" Thomo quizzed.

"Let's get back to the nick and check for her car."

"How do we do that? We share a car park with ASDA. There must be a hundred 'big blue' cars on there."

"There's a way."

"Well?" Thomo asked, fairly young in service and unfamiliar with all the searches available on the Police National Computer (PNC).

"Warren to Atticker. Are you on the air yet?"

The biggest advantage of using an unmonitored back-to-back radio channel was the lack of a need for formality. Using personal names and knowing everyone who was on the air within a small team made for shorter and more easily understandable transmissions.

"Go ahead Wazzer."

"I need a postcode to vehicle check on Lizzy's home address. We need to know what sort of car she drives."

"Roger that. Standby."

Atticker knew enough about radio etiquette not to ask for the details over the air. Despite being an encrypted, secure channel, it was considered *bad form* to pass personal details of colleagues by radio. Atticker quickly retrieved Lizzy's home details from the constabulary address book and inputted the postcode onto the relevant page of PNC. Seconds later, Thomo's mobile rang. Atticker may have been a desk jockey but he still had enough *bobby* in him to have noticed that Wazzer had picked up their particular pairing's car keys and that, as such, was likely to be driving and, therefore, not in a position to use a phone.

"He's good," Thomo commented to Wazzer as he accepted the call.

"She's got a blue Ford Maverick, index Mike, Foxtrot, Five, Four, Alpha, Zulu, Hotel. I think it's a couple of spaces away from my red Clio on the ASDA car park, in the second row down from the petrol station. I saw one there on my way in tonight but didn't realise it was hers."

Thomo noted the details and passed them to the waiting Wazzer.

"Cheers Atticker," Wazzer replied via the vehicle's hands free radio. "Contact the Sergeant and let him know we're on our way to ASDA to check for her car now. I've got a very bad feeling that she might be in trouble. She never got home tonight."

"Wazzer, this is Backhouse. I've been monitoring and I agree. Get there ASAP. Atticker, text me the DI's home number straight away."

"Roger that Sarge. Will do."

Wazzer depressed the accelerator of his three litre crime car and the pair began an almost pursuit pace drive back to the police station and the adjoining superstore car park.

***

"Sir, we have a situation. Do you recall the e-mail you sent me? The *PS* about Murray? Do you remember any details of where she was going because she's missing and Wazzer has just found her car on the ASDA car park. I think she's in serious trouble. The last information we have on her is your sighting in the rear yard at fifteen hundred hours."

"Sorry Steve. She didn't say where she was going but she did mention it had something to do with someone she'd interviewed earlier in the day. Has she got her mobile on her?"

"Yes sir, but we've already tried it and its answering as switched off."

"Well, get it 'pinged' anyway. I'll authorise. Has an incident been raised yet?"*

"Not yet Sir. You were my first call."

"Right, I'll sort that and I'll ring the Super' too. Get everyone back to the office and get the TPT in as well. I'll contact Air Support. You get on to the search team and dog handlers."

"Will do, boss. See you back at the office."

"Twenty minutes."

"Understood."

Chapter Eight

"Time to go, DC Murray."

The more she heard the voice, the more she convinced herself it belonged to the peculiar David Lewis. Everything she knew about him was a paradox. Meek then bold, calm then violent, even injured then cured. If she'd been told about the characteristics by someone else she'd have thought they were talking about two different people.

However, she had seen the changes, most dramatically those wrists which had blistered before her very eyes and then healed with neither time nor treatment. Something unnatural was going on here but for the time being Murray had worse prospects to consider. Her captor had re-bound her mouth now; not so tightly that she would start choking as she had earlier but enough that, should she choose to, she would not be able to call out for help.

He pulled up on the prone officer's upper arm to lift her to her feet. She let out an objectionable squeal and he reduced the pressure.

"Come on, get up."

Murray tucked her legs up and rolled onto her face to shift her body's weight over her knees. He reapplied the pressure to her elbow and, now prepared, Murray raised herself to her knees. From here on up, the rest was up to him. Seeming to realize her inability to elevate herself further, he moved around ahead of her and placed his hands under her armpits. He grunted slightly at the effort to lift her petite body to fully vertical. The noise served to tell her that this guy was hardly muscle-bound. However, this conclusion only hardened her opinion that this was indeed the insignificant young man that she had spoken to earlier that day.

Now vertical, she found her feet were no longer bound. She hadn't realised this earlier as the tightness of the bindings around her knees had numbed her lower legs. It had begun hours before with pins-and-needles but now her legs were totally devoid of feeling and as capable of taking the tiny load of her bodyweight as a couple of wet ropes. As soon as he released his lifting effort, her legs began to give way. He caught her but it was too little, too late. She painfully crashed back down to her knees and crumpled over to the prone position from which she had begun.

Murray heard a frustrated "Shit" from her captor and lay still and quiet, awaiting his next instruction. She knew, now, that he was not a strong man. The fact could prove useful later if she could gather enough of these weaknesses together to give herself the upper hand. His next effort was to lift Murray to a seated position and try to drag her backwards toward the stairwell. Murray did not relish the idea of this less-than-capable man being her only support as she was dragged backwards, bound and gagged, down a flight of debris-strewn steps. In addition, his efforts to drag her by the armpits sent bolts of agony raging from her bleeding and torn wrists. She let out an increasingly violent squeal until he stopped and gave up the plan.

"Well, you're not helping," the frustrated assailant said.

Murray considered this comment for a moment. Had he really just blamed her for his inability to transfer her to what might turn out to be her grave? She briefly saw the dark satire in his retort but then it occurred to her that this was an opportunity to gain that second rung toward an advantage. She grunted and nodded her head at her bound legs and wriggled them to gesture he should untie them. She continued the action for a short time, unable, in her blindfolded state, to gauge his response.

Then she felt him releasing the bindings from around her knees. As the last restraint was removed, she felt the rush of circulation begin to return to her lower legs. Only then did it occur to her that this may cause more of a problem than she was ready for. The lack of oxygen to her lower legs had built up toxins which she knew from her police training could cause organ damage if released, unchecked, back into the bloodstream.

Even as she considered this dilemma, the first painful sensations began to surge into the limp limbs. The raging cramps grew and grew until she could barely stand the agony. Bravely, Murray held the pain inside, her eyes streaming with tears. She did not want to writhe, agonising about the floor for fear that her captor would misconstrue the display as an attempt to make an escape and tie her up again. That intention was for later. For now, she silently held the pain at bay giving no indication of an intention to struggle free. Her efforts were not in vain.

As the cramps began to pass and a sense of some control returned to her legs, her attacker again tried to lift her to her feet. This time she managed to remain vertical and without further pause for thought he guided her toward, she assumed, the stairwell. As they approached the stairs, she felt him manoeuvre her around a corner and stop her short of the top stair.

"Steps ahead," he said calmly.

She had considered trying to push him down the stairwell. It was narrow and without handrails. Once falling, he would probably stumble at least to the halfway turn. That said, she couldn't be sure this would incapacitate him and, besides, from his voice it was obvious to her that he was now behind her. Instead, she carefully protruded a foot forward until she felt the lip of the first step. Once aware of it, she stepped forward and, extending her heel over the edge, solidly placed it against the first upright and lowered her foot until it touched down on the first flat.

Now more aware of each stair's size, her subsequent steps were more confident and she repeated the same testing manoeuvre after reaching the half way turn. He had been behind her throughout the descent. She could feel his hand on her shoulder. She reached the ground floor and he guided her out into main floor space of the warehouse. She then heard a jingle of metal, a familiar beep and the doors of the vehicle he had arrived in earlier click unlocked. He again took hold of her arm and guided her in a quarter circle. She heard another click and the boot of the car jolted open. A swoosh of extending hydraulic struts was followed by him saying,

"Get in."

She didn't like this at all. A trip to a potentially deadly destination was one thing if she had been travelling in the passenger compartment but to do so laying trapped in the vehicle's boot, from where she had no escape, was another. The former left the opportunity for escape at the journey's end, or even during it, but entrapment in the secure boot meant that this could be her last moment to change her misfortune. He might intend to use the vehicle's exhaust to smother her once she was trapped inside. Parked in a remote location, or even left here in this disused factory, it would be highly unlikely that she would be found before fatally succumbing to the noxious fumes.

Then again, what choice did she have? She sat onto the lip of the boot and slipped backward until her backside contacted the boot-space floor. As she did so, her head knocked against the moveable parcel shelf and she made a mental note that she must have been getting into a hatchback. As she began to half-fall sideways, he cupped her head in his hand and lowered her into the confined space. She tucked her legs up and folded them into a horizontal crouch.

As the boot lid was closed down, she stretched herself out as far as she could. Firstly, to blindly test the limits of her confine and, secondly, to brace herself against the forthcoming journey; one which she hoped would shortly begin and put an end to her fears that he intended to suffocate her right there in the factory. She then heard the rattling of the shutter doors and felt oddly relieved that the journey, which could easily be her last, was about to begin.

The engine started, a diesel she noted, and the car slowly moved out of the factory door. She heard the echo die away as the noisy engine passed through the opening and out into the industrial estate. This gave her the idea that, if she continued to listen carefully, she might be able to determine the route they were about to take, however *that* might help. Then they stopped again and her captor left the car, engine running, to close the shutter doors behind them. She thought for a moment and surmised that he must have intended to use the factory again and wanted to close the door to conceal the fact from passers-by that it was occupied, that he actually lived there. The fact that he may have only used it for hiding, whilst taking heroin, had not occurred to her.

Other than the Sergeant's hunch that the mugger may be an itinerant drug user, she had experienced no other indications that drugs were involved in this individual's life. David Lewis certainly had none of the regular indicators associated with heroin use: no drawn, gaunt features; no visible track-lines in his veins; no misshapen and discoloured teeth from the overuse of methadone, the prescribed alternative to heroin. No, the profile of a drug user definitely didn't fit David Lewis. Murray sincerely hoped that, if Backhouse had been wrong about the mugging suspect, it would be his last mistake for some time. After all, it was he and her other robbery squad colleagues that she was going to have to rely on to find and save her.

The clattering ended and moments later the car gently rocked to signal the driver's return before the offside door was once again closed. The vehicle pulled away and Murray began mentally noting as many sounds as she could. Initially, the tyres rumbled over the coarse, concrete-panel construction of the factory access road. Then there came the 'click-click' of a tar-strip that sealed the concrete to the more advanced, but still uneven, tar macadam surface of Link One. She could be fairly sure of the road names at this stage because, if they had started at the factory, there were few, if any, alternatives they could use to leave the area.

Her sense of balance and inertia told her they were turning left. This would lead from Link One to the nearby dual carriageway of Midland Road. The vehicle's speed increased and the surface became smoother and more even. A sudden slowing was followed by the familiar jump-pause-jump of a speed hump. After a few seconds, there was another; she counted five in total. They were definitely on one of The Link

Estate's eight parallel thoroughfares; she recognised the layout. A sharp right turn was next; followed by an increased speed and then braking, signalled by the red glow that filled the dark compartment so brightly she could see it through the masking tape covering her eyes. They moved off again, a left and then an accelerating, sweeping right. They were on the bypass junction roundabout. Sure enough, she felt the car rising up the on-ramp of Midland Road.

If she'd read the turns correctly they were headed west, out of town toward Little Dunsford. She thought of her home there, warm, comfortable and welcoming. Would she ever see it again? She knew the drive-time was just twenty minutes, normal speed, to the Little Dunsford turnoff. She began to count to herself to judge their approach. If he exited there, she would have a good chance of keeping track of the turns as she'd done so far. Nine hundred, a thousand, eleven hundred seconds passed by. She left it to thirteen hundred to be sure that her adrenalin powered body clock wasn't running too ridiculously fast but, after that, began to lose hope that she would be able to recognise their ever extending route.

The next junction was another four miles away and beyond that was the A1(M) motorway. If he joined that, or continued past it on the dual carriageway, she was in trouble. She barely knew either direction. The smooth, turn-free journey carried on for too long to be what she had guessed might be the distance to that last, pre-motorway junction. Finally, she recognised the descending sensation of an off-ramp and the car came to a full stop at its end. She heard the heavy, rumbling passage of a large lorry and the car was away again. A long accelerating right bend was followed by a left; another roundabout junction? The extended Midland Road, whatever it was called this far west of Hopefield, was basically a west to east route so a right turn off it would, she determined, take them north.

She didn't know why she was keeping track anymore. She expected to be dead within the hour. Maybe it was her way of maintaining her sanity in the face of that woeful prediction? This road, however, was far more meandering than the expected motorway and she soon lost any sense of north and south. After ten or so minutes, she gave up trying to recall the stops, starts and turns. The pointlessness of the exercise began to dawn on her until finally she sensed the road surface change. The wheels began to crunch on a gravel track of some kind and the car slowed to an almost walking pace. Murray was rocked and buffeted as the suspension battled with both undulations and potholes alike.

Eventually, the track seemed to run out and, with a final turn to the right, the car came to a stop. The brake lights remained illuminated as the engine noise died away. However, they too were quickly extinguished and the young detective feared she was to be next.

Chapter Nine

The station canteen, the largest open area in the building, had quickly been turned into an ad-hoc briefing room. Atticker had been busy at work since his Sergeant's call and, to his credit at this late hour, had managed to set up a laptop-driven projector. The white receiving screen had been erected in front of the restaurant's serving area and showed a large-scale map of the area divided into potential search zones.

The room's twenty or more tables had been side-stacked and replaced with as many additional chairs as the old specialist could muster from the surrounding offices in the time allowed. However, the briefing was still a standing-room-only affair. The dozens of hastily assembled officers sat and stood in groups of close colleagues from the various teams and squads which had been summoned for this urgent, night-time task.

A single table was left at the head of the room in front of the projection screen and the three seats behind it were occupied by Priest, Backhouse and Atticker. The latter was intently concentrating on the laptop in front of him and still arranging the various pictures and maps he had rapidly prepared in the previous hour. The Divisional Superintendent was also present, but was obviously absent from the briefing table.

However, his choice to stand as innocuously as he could, just inside the canteen door, was a deliberate one. He may have been a Superintendent but he was still a bobby's bobby. He knew that the very nature of Command Team rank created a subconscious feeling of derision amongst the lower ranks and, as the vast majority of those present were constables, he didn't want his presence to detract in any way from the

71

following briefing. In short he wanted them to listen, and listen 'bloody well'.

The force helicopter had already been scrambled and had commenced a search of The Link Estate area for Murray's SIU car. The short distance, of only a few miles, between the estate and the station allowed the hundred-plus officers to hear its distant twin gas turbine engines and rotor wash; even over the low pitched mêlée of mumbled, questioning conversations which were carrying on amongst the gathered officers of the Wrenshire Force.

"Quiet please everyone," DI Priest interrupted them, rising to his feet.

The conversations died away in a reactive wave toward the back of the room. The officers fell silent in anticipation of a full explanation for their recall to duty at this late hour and the high pitched whine of the helicopter was the only noise that could still be heard.

"Okay," the Inspector continued, "firstly thank you to you all for attending so quickly. I know some of you have come some distance."

The Forces search teams and dog handlers were not part of the Hopefield Division and, as the station was situated in the north-west quadrant of Wrenshire, some of the assembled officers had travelled upward of forty miles to arrive for this 23:30 briefing.

"For those of you still unaware, this situation has been classified a crime-in-action and should be considered as of threat-to-life importance. An officer of the Hopefield Pro-active Robbery Squad, DC Elizabeth Murray, has gone missing."

Atticker projected a large file picture of Murray onto the screen.

"It is believed she may be in the enforced custody of a male called David Lewis. In brief, it seems that this male handed himself in as responsible for the recent series of street robberies this division has been suffering and was interviewed by DC Murray around ten hundred hours this morning. It seems the male was agitated and displayed some peculiar medical symptoms that are, as yet, unexplained. We are fortunate in that, because of his odd behaviour, PC Peterson here," he nodded to the front row uniformed officer, "was asked to stand in on the interview. Now Lewis was not arrested as it was deemed his *confession* was flawed by doubtful accuracy. His details were only taken by DC Murray and, for whatever reason, which can be poured-over later, DC Murray decided to follow up whatever enquiries she had developed from his story during the day on her own, and without leaving any indication as to where she was going."

The reasons for Murray's total disregard for proper procedure had already crept into Backhouse's mind. He was beginning to feel responsible for his fatigued dismissal of Lizzy's belief in this Lewis guy's guilt. If he hadn't put pressure on her to conjure up some *real* leads, she may not have felt the need to bend, no, totally break, the rules. She may have arrested him, interviewed him in the relative safety of a custody suite interview room and either remanded him to a secure cell or bailed him for further enquiries which she would have been happy to leave to the following day, to follow up with an accompanying officer.

Instead, she had been bullied by him into being rash, even stupid, in her thought processes. She had gone off alone to prove a point and he knew exactly who was *really* to blame for *that* indiscretion; him. His head was already bowed in guilty contemplation and he knew full well that the subsequent investigation into the whole sorry episode would critically highlight his actions. However, that was for later. Considerations of his remaining career's prospects took a back seat to the imperative nature of the moment.

"Now, I saw her leaving around fifteen hundred hours," the Inspector continued, "and she indicated to me that she was following up information from what she referred to as 'an earlier interview'. Our only lead is to assume that she was referring to the interview with Lewis. Computer records of her door pass-card show she didn't leave the building between ten and three and the helpdesk log shows no other record of visitors asking for her by name. What is curious is that this character Lewis has no previous form. In fact, some of you may know him as the local Job Centre's Police Liaison Officer. I've got a patrol on its way in now with his immediate supervisor," he referred to his notes, "a Miss Seymour, in order to get a firsthand account of his recent mental state. We have a shot of Lewis as he entered the helpdesk this morning."

Atticker switched the screen's picture to an obscure, pixelated image of Lewis from that morning's in-station CCTV recording.

"I appreciate it's not a great shot but as you can imagine when we fitted the system we weren't expecting to use it for evidential grade photography. Miss Seymour has been tasked with obtaining Lewis's home details via her office en route so we'll be sending a team there as soon as that arrives. Now, as for PC Peterson's other involvement. It seems that Lewis described an area of The Link Estate to which he, allegedly, took the most recent robbery victim's bag. Now, although PC Peterson wasn't taking notes at the time, he can remember that the route described by Lewis seemed to end around some kind of disused factory on The Link Estate. It's a big area so we've got our work cut out."

Backhouse was feeling increasingly guilty about his dismissive treatment of his subordinate. If he'd known that the 'version of his story' he instructed the young detective to take from Lewis was going to include such detail he would have treated the matter altogether differently. He had allowed his tiredness and his frustration at the undisciplined section officers patrolling the surveillance area over the previous weekend to cloud his judgement. In short he had failed young Lizzy.

"As you can all hear the helicopter is already up searching for the unmarked car we believe DC Murray left the station in. Okay, I don't want to go on, but needless to say I want to ask the very best of each and every one of you tonight. Let's remain optimistic about DC Murray's condition but, at the same time, I want everyone here to understand the urgent nature of this search. As it stands, we can consider this Lewis individual to be an unknown, potentially unstable quantity and, as such, very dangerous. I want Elizabeth back with us by morning."

In this final reference to the young detective he purposefully personalized her by using her first name to emotionally connect each officer present to the unfortunate woman.

"Now, I'll hand you all over to your individual supervisors who have been given your respective search areas. Are there any general questions for now?"

"Sir," a voice called from the back of the room, "has DC Murray's phone been pinged?"

"Yes, thank you, good point. That has been done already but the phone is still switched off so we're having no mast hits as yet."

The officer nodded acceptingly.

"Anything else?" Priest asked. There were no takers and the Inspector glanced finally at the Superintendent. The Divisional Commander, standing with his arms crossed in an official and attentive manner, nodded approvingly. The group of officers began to break up and exit the briefing to locate their respective team rooms which had all been carefully signed off the main corridor by the spookily detailed Atticker.

Before midnight, the teams had begun to leave the overcrowded station yard and head off in the direction of the beam of light that the helicopter's night-sun lantern was scanning backward and forward across The Link Estate. Like some biblical exodus from Pharaoh's Egypt, the convoy of vans and patrol cars followed the aircraft's pillar-of-fire to their own promised land.

By this time, Janet Seymour had arrived at the station and was seated in the Inspector's office wearing the smartest throw-ons she could manage to grab when hurriedly jolted from her bed by the officers sent to collect her. She watched patiently through the glass-panelled door as the DI chatted quietly but intently with the Superintendent outside the office. Priest nodded in finalisation of the conversation and opened the office door.

"Sorry about that Miss Seymour and can I first apologise for getting you down here at this time of night. However, I'm sure you'll understand my reason for urgency in a moment."

He went on to describe the day's events and, as he continued, the spinster's jaw dropped lower and lower.

"I can see from your reaction that this doesn't seem to ring true with you."

"Well, no. In fact I'm astounded. I know he was having a few medical issues in the last week or so but this is unbelievable."

"Medical issues?" the Inspector quizzed.

"Yes. He's not been in work now for, what, a week, and he's off for another fortnight pending a medical review board."

Priest suspiciously picked up on the reference to a week off work and noted the coincidence in timing to the last reported street robbery.

"Sounds serious," he feigned sympathetically, wanting to draw as much personal information from the guy's supervisor before damning him as a psychotic kidnapper. "Mental problems?" he prompted.

"Not in the way the stereotype might suggest, but he has been diagnosed as epileptic which I suppose is a condition of the mind. He was apparently unconscious for three days after his first attack last Tuesday."

Again Priest's suspicions were peaked. Last Tuesday? That was the day of Mrs Nugent's robbery. A stretch in hospital would certainly account for the sudden cessation of subsequent offences.

"Do you know what time on Tuesday he suffered the attack?" he asked, already formulating a timetable of events for the pensioner's last day on her feet.

"I'm not sure. I think it was sometime mid-morning."

'Bingo,' thought Priest. This was definitely our man, he hastily concluded.

"Has he shown any signs of deteriorating health over the last few months?" he continued. 'Since the robberies began,' he simultaneously thought.

"Well, he did seem to be increasingly depressed since the breakup of the relationship with his girlfriend. Lucy was her name, I think. She came to last year's Christmas party and it was obvious he was besotted with the girl."

'*Christ*', Priest thought, '*this guys a classic mind-melt patient.*'

"Okay, well let's have a look at the address details you've retrieved for us and we'll take it from there."

***

With a swoosh, the boot lid swung open.

"Out," he ordered with a less concerned tone than he'd used earlier, after Murray had suffered at his efforts to lift her from the factory floor.

Still gagged and bound, Murray thought the order pretty mute. She vainly attempted to lift her legs from their curled position beneath her but again found herself relying on her, now more assertive, captor. It occurred to her that he had been dwelling on her predicament during the long uneventful journey and concluded, by his tone, that he had hardened his resolve to rid himself of this legal inquisitor. Her suspicions were confirmed by the manner in which he grabbed her upper arms and tugged harshly at her aching, folded body to wrench her from the enclosed space of the car's boot.

She again let out a muffled squeal as the bindings around her wrists tightened with his efforts to remove her. However, this time he did not release her to relieve the pain. He wanted her out of the car and continued to drag her twisted and tortured body over the boot-lip and onto the floor. She landed in a heap and knew now that the end was coming. His increasing disregard for her was, she decided, an obvious pre-cursor to the final act of murder she had feared since first regaining consciousness some hours before.

If she was going to somehow survive the night, she would have to act within the next few moments. As he lifted her to her feet, she realised that the effort of dragging her from the car had dislodged the bottom of the tape from around her eyes. She could see a slither of detail down toward the ground. She momentarily found herself lifting her head in order to see her attacker's face but stopped herself, realising that doing so would divulge this additional benefit to her captor who would then reset the tape and take it from her. Instead, she satisfied herself with the ability to see the floor a few feet ahead of her. It was dark and she could see that the ground around her was made up of large, coarse gravel. It was reminiscent of a railway and, sure enough, she soon found herself being led across the first metal rail of a concrete-sleepered track.

"Watch your step," he directed.

Unbeknown to him, of course, Murray had already seen the rail but, intentionally, she kicked a foot against the metal and jerked her body, as if tripping, to reinforce the impression she was still fully blindfolded. As they continued, now along the line, Murray sensed a change in the crunching tone of the rocks beneath their feet. It had begun to echo and she realised they were approaching a tunnel. It was now or never. Her only weapons were her untied feet and she decided upon the only target she felt would prove capable of incapacitating her enemy.

He was in front of her, facing ahead as he led her along the track. She feigned a stumble, dropped to one knee and broke free of his grip. Then she rolled backward onto the sharp, inter-concrete ballast. In reaction, he span to regain control of her and, as she had hoped, stepped quickly toward her prone body and straddled her feet to bend down and make a grab for her upper arms. With all her reserve strength, and carefully marking her target from her restricted field of view, she coiled her right leg high into her chest before arching her back, aligning her body and driving her sole deep into his groin. There was a sudden expelling of air and the change from superior to inferior was almost instantaneous. He crumpled over to one side and, with his diverted hands failing to break his fall, his head hit the far rail with a thud.

Her own agonising injuries were forgotten in her moment of triumph and she gymnastically threw her legs over her own head and into a swift backward roll to bring herself into a crouched, kneeling position. She pushed up forward and was quickly standing over the sprawled, groaning heap of a man. Although her adrenalin was through the roof, his diminished, but conscious condition was not going to provide her with enough time for a realistic prospect of escape. She held her head back in an unnatural arch to partially see her target and repeatedly kicked until the groaning stopped. Then she turned and ran. They had walked about two or three hundred metres before the mouth of the tunnel but, in her state of excited delirium, she soon lost her bearings as to where the car was.

She stumbled on toward where she thought it might be but, in her haste, overran the site of the abandoned vehicle. Her heart was pounding and, hyperventilating, she soon became dizzy and disoriented. She wanted to stop and remove the bindings but she had already failed to do that when calm and controlled back at the factory. She didn't want to lose time here. Her attacker could be conscious and after her already. The thought powered her lead-like legs onward and she scrambled forward along the line toward where she believed the car would be.

'Must be close,' she desperately thought as she turned sharply to get off the line.

There was a sudden sharpness across her thighs and she tumbled forward. Unable to stop herself, with her hands tied, she rolled on to the cold, iron girder and, briefly feeling the large, mushroom-headed rivets against the soft tissue of her abdomen, continued over the parapet and into a silent nothingness. A gut-churning weightlessness followed by a sudden, breathtakingly cold immersion and Murray was gone.

Chapter Ten

Gradually regaining consciousness, he heard a distant and peculiarly synthesised buzzing, its tones hypnotically rising and falling. Next, he felt the cold of the narrow metallic pillow beneath his head. The increasing vibration evolved into a low rumble and he began to feel the swollen contusions on his face and head, the taste of blood in his mouth. In the darkness, his returning sight initially had him believing he was standing close to some roughly rendered wall. His mind re-focused and his pupils widened to capture the full gravity of his situation.

'Bitch,' he thought. He had brought her here to be rid of her but instead *he* was the barely conscious victim. He admired her tenacity but it was a short-lived respect. She had found him at the factory and knew he was called David. With the information she must have had linking him to the muggings, she could put him away for a very long time. The ramifications of her escape suddenly took a back seat to an ear-splitting, high-low siren-blast.

It was the warning alert of a train entering the other end of the tunnel and lying within the rails of the outgoing line was definitely the wrong place to be. He had mere seconds to clear the track if he wasn't going to be crushed and dismembered into a dozen or more pieces. Turning to face into the tunnel, his worst thoughts were confirmed. The bright, single headlight of the oncoming train was practically on top of him already and the previously hypnotic vibrations had erupted into a violent cacophony of deafening sound. Gripping the nearest rail with both hands, he jerked his body in line with the edge of the track and span violently over it to the barely relative safety of the outer sleeper limits. With hardly a split second to spare, the engine's first wheels roared past his head.

He had never heard anything as loud. Then again, the noise was more *felt* than heard. The accompanying blast of wind tore at his clothes like a giant beast slashing at its pinned prey and he froze to the spot, terrified that the slightest movement would allow the creature to snag a hold of him and drag his insignificant body into its gnashing, deadly teeth. Seconds seemed to slow into minutes and, as the tumultuous roar of the giant diesel engine was replaced by the more rhythmic rumble of passing dolly sets, he found the breath, which he'd unwittingly been holding, was running out. A gasp for air only sucked in a distasteful lungful of oil vapour that was being strewn from the hundreds of greased wagon axles and he felt a sudden nausea.

Desperately rolling away from the line, he reached the limit of the ballast and, once into the rough grass of the parallel embankment, arched up onto all fours and brutally vomited until his stomach could offer no more. The train had become a distant red speck and the air around him grew still. The diminishing whistle of the vibrating rail was exchanged for a ringing tinnitus and he slowly lifted himself to his feet. Roughly wiping the vomit from his pained, bruised face, he began to walk back toward the car he had stolen to bring that troublesome copper to this thwarted execution.

Reaching the abandoned vehicle, and assuming that Murray was long gone, he decided a number of loose ends needed tying up before he left the Hopefield area for good. He sat in the dim glow of the vehicle's interior light and retrieved the phone and notebook he'd taken from the detective earlier. The phone's battery was dead and he cast it aside, slowly re-reading the officer's note book for any clue as to his next move instead. Twenty or so miles back to the outskirts of the town, he could leave the car at a large shopping centre. It would remain unfound there for days, hidden without suspicion amongst the hundreds of other cars. It was a plan, or at least the start of one, and he turned the ignition key, resolving to add to it as he drove.

Arriving at the large retail park, he locked the car and walked away toward the exit. He considered returning to it to

81

make his final departure but for now it was too risky to use in the imminent daylight for the remaining journey into town. The buses weren't yet running so he turned up the collar of his coat and stuffed his hands deep into his pockets to spare them from the day's pre-dawn chill. He strode purposefully toward The Link Estate once again wondering how he had become an overnight fugitive.

Ahead of him, high enough to be lit by the rising sun, he noticed the black and orange body of the police helicopter circling the distant industrial zone. Considering the likelihood that it was looking for him, he turned into the entrance of the Westgate Park to avoid a direct path beneath it and as the large disc of the sun's orange light broke the horizon he strode across the open playing fields toward Trojan Way.

His lip was fat and his head was aching with the blows which the escaped Murray had rained down upon him. That crushing blow to his family jewels wouldn't be forgotten either. As he reached the park's exit onto the adjoining housing estate, he began to feel dizzy. Whether from the effort of the fast-paced walk, the blows to his head or a combination of the two, he became increasingly light-headed. His vision smoothly tunnelled inward toward blackness and his final image was the ground rolling out of sight in favour of the dawning skyline.

***

"Any update Sergeant?" the Inspector's voice struggled over the air against the whining helicopter engines.

"Nothing yet Sir," Backhouse shouted the reply. "There've been no sightings of DC Murray's car. Searches of all premises on Links Eight to Four have been completed. We're moving on down toward the by-pass and the waste ground now that we've got the daylight."

"Anything from the helicopter's thermal imager?"

"Nothing at all I'm afraid. In fact the chopper's looking to stand down, now that the sun's up, in favour of a more thorough search by the ground teams. The fact is, they've been up and down now for the best part of eight hours and the pilot is concerned about the flying time for the month."

"I don't care about their hours. Keep them there Steve. This search is far from over."

"Roger that Boss." Backhouse turned to Barnes at his side and passed on the news for him to relate to the hovering aircraft on his radio. Barnes had been on the Air Support Unit's channel throughout the night and was becoming increasingly demoralised at passing the updates of their progress, or rather lack of it, to his supervisor. He could hear the rising frustration in Backhouse's voice and was beginning to sense that, in some way, the veteran detective was bearing a greater proportion of responsibility for the missing officer's situation than Barnes thought he should.

'Had he sent Lizzy out alone?' Barnes pondered. As quickly as he had formed the thought, he dismissed it as ridiculous. If Lizzy was missing as a direct result of an instruction from their supervisor, Backhouse would have had a better idea of where she had gone. No, Backhouse was as perplexed at the young woman's disappearance as the rest of them. His growing frustration was simple concern, he concluded. Lizzy was part of his team and no-one wanted to lose part of a team, part of a family.

"Lima Golf Two Six to DS Backhouse." The call, coming across Backhouse's radio, immediately attuned the pair's attention.

Lima Golf patrols were dog handlers and when they shouted up it was for a good reason. Two Six, PC John Evans, had found something, something relevant, something important.

"Go ahead," the Sergeant eagerly responded.

"Sergeant, I'm down on Link One with team seven. We've been searching around a disused factory at the end of the road and the dog has picked up a trail from the roller doors to a side entrance. It's the detached unit on the right with the tall chimney. Do you want us to go in or standby for you to get down here?"

"Standby there. I'm two minutes away. Good work."

Backhouse dropped from his standing position in the open doorway of his car and started the engine in one smooth movement. The vehicle was in gear and rolling before Barnes's door was even closed and the car wheel-span away toward Link One. As he drove, Backhouse barked into his radio, calling in other dog units and search officers to surround the desolate factory. Then, with his free hand, he swerved the speeding car into the access road to the disused building and drew the vehicle to a sharp halt outside the roller doors. He flung the door open and strode briskly to the group of officers making up search team seven that were waiting toward the right hand end of the building with the dog handler.

"Hi Pete," he said, acknowledging the uniformed Sergeant leading the team.

"Long time, no see," he added. However, without waiting for the pleasantry of a reply he began to direct the team along with the other officers arriving at the factory.

"Pete, as you were here first I want you to take the lead once we're inside. It looks like a three storey set-up so take team two with you and have them secure the stairwells as you find them, at least two officers to each. Understood?"

The attentive Sergeant nodded the affirmative.

"Giles, I want you to take your team and team six and cover the exits around the building. I noticed at least one other entrance similar to this one at the other end and while I appreciate they're shuttered at the moment there's nothing saying they can't be opened from inside. In addition, I don't want this character coming out of a first floor window or any of the fire escapes and slipping by us, okay?"

The young search team Sergeant also nodded in agreement and Backhouse turned his attention to the dog handler who had led them to the factory.

"Nice work John. I want you to take 'Pookhams' here and go in first with Pete's team and team two to see if you can pursue the track you got out here. Hopefully that'll narrow down the search area. Right, listen very carefully everyone. Taking our lead from John here I want a room-by-room search of the entire building, ground floor up. If this Lewis guy is inside with Lizzy, he's going to know we're here already so I'm not going to give him the time to draw this out into a hostage situation. I want a fast search and, unless we come up against him with a knife to her throat, I want a swift and hard take-down. No pussy footing around. This *tosser* has kidnapped a colleague and is to be treated accordingly. Am I understood?"

The group of officers heartily agreed with the Sergeant's plan of action, all but one. Backhouse's reputation for action was alive and kicking and the assembled officers, tired of having their hands bound by the bureaucracy of modern day policing were more than happy to give Mr Lewis what was coming to him. All that is, except Barnes. As the teams broke away from the hasty briefing, he tugged the Sergeant's coat sleeve like a small child might approach a disapproving parent and meekly suggested,

"Sarge, if we believe that Lewis is actually here don't you think we should notify the FIM* and wait for a negotiator?"

"Nah, bollocks to 'em," Backhouse snapped in response to the young detective's adhesion to policy. "I'm not giving this bastard any room for manoeuvre and waiting for those three-ring clowns will give him just that."

Barnes realised any further suggestions would be unwelcome at best and kept his thoughts on the response to himself. Yet again though, he found it curious that Backhouse seemed so driven to bring this operation to a rapid conclusion and he made a mental note to include the reply in his notebook later in case this course of action went severely pear-shaped. Should Murray, or even Lewis for that matter, get injured or worse as a result of Backhouse's haste, he was going to make very sure that he could account for his actions and distance himself from the Sergeant's cavalier attitude.

The dog handler entered through the small, lower-panel opening in the recessed doorway and reached out to the search team officer behind him. He retrieved the lead he had given the officer to keep his dog, Satan, outside until he was in a position to control him inside the building. When considering the bulk and long black coat of the specially trained Alsatian, the real name was certainly more appropriate than Backhouse's moniker for him but his handler, John, wasn't so specialised that he failed to see the humour in Backhouse's earlier quip.

The remaining team members waited patiently for the handler to give an all clear before making their entry. Satan could be heard shuffling through the broken safety-glass inside the doorway.

"Let DS Backhouse know. There's a stairwell immediately to the right and the dog is indicating a track to the first floor. Does he want me to take it or let the search team go ahead?" the experienced handler asked.

Backhouse was close to the narrow opening and answered for himself.

"John, you go on but, Pete, keep your team close behind him in case there's a welcoming committee."

Team seven, led by their Sergeant, filed through the doorway and assembled briefly inside before being directed by the competent search supervisor as to the order in which they should follow the dog handler. John allowed his charge some lead-slack and the dog bounded up the stairwell and promptly disappeared out of view around the half way turn of the whitewashed concrete rise. The handler gripped the rope and drew it in as he climbed the steps to the turn in order to stop the dog getting any further ahead. As he reached the turn himself, he repeated the action and Satan again bounded to the first floor landing. John followed him up and saw that the sensitive nose of his loyal companion was centring on the open area of the dusty office floor. Sensing the track had come to a conclusion, he pulled the dog away, back under closer control, to ensure no forensic clues might be destroyed by the inquisitive beast's snuffling nose.

There was no-one present and he could see for himself that the grime and dirt on the floor had been disturbed by what appeared to be some sort of struggle. However, he knew his role was over for now and he dutifully stood aside to let the search teams do their work. He reached down and gave the now seated Satan some well deserved praise by heavily stroking through the dog's thick mane from head-top to mid-back. "Good boy," he quietly commended.

Backhouse had joined them on the middle floor of the factory and he scanned the room in a quick but precise manner. He looked toward the dog handler.

"Track end here does it?" he enquired.

"Seems to Sarge."

"Okay, nice job. Go and join team two downstairs and once the ground floor's done check the second floor. Remind team two's Sergeant to keep the stairwells covered as you move on. I doubt this can be the only set of stairs in a place this size."

"Will do Sarge," the handler said, and with that he gently tugged Satan to his feet and back into action.

Turning his attentions back to the open plan office, Backhouse again checked around to get a feeling for the minute details that may tell a story of what had occurred. The disturbed floor dirt was obvious enough but there were other indications of previous habitation as well.

"Sarge," one of the search officers interjected, pointing across the room at an old table. "Is that blood over there just near to that desk?"

Sure enough, he was right. Backhouse carefully picked his way between the potentially tell-tale footprints spread across the floor and approached the tiny pooling of blood the sharp-eyed officer had spotted. Although its edges were congealed, it was still liquid enough to tell the seasoned detective that it had only been here a matter of hours.

"Get CSI in here," he called back to Barnes, who had just finished the short climb from the ground floor. "I want this swabbed and taken to the Lab straight away. See to it yourself and make sure they test it for Lizzy's DNA while you wait. I want a result within the hour so don't let them fob you off with any *'too busy'* crap. Got that?"

"Yes Sarge," Barnes replied setting off back outside to make the call.

Backhouse continued his search of the room. On the table, above the blood, there was an old tool box. The lid was up and a roll of beige masking tape was precariously balanced on the edge of one of its internal trays. Pulling on a pair of latex gloves, promptly handed to him on request by one of the search team officers, he carefully lifted the box and, seeing no difference in the amount of dust beneath it to that of the surrounding table he confidently announced,

"This hasn't been here long either. I'll bet a pound to a pinch of shit he's tied Lizzy up with this tape. And, if she's bound but not here, he must have... JOHN." His shout echoed down the stairwell to the dog handler on the ground floor.

"Sarge?" came the distant reply.

"Check down there for tyre marks. He's driven out of here."

Chapter Eleven

Pinpoints of light began to grow beneath the swollen eyelids of the prostrate David Lewis. Like a soon forgotten dream, the fleeting memories of restraining a woman, of bundling her into a car's boot and walking into a darkened ... something ... pain ... no, it was gone. David could no longer recollect what he suspected were the events of the previous night and he released a frustrated groan through what felt like the cotton-packed mouth of a dental patient.

His mind had been enduring a festival of confusion over the last week or so and he was growing increasingly desperate at the feeling he was losing control of it. Worse still, with the images of violence he had been recalling as his own, he feared his actions were as equally lost.

"Oh, so you're back with us again David. And a little quicker than last time; that's a good sign."

The now familiar voice of Dr Reynolds reached into David's dazed senses. He was back in the hospital and the good doctor was leaning inquisitively over the groggy young man shining a small bright torch into his eyes in order to test his returning reactions.

"Well, I'm not sure I want to know how you came about all these cuts and bruises but I do know that you appear to have suffered another seizure. Have you taken the medication we had settled on or did you not get the chance?" the doctor quipped, referring to the short time David had been out of the ward since his release the previous day.

David tried to speak and inform the bemused physician that he had taken the veritable cocktail of drugs as instructed but again he found himself blubbering through a stinging pair of fattened lips. As his senses regained their full strength,

David began to taste the dried blood inside his mouth. His tongue rolled lazily across his teeth and he realised that at least one pre-molar was missing from the right side of his jaw. He carefully moved the swollen mandible from side to side before the doctor interrupted the action.

"Careful there, we think that may be broken. You took quite a beating. Do you remember anything?"

David did have some vague recollections but none he wanted to share with the friendly medic. Instead, after a small pause for thought, he released a low groan and shook his aching head.

"Well," the doctor continued, "whatever happened, it seems to have triggered another episode. If it hadn't been for that chap walking his dog finding you, you may have laid out there in the cold for a great deal of time. Despite your appearance, you're actually very lucky."

Lucky or not David couldn't help but feel troubled by the images which had left him moments earlier. He had already run the gauntlet of desperate guilt over the mugging of the old lady. He'd been so sure that, in some bizarre way, he had been responsible for that horrible crime. However, that female detective had dismissed his confession, his very memories. Now he was seeing more terrible acts. He struggled to make sense of it all.

His mind suddenly flashed an image of the young detective, but not from the interview room. He saw her lying, curled like a sleeping animal, calm and quiet. The image sharpened. She was bound and gagged. These were his eyes looking down at her, his hands reaching from his torso to search her clothes, to retrieve a phone, a notebook and some keys. A sense of screaming pierced his silent contemplation of the witnessed horror and as instantly as it had appeared the image was gone. It couldn't be true. Had he really lost control of his mind? He winced at the realisation he had again committed a crime, a violent crime.

"Are you alright David? You weren't with us for a moment there."

He was not alright, not alright at all, but he doubted it was

90

anything that the doctor could help him with. He drooled a barely coherent, "Tired," to the attentive young man and rolled his head and body away in a shameful dismissal of any further assistance.

"Very well," the doctor acceptingly announced. "We'll talk again later."

David made no response. His mind was slipping, fast, into a gravity-well of despair, spiralling ever downward into a pit of guilt and pain. He ignored the painful swellings about his head and face. *'No more than I deserve,'* he thought. The quiet ward grew heavy on his mind, like a crowd of faces were staring deep into his very soul. Then the images began to return and he re-witnessed the whole sorry episode of the previous day's events. A tear of remorse rolled from his cheek onto the crisp white sheets of his hospital bed; or was it a droplet of fear that he was no longer David Lewis, no longer the bored-but-helpful civil servant of just a fortnight before? What was he to do next? Did he even want there to be a next? He tried to close his slit-lid eyes and drift away to sleep, but the images kept replaying themselves over and over and his tortured mind ached with regret.

***

"Lucy, can you pass me the pink, floral cellophane please?"

"There you go," the pretty young brunette replied as she reached under the counter of the single-fronted flower shop.

"Thanks," her boss said as she leaned through the adjoining door, took the roll and, one handed, flung it unravelling across the wide preparation table of the rear work room. "You know this guy's been buying a dozen roses a week for his wife since we opened," she commented as she arranged the deep scarlet flowers she had been holding across the unrolled wrapping.

"Really?" Lucy quizzed.

She had only been working at the shop a few months, since her break up with David. She caught herself still gauging her life in periods of *before* and *after* the split but she couldn't help thinking that she still loved him, despite the nasty habit he'd developed. Maybe she could have, even should have, stayed with him and helped him through the problem? Her lingering thoughts were drawn back to the moment.

"Yeah, and we've been here, what, nine years now," her boss continued, oblivious to the young girls wandering mind. "You know the dope must have spent a bloody fortune on her," she joked, laughing out loud.

"Still, must be nice to have someone willing to devote themselves to you that much," Lucy replied in a long sighing breath.

"Ooh dear, you've got it bad. What's his name then?" her boss asked intrusively.

Lucy's new boss was a terrible gossip and found the social lives of her customers and employees alike intensely interesting; and fantastic chat-material to boot!

"Oh, no-one," she lied. "I'm on about the rose guy."

"Sure you are," her boss said sarcastically. She left it at that though. There would be plenty of time to delve into her apprentice's private matters later. Besides, the door chime rang-out the arrival of a new customer and the inexperienced assistant could only concentrate on one thing at a time, for now.

"Morning. Can I help you?"

"Yes. I'd like to order a bouquet for delivery to the hospital please."

"Certainly. Any favourite blooms and how much would you like to spend?"

"Thirty pounds please, I'm not sure about the flowers. What would you recommend? My sister's just had a little girl."

"Oh, how lovely," Lucy exclaimed. She again found herself thinking about David. Before they had split, their relationship had reached a point where she had been considering a baby herself and the thought of a newborn baby girl made her feel broody again.

"Yeah, she's gorgeous." The woman screwed her face in a gooey expression. "She's all wrinkly and serious looking but she's so cute."

Lucy pondered, "Well... Margaret," she called through to the back room "what would you recommend for a baby girl?"

"What about some lovely powder pink, thornless roses with some white chrysanthemums and a sprig of gypsy?" the store owner called through.

"That sounds lovely."

The woman completed the order and Lucy took the details of the recipient at the local maternity ward.

"I'd deliver them myself but we're off on holiday in a couple of hours and you know what it's like trying to organise the kids. Can you get them there today?"

Lucy glanced over at Margaret for an answer on the query.

"The flowers or the kids?" Margaret and the woman laughed shallowly. "No problem," she assured the customer. "Lucy, how do you fancy a trip to the maternity ward?"

"Do I!" the young assistant eagerly replied. The chance to surround herself with babies was an opportunity not to be missed.

***

It was early afternoon and David Lewis was again ready to be released from hospital. His latest seizure had only left him unconscious for a couple of hours that morning and Doctor Reynolds was happy at his diagnosis that the episode was a result of the assault David had suffered and not any sort of problem with the medication he had prescribed the previous day. In addition, the latest x-rays of David's jaw had shown no fractures but just a swollen ligament. Without the need for further treatment, David was free to leave with a pocket full of anti-inflammatory tablets and a 'be careful' warning from the doctor.

"Are you going to go to the police about the assault?" nurse Mills asked David.

"Not sure yet," David responded, using as few words as his swollen jaw would allow.

"Well, take care of yourself... this time," she added.

The nurse was barely older than the young patient but her

93

tone was almost as condescending as a parent chastising a naughty child. David, however, saw the gentle concern from the mild-mannered nurse in the way it was intended and smiled as well as his contorted lips could manage. He picked up his coat and left the ward by the now familiar route to the reception area. He turned the last corner to the large foyer area and almost knocked straight into a large bouquet of pink and white flowers. He snapped his body into an abrupt rearward-leaning halt and automatically blurted out,

"Excuse me."

As he did so, his left hand reactively raised up to steady the stalling approach of the fragrant-arrangement's bearer. His fingers touched the delicate wrist of the petite courier and he suddenly felt a searing hot flash of agonising pain in his right temple. He lowered and snapped his head to the right, reaching up with his hand to cradle the superheated spot. His eyes instinctively clasped shut in response but before his hand even reached the seemingly punctured flesh the pain was gone and he was left with a sense of terminal darkness.

"Are you alright?" the young delivery girl asked as she lowered the bouquet. "David!" she added, half shocked, half excited by the chance meeting.

David opened his eyes in reaction to the use of his name. "Lucy," he exclaimed. There was an awful pause.

"My God," Lucy exclaimed. "What happened to you?"

"Err, I was mugged last night," David meekly offered. He didn't want to divulge the onset of his epilepsy at this stage in the conversation. In fact, he vainly hoped the chance meeting would prove to be the opportunity he wanted to win Lucy back.

"How awful. Did I catch your face with the cellophane?" she asked referring to David's short-lived wince as they had collided.

"No, no, I don't know what that was." This was a more truthful response. "Are you visiting someone?" he asked, changing the subject to the impressive arrangement Lucy was carrying.

"No," she replied, diverted from the beaten appearance of

her ex-boyfriend. "I'm delivering them to someone in the maternity ward. I work at Blossoms Florist on the High Street now."

"Oh, that's nice." David was struggling for conversation, for reasons to keep Lucy from her task; and here, talking to him.

"Well, I'd better get these to the maternity ward," she said waiting for any sign that David wanted her to stay. There was an awkward silence before David offered,

"Well it was nice seeing you again."

"Yeah, nice," she disappointedly replied. They began to part ways but Lucy wanted to say something more. "Listen, David. Do you want to meet later on for a chat?"

She had put her heart at the very limit of her sleeve but was prepared to take the risk. David paused for a moment, surprised into silence by her unexpected and reconciliatory tone but was more than happy to accept the invitation. It was more than he could have hoped for. *She* had left him and now *she* wanted to meet again. She had opened a door back into her life and he was utterly ready to step through it.

"Yeah sure, that'll be great," he said, ignoring the stinging stretch of his inanely grinning face.

"I'll call you," she replied, equally as happy with the outcome.

With that, they parted ways and for the first time in weeks David felt an upturn in his mood. He walked away toward the exit doors and turned back to admire the shapely figure of the girl he hoped to be holding closely again in the not too distant future. However, she had already turned the nearby corner and was out of sight. He left through the sliding doors and happily strode toward the bus stop he had used just the previous day. However, with each pace, the balance of his thoughts began to sway back from the pretty Lucy toward the belief of his involvement in the recent crimes.

'It's a very complicated organ,' he recalled the doctor's words. How complicated could it be? Could he be committing these offences while being unaware of them? Could he be somehow affected by the epilepsy into unconscious bouts of violence

which he could only recall after the seizures; some sort of temporary memory loss? The doctor had said that was possible, even likely, but that didn't explain the symptoms he was experiencing, the blistering wrists, the sharp, short-lived pains.

He remained as confused as ever but what should he do now? He didn't know what had happened to Murray after the railway tunnel. Was she alright? Should he go to the police station to find out? What if she hadn't reached the town?

'My God,' he thought. *'What if she was dead?'* If she *was* he was now a murderer, not just a mugger. *'Just a mugger!!'* What was he thinking? Could he really have just belittled a crime which a fortnight before he would have found abhorrent? How could he know for sure?

It occurred to him that the death of a police officer would be big news. He walked away from the bus stop and approached a nearby paper shop. He scanned the headlines to look for some clue as to the detective's demise but he could not find any reference to it. Then again, it was only three o'clock. If she had collapsed somewhere between the tunnel and the town the previous night she may not have been found in time for the papers to have printed a story that morning. He thought for a moment. Television was more likely to be up to date.

He glanced up and saw a screen high in the corner behind the newsagents counter, but it was just a closed circuit monitor and he found himself looking at his own recorded image. He left the shop and walked along the small promenade. Four shops along he found what he was looking for. He stood watching the multitude of varying sized screens. After what seemed an eternity, the local news programme finally began; and there it was.

Even without the sound, he instantly knew the subject of the opening story. A file picture of DC Murray was followed by a short interview of a high ranking officer outside the police station. Then, what he'd been dreading; a poor quality, but none the less discernable, photo of him; of David Lewis.

His mind raced into acute paranoia. Out of the corner of

his eye, he caught the shop assistant approaching the front of the store. The suited assistant opened the door and spoke to the transfixed young man.

"Anything I can interest you in Sir?"

Without the courtesy of a response, David turned and walked quickly away. He was a wanted man and he knew his life was now completely inverted. What had begun as a curious sensation of disjointed guilt had now become a manhunt; with *him* as the prey.

***

Lucy turned the wheel of the small, floral-liveried van and pulled into the narrow alleyway leading to the rear of Blossoms. Parking it neatly against the rear wall of the tiny yard, she stepped from the driver's door and happily flung it closed before briskly walking to the shop's rear staff entrance.

She was delighted with her chance meeting with David. It had made her realise how much she had missed him and she was determined that she was going to make good her hasty departure some four months before. She decided that she was going to help him kick his habit and then they would pick up where they left off. Then, who knows, maybe she'd be the one getting flowers at the hospital?

She walked through the shop's rear staff corridor, narrowed by piles of wire-reels, ribbons and oasis, and called ahead to her boss.

"Hiya, I'm back."

"You're chirpy. Did all those babies take your mind of your love-life?" Margaret said, taking another deliberate stab at her earlier supposition that Lucy had recently ended a relationship.

"I don't know *quite* what you're on about," Lucy replied in a humorously sarcastic way. However, as she reached the workroom her faced dropped. Over on the worktop, she saw an image of David on the television screen.

"Was the baby lovely …?"

Open mouthed, Lucy held up a dismissive hand and Margaret instantly knew there was something important about the young man pictured on the screen. She reached over and turned up the sound and with the mention of David's name a shattered Lucy was in tears.

Chapter Twelve

David was confused and increasingly desperate. From the television broadcast, it was obvious, at least to him, that Murray had met an untimely end and that he was responsible. Even the niggling doubts that remained in some dark recess of his mind couldn't argue with the connection the police had made between him and her disappearance, as portrayed on the multitude of screens in the high street television store.

He had resolved to hand himself in over the street robbery of the old lady from the bus stop but this was altogether something different. He damned the detective for not having believed him in the first place; for not keeping him in custody to face the appropriate punishment for his crimes. She had let him go and his alter-ego, as he had now decided it must have been, had sought her out for some wicked revenge. How could he regain control over the beast his self-tortured mind had created out of its struggle with his newly developed illness?

Wandering on, away from the town and out toward the Westgate Park, he felt that amongst its acres of copse-dotted parkland he could find the quiet his mind needed to make some sense of the past few days' events. Besides, it was in the direction he last recalled seeing DC Murray. If he could search for her, even find her, his mind could have at least one answer; a direction to give his upturned life.

He also knew that he couldn't return to the place he once called *home* or, indeed, any of his other regular haunts. They would surely be crawling with police by now. Options, both plausible and ridiculous, plagued his every thought and, as he walked staunchly on, he began verbally arguing with himself, his conscience split between morality and self-preservation.

The duality of it was suddenly confirmed, to what small, logical corner of lucidity his brain still possessed. He had indeed taken on some sort of Jekyll-and-Hyde persona. He was, in fact, losing his mind!

David entered the park and continued across its expansive grassland before engulfing himself in the thickening woods that made up the west edge of the park. He found a quiet clearing and sat down at the base of an ancient oak tree. He leaned back against its broad trunk, closed his eyes and allowed the diminishing figure of his remaining sanity to dwindle away from his mind's eye, like some freefalling parachutist, into the oblivion that was the chasm of doubt below.

***

He slowly opened his eyes to be greeted by a large, black, wet nose sniffing at his shallow breath.

"George, come away," the dog's owner called. The giant, drooling Great Dane lifted his head back toward his mistress and trotted away with a pendulous gait.

"Are you alright?" the owner asked.

"I'm fine," he sharply replied raising his own head from his horizontal sleeping position.

"Ooh, that looks nasty," the woman exclaimed, referring to the swollen face of the recumbent stranger. "Would you like me to call an ambulance, or the police? Has someone beaten you up?"

"No. No police," he said. "Thank you," he belatedly added, hoping that a more pleasant tone would dismiss the over interested rambler.

"Oh, okay," she replied in a curious tone. "Are you sure you'll be alright?"

"I'll be fine," he said dismissively.

"Okay," she concluded. "Come on George. Let's leave the young man alone." The woman retrieved the lumbering canine from the nearby bushes and continued on her way.

Now fully awake, the dog's pungent breath still strong in his nostrils, he rolled onto all fours and raised up onto his knees. He didn't know how long he'd been asleep but from the position of the sun he decided it was late afternoon. Besides, the craving for another score was powerfully present so he knew for sure it was well after midday.

He reached into his underpants and fumbled for the remaining cash from the old lady's bag. It was still there so he reached into his pocket for his phone to make the regular call to his dealer. It was late in the day so he knew he may struggle to be served-up. He hoped his dealer was busy enough to be flush with a second or even third batch for the day.

However, the phone was missing. He quickly padded down his other pockets. 'Shit', he thought, concluding he must have lost it back at the railway tunnel. It wasn't a problem though and he set off, walking the short distance to the wood's parking area before dialling the memorised number into the public payphone. He waited for the usual response.

"Go."

"Two brown."

"Where?"

"Westgate Park, rangers hut car park."

"Twenty minutes."

"There's something else."

"What?"

"I need a twizzer." There was a curious pause from the dealer.

"For?"

"To take care of some unwanted attention."

"Expensive."

"How much?" There was another short pause.

"One fifty. Hire only."

"Okay, twenty minutes then," he answered, accepting the no doubt inflated figure.

"One hour for the piece."

"Okay, one hour." He ended the call, moving back into the trees and out of sight to wait for his associates. He tugged the copper's notebook from his pocket and re-read the final pages to confirm his full understanding of the entries.

***

"You're going to have to stand your team down Steve," the Detective Inspector said in a sympathetic but nonetheless directive tone. "I know they don't want to leave the search but they've been on duty for over twenty hours now and I can't see how they can be much use to the search for much longer. They must all be shattered; I know I am."

It was Tuesday and past six in the evening. The DS, now back at the station and supervising the silver-command office which had been set up to co-ordinate the search efforts, raised his eyebrows in an accepting expression of his supervisor's assessment. He nodded,

"I know you're right boss but Lizzy is still out there somewhere and, apart from the items found at the factory that confirm she was right to have suspected Lewis, we've not got much to go on."

Earlier that day, in a side room off the open-plan first floor of the factory, the search team had recovered the handbag and purse belonging to Mrs Nugent, minus its cash of course. CSI had swabbed the drops of blood and it had indeed proven to belong to DC Murray. The lab were about to start testing the numerous syringes and other drugs paraphernalia recovered near to the pensioner's stolen items and the urine soaked duvet found in the open plan workshop was also waiting their attention.

Results were due by morning but Backhouse wasn't expecting a hit against the national DNA database. He already knew that Lewis had no form, no previous convictions, and as such would not be 'DNA confirmed', a prerequisite to being identifiable by use of the ever-improving investigative tool.

In addition, the tyre tracks found in the ground floor cargo bay by the dog handler, John, and his trusted partner, Satan, had been confirmed to match the standard tyres fitted to the Division's unmarked fleet. It had been concluded, by the lack of it being found anywhere else on the estate, that Lewis had used Murray's plain car to take her from the site.

This unfortunately meant, as the majority of police vehicles were kept fully fuelled when not in use, that she could be anywhere within a three to four hundred mile radius of

Hopefield; and that was only if Lewis hadn't found the fuel card. Its usage was a possibility already being monitored by Atticker in the hope of pinpointing the car's location and giving a direction of travel for the captive officer. So far, though, it was another dead-end enquiry.

"I appreciate your concern Steve but you've got to face facts," the Inspector continued. "The track's gone cold for now and you need to rest if you're going to continue to help DC Murray."

He needed rest? Backhouse was happy to let his staff go home for some well earned sleep but *he* was going nowhere.

"I'll get my head down for a couple of hours in my office but, if it's all the same with you, I'll not be going home. Besides, I doubt I'd get any proper sleep anyway."

The Inspector wasn't overly keen on letting his subordinate *crash down* in the police station but he could see in Backhouse's eyes that he was not for dissuading on the matter.

"Okay, but I want you to book out a proper camping cot from the emergency shelter stores in the basement. At least that way you'll have the chance of some proper rest. I don't want you just dumping your head on your desk for an hour."

Backhouse nodded, thankful for the useful suggestion and turned to leave the office to retrieve the sprung-steel framed put-up. The Inspector paused for a moment and then added,

"While you're at it Steve, get me one too will you?"

"Will do," Backhouse replied, his respect for the recently promoted officer growing tenfold with the request. He dropped in on the robbery team office and spoke with the surprisingly alert Atticker.

"Atticker, have the search teams been fully rotated yet?" he asked.

"The third shift has just arrived, Sarge. They're in their briefing now but should be on plot for eighteen thirty. The second shift will stand down and be away for nineteen hundred."

"And where are our guys?"

"They're helping with the search around the Trojan Road area, house-to-house and the like."

"Okay, call them in and stand them down for the night. I'm

nipping downstairs to the shelter store. Give me a shout when they're all back. I want a quick word before they get off."

"Understood," the officer replied.

With that, Backhouse wearily made his way, via the front desk's key-safe, to the stairwell at the far end of the building and descended the concrete steps into the murky bowels of the station.

He turned the heavy key in the steel, fireproof door and pulled it open. As the basement stairwell air rushed into the room, Backhouse followed it into the darkness. The air settled and the cool stench of mould filled his nostrils. He groped around for the light switch and, upon finding it, was greeted by a chorus of pinging and popping as the hundred or more fluorescent tubes flickered into life for what must have been the first time in months, if not years.

Hopefield station was the only one in the county with a full-size basement level and, as such, the store here held the vast majority of the constabulary's stock of emergency kit. Makeshift ex-military tent-shelters, dry-pack ration boxes and empty hessian sandbags were amongst the first items he could see that added to the musky odour in the air. The store was enormous. Shelves stretched away into the distance, filling the entire building area of the whole station in one giant room. He could see that, without guidance, finding a cot-bed amongst the dozens of rows of shelves was not going to be easy. To his left, just inside the door, he could see a long bench-like table.

The scene was reminiscent of his days in the army, years before, when raw recruits would be herded, single file, along the store's counter and issued an ever-growing pile of personal equipment and bedding before being spat out the other end, unable to see where they were going and expected to then blindly find their new barracks. The military-mould smell reinforced the picture and Backhouse found himself instinctively searching behind the counter for a stock-list manual.

It was obvious, by the fact he found one, that this particular store had been set up in an era when the police were a *force*, modelled on military standards, rather than, in his view, the more namby-pamby *service* it was now portrayed to be. The transition from authoritative to business-led never sat well with the veteran officer. Most of the police joining with and before him were ex-forces: disciplined, motivated and forceful.

Nowadays most were straight out of school and had be led around by the nose, unable to make a decision on their own initiative because they were too scared of the kick-back from an ever-more litigation-mad society. Sue for this, claim for that. He was sick of it, and glad to be leaving within the year.

He scanned the stock manual and then easily traced the requisite shelving. Taking two beds, he signed the old pre-computer, handwritten log book; checking the items out of the store. He extinguished the lights, returning the huge room to its darkened, time-warp state and locked the door behind him.

As he reached the office, the first of the robbery team were returning, informed of the official stand down by Atticker, as instructed. Backhouse filled himself a plastic cup of water from the cooler plumbed into the corner of the room and waited silently for the remainder of the team. Wazzer and Thomo were the last through the door having been out on a perimeter drive, west of the town, searching for Lizzy's errant vehicle.

"Okay everyone thanks for your efforts today. Well," he caught himself in the error "since last night in fact. Back for seven in the morning, please," he more suggested than ordered. "And bring your butties and flasks. We're going to take over the obs on Lewis's place in case the little shit turns up back there."

There were no objections. The detectives and constables alike arose slowly to their feet and filed out of the room. Atticker was the last to leave. Still busy on his computer, he informed the Sergeant of the day's actions before shutting down the plethora of open programs one by one. He too then followed his colleagues to the locker room and the rear staff exit beyond.

With the possibility of Murray's car being used by Lewis to take her almost anywhere in the country, Atticker had placed an urgent *marker* against the vehicle's PNC record. This meant that any officer in the country that checked the vehicle registration against the national database would be aware of the wayward detective's predicament and would take the action indicated by the free-text portion of the report.

In addition, he had also created a *hot-marker* on the surrounding forces ANPR* systems meaning that any automated camera checks against the registration would generate a text alert to both himself and DS Backhouse, twenty-four hours a day, to inform them of the sighting of the passing vehicle. There had still been no use of Murray's phone so the active cell-site-location check was still a none-starter.

As he set up the folding bed in his first floor office, Backhouse mulled over the day's events and scrutinised the enquiries he had set into motion in the attempt to trace his missing officer. He didn't want to wake up from his narrow but strangely comfortable-looking canvas bed only to think of something he could have already done. He snapped the last sprung-steel leg into place and stepped into the corridor with the second bed.

"There you go boss," he said as he propped the green roll-up against the Inspector's door jamb.

"Cheers Steve," the Inspector thanked him. "See you in the morning."

Backhouse glibly acknowledged the comment but believed he would be awake long before then. With that, he returned to his own adjacent office and moved the set up camp bed behind his desk, away from the direct light of the corridor. He slipped off his now potently odorous shoes and lay back onto the canvas matting. Like his team, his body was also shattered but his mind raced on. He continued pouring over every detail of his actions in the previous thirty six hours until, finally, his fatigue took over his thoughts and he drifted into a deep but troubled slumber.

Chapter Thirteen

The hour passed quickly and without further incident. The park was devoid of visitors, no more dog walkers or kids playing football. As in life he was alone, apart from, that was, his increasingly tenacious cravings. However, he was content in his isolation. In fact, he had often considered had it not been for his distinct lack of friends to supply him during visits he would happily be incarcerated for a lengthy stretch.

He had no responsibilities on the outside and the overbearing beauty of the world about him, even here in this idyllic spot, held no place in his cold and indifferent drug-stained heart. Apart from a distant ex-girlfriend, the only passion he'd ever held was found at the point of a needle and, in his totally corrupted state, he didn't even see the tragedy of his situation. Other than the ease at which he could sustain his habit, he had no real reason to remain at liberty.

Hearing the crunching of gravel in the nearby car park, he eagerly glanced out of his temporary hide of rhododendron bushes to see the familiar blue hatchback arriving as arranged. He stood and clumsily made his way to the undergrowth's edge. He caught the eye of the car's passenger and, in a feigned impression of actual friendship, half raised a nonchalant hand in recognition of their arrival. The passenger turned and made some unheard comment to the driver and the car swung steadily around the edge of the empty arena.

Now standing adjacent to the driver's side rear passenger door he stepped out of the semi-cover of the tree-line and strode the two or three paces to the car. He opened the door and stepped in. However, the vehicle didn't move away, as was the normal routine for his daily deal.

"What's wrong?" he asked.

"What's wrong? What's bloody wrong? What the hell does a low-life, ten pence, piece of shit like you want with a gun? And where did you get a ton fifty to pay for it so easily?"

He sensed that he was about to be taxed. As a non-dealing user, he may have been at the bottom of this particular food-chain but he wasn't going to be pushed around by a couple of Manc toe-rags only one rung above him on the heroin ladder.

"Listen," he cut in, in a dominating tone, "if you haven't got the twizzer just say so and I'll take my business elsewhere."

"Will you now?" the front seat passenger said in a surprised yet condescending tone. Rather than maintaining the belittling connection to his customer in the rear view mirror, he turned to look at him face-to-face.

"And that goes for *all* my business," he pathetically added, as if one user would make any actual difference to the pair.

"Oh!" the passenger remarked sarcastically, looking to his driver for an equally bemused chuckle. "*All* your business?" he quizzed. "I tell you what. Why don't you just give us the ton-fifty and whatever else you've got in those smelly gruds of yours and we'll *think* about getting you a piece to go *pop-pop* at your friends."

He knew now that his dealers had not come to supply him with either his daily two-bag or the weapon he had requested. He knew they indeed intended to tax him, to turn him over for *his* money, and he was too involved with the intrusive DC Murray and her informant to let them do that. Wherever he ended up running to, he would need that money to get started again; to get into a new dealer to keep his cravings at bay. No, these two clowns had overstepped the mark and he had to act fast if he wasn't going to become their latest windfall.

The utter frustration, brought on by the recent events, welled up inside him, quickly passing through fury to an overpowering rage. As the front passenger returned to facing forward, motioning to get out of the car and come round to pull him from the rear compartment, he quickly reached down to his left boot. From the inside edge, he pulled the work knife he had found earlier in the factory and lunged forward at the first man. With his left hand, he reached around the seat's headrest and grabbed at the unprepared youth across the face.

Pulling back on the dealer's head, he swiftly drew the rusty, yet still sharp, blade across his throat. The passenger went to give out a shrill scream of surprise but the blade dug deep, widening his windpipe, and the noise quickly degenerated into a low gurgling exhalation of bubbling blood.

"JESUS!" the driver exclaimed in shocked horror as his right shoulder bolted pointlessly into the driver's door. His previous quiet confidence was suddenly replaced by shear panic as he frantically fumbled for the door handle.

The passenger, still alive and now wide-eyed, reached for his neck hopelessly attempting to stem the now spurting blood from the gaping wound in his throat. His legs thrust outwards into the foot-well of the small car causing his body to arch sharply upward toward the windscreen. In a vainly brief attempt to flee the closing moments of his life, he writhed in silent violence before his draining life-blood left his brain sinking into the blackness of inevitable hypoxia. The body slumped back into the seat and the crumpling action sent the last gurgling exhalation of pointless air gushing from his lungs.

The driver's desperate fingers finally found the door release and his upper body fell from the opening doorway. In his panic, he had forgotten to release his otherwise life-saving seat belt. He gave out a child-like squeal as he desperately swung around to reach the cruel mechanism's release button. As he turned to face back into the car, he saw the crazed face of the rear seat passenger lunging at him, high from between the car's front seats.

The knife, his brother's blood trailing in a high arc from its blade, was diving fast at his now horizontal left side. The belt's release button gave way and, as the knife stung deep into his upper arm, his overbalanced body tumbled from the car. The motion involuntarily drew the blade, already deep into the flesh, across his arm and into his torso just catching his last floating rib before it passed out of reach of his attacker. The thin t-shirt and track suit bottoms offered no protection and the knife continued on, splitting the flesh of his abdomen down toward his left buttock.

His head hit the floor hard and he bounced off the fully open panel, collapsing in a heap in front of the rear door. The inch-deep gash roared in agony but he knew, if he was to avoid the same grizzly fate as his brother, his only chance was to get up and flee into the woods while his assailant was still half trapped; drawn between the front seats by his frantic escape.

He desperately scrambled for the gravel's edge just ahead of him and somehow managed to get to his feet to run. However, as the first step of his unzipped flank hit the ground a crippling shockwave blasted him from hip to armpit and he collapsed into the trees. Again, his head suffered a crushing blow and he span as it collided with the first tree trunk in the wood-line. Falling onto his back, he saw the wide-eyed face of his doom lunging down at him from the open rear door of the cheap, blue hatchback. Pinned by the blooded hands of his attacker, the blade sliced across his eye-line and a searing hot bolt became his optic nerves' last impulse. Within a second, he felt the same gurgling breath his brother had offered up leaving his own body as he too succumbed to the senseless void of death's dark veil.

The killer paused for a moment. The frantic noise of scrambling bodies abated and, with his heavy breathing the only remaining sound, he checked around for witnesses. There were none and he was alone; alone, that is, with the two blooded corpses of the heroin-dealing brothers. Even his debauched lifestyle had not sunk to murder before. However, with his intentions of ridding himself of DC Murray returning to counter the thought he hurriedly searched the blood-spattered car for the possibility that the dealers had in fact brought a weapon with them. After all, they had taken an hour to get there. If they'd had no intention of supplying him with a pistol they would have, surely, stuck to their initial twenty minute arrangement? In addition, there had to be at least part of a batch in there; a bonus, he thought, to their unplanned demise.

The daylight was fading fast as the sun sank over the trees but, sure enough, he quickly found the golf-ball-sized package tucked neatly under the driver's seat lining and immediately recognised it as the brothers' dealing wrap. He didn't bother to count the individual corner-bags of brown powder. He knew from its bulk it would last him a week. That is, if he didn't end up taking it all in quick succession, as most users would, given the opportunity. Stuffing the batch into his trouser pocket, he continued a more cursory search for the gun. A pistol should be easier to find and besides, he had to be out of here quickly. Mugging old ladies was one thing but kidnap, and now murder, were going to bring a lot more attention than he needed right now.

He reached between the legs of the front seat passenger and found the cold, metallic barrel of the ordered weapon.

"Jackpot," he muttered to himself as he tugged the pistol from its strapped position on the bottom of the seat.

Peeling away the tape, he briefly examined the weapon, a self-loading slide barrel of some type. He tipped the muzzle to his forehead in a nonchalant salute and looked into the staring eyes of the deceased dealer.

"Why thank you," he sarcastically remarked. "Just what the doctor ordered."

As he withdrew from the compartment, he spotted an expensive watch on the dealer's wrist. 'Waste not, want not,' he thought as he unclasped the metal band and slipped it onto his own arm. He raised the timepiece to admire the additional prize and, in doing so, glanced up into the rear view mirror, dislodged downward from his earlier fall into the front seats of the car. For the first time, he noticed the amount of blood his efforts had spattered, not only on himself, but throughout the car's interior. No chance of clearing any evidence he'd left here. He would have to torch the car.

Noticing a discarded and relatively blood-free jacket on the car's back seat, he opened the rear door and grabbed it to replace his own blood-stained coat. He stuffed the pistol into the rear of his belt, pulling on his newly acquired jacket to cover the protruding weapon, and stepped the short distance to the collapsed corpse of the driver. Dragging the heavy body across the now blood-stained gravel, he struggled the dead-weight back into the driver's seat. He quickly searched the dead driver's coat and pulled out his lighter. Then, tearing a strip from the body's already sliced t-shirt, he opened the cover and stuffed the cloth deep into the spout of the vehicle's petrol tank. He then set about lighting various flammable items within the car, including the two brothers' clothing, before finally igniting the makeshift fuse and retiring into the trees.

He casually walked away checking further through the dead dealer's coat. His luck was definitely *in*. It hadn't even occurred to him that the amateurish dealers would still be carrying their day's takings but there they were. As he counted the wad of notes past three hundred, four hundred, five hundred, he let out a low, self-contented laugh.

'*What a pair of tossers,*' he thought to himself. He now had the wherewithal to elevate himself to *dealer*, should he choose to do so once he'd dealt with that interfering copper. As the notion lingered in his mind, the cloth fuse finally burned down into the car's tank and the brightening fire behind him exploded into a more raging inferno.

He turned to watch for a few moments, satisfying himself that the flame-engulfed car was fully alight and that the entombed brothers' identities were becoming increasingly difficult to determine. Then he walked on toward the pond, which he knew from fishing there as a child lay just ahead, in order to clean off the more obvious marks of the recent slaughter.

After that, he decided, he would return to the abandoned hatchback he had left in the shopping centre car park that morning and use it, under the cover of darkness, to go and find the bitch who had escaped the previous night. She wouldn't be naming him in any court hearing. First things first though. Before anything else he would stop right here and shoot up.

Chapter Fourteen

Lucy had called David's phone a thousand times, or so it seemed to the distraught young girl. She was still getting the automated message that the missing man's phone was switched off but she had to know the truth. She needed to hear from his owns lips that he wasn't the one who had kidnapped that female police detective. She couldn't believe it was him. She didn't *want* to believe it but the news had mentioned him by name, had shown a picture of him at the police station. She began to doubt her own judgement.

He had shown no sign of any secrets at the hospital; no duplicity, no concealment. It had only been four months. Could he have changed so much? Then it occurred to her that she had an alternative line of enquiry. She scrabbled through her side table drawer for the discarded invitation to last year's Christmas party. She was a terrible hoarder. Even after leaving him, she had kept things that reminded her of their life together. Only now, her peculiar habits may pay off. She found the card and quickly turned to the back of the folded note. There it was, the number of Lisa Turner; the organiser of the Benefit Office party. If she still worked with David, she might know what was going on since their break-up. She hastily dialled the number.

"Hello," the recipient answered.

"Hello Lisa. Sorry to call you so late. It's Lucy Short here. I'm not sure whether you'll remember me but I was with David Lewis at last year's office party."

"Hi Lucy, of course I remember you. I thought you and he had split up. Is everything alright?"

Lucy began to blubber but managed a coherent,

"I don't know what to do. You're the only person I had a number for that knows David. Sorry," she repeated.

Lisa could tell the young semi-acquaintance was obviously upset. Ever the office socialite, she easily slipped into concerned mode.

"It's alright sweetheart. Don't cry now. What's wrong?"

"I'm not sure." Lucy sniffed back the tears. "It's David. I bumped into him at the hospital this afternoon. I was taking some flowers in for a customer. He was really roughed up. He said he'd been mugged but then I saw him on the telly and the police are after him for *kidnapping*. I couldn't believe it but I don't know what to think. Do you know anything about it?"

"My God, no! Janet was late in this morning and mentioned the police had had her out in the night about David but she didn't mention anything about kidnapping. Who's he kidnapped?"

"A police woman, they said."

"A police woman? Jesus." She thought for a moment. *"I don't know whether it has anything to do with it but did you know he's been off work all last week?"*

"No. Why?"

"Janet said he's been having epileptic seizures. He was unconscious for days apparently."

"Seizures?" Lucy was shocked by the news of David's illness. He'd always been so healthy, barely even a cold. That said, his drinking had become a problem; enough, at least, for her to have left him; but this? She wanted to help him but what could she do?

"I don't suppose you know where he might be? He's not answering his phone," she desperately asked his work colleague.

"No, sorry," the otherwise helpful woman replied.

"Okay. I'm sorry to have bothered you."

"Listen. It's fine. Tell you what, call me in the morning around ten and I'll ask around the office in case anyone's spoken to him, okay?"

"Thanks Lisa, that'll be great. I'll speak to you then. Thanks again. Goodnight."

"Goodnight," Lisa answered before hanging up the phone. Lucy held the now buzzing handset at her ear, confused at the news that David was now ill, as well as missing and wanted.

She snapped out of the daze and returned the cordless device to its base. She didn't know what to do next. She just knew she had to do something.

She tried his number one more time but, getting the same response, decided her efforts would better be served in the morning with a refreshed, more logical mind. She pulled back the sheets of her crisp, clean bed and slipped her feet down to the cosy, tucked-in foot of the heavy, woollen blankets. She wiped the drying tear streaks from her face and stared at the smooth, pale ceiling until the weight of the day's events finally closed her fatigued eyelids and she drifted away to sleep.

***

The dancing darts of light faded away, spinning downward to meet an imagined floor of darkest black. David's periphery view collapsed outward to reveal the star filled sky above the clearing he had retreated to in order to consider his dwindling options. It was dark. Had he had another seizure or had he just fallen asleep in the park? He felt dizzy and could sense that metallic taste again.

Reaching into the water, he splashed his face to reawaken his senses. The water was refreshingly cold on his face. He looked down into the settling ripples of the moonlit pond and saw the tortured face of a barely recognisable man. The stitches to his forehead had reddened into immunity-fired wheals but these paled insignificantly against the swollen lips and bruised cheeks. His eyes were partly closed and his mind ached. His neck felt like it could barely hold the weight of his battered head and he struggled with images of a gang of young hooded lads reigning kicks and blows down upon it. Or was it a single young woman, bound and desperate? He could barely distinguish the images anymore. Was one a dream, a vision?

As his mind staggered to a poor impression of focused, he recalled the full weight of his situation. Murray was dead. He was on the run, wanted by an entire force of the fallen officer's enraged colleagues. He stood and walked around the small lake. Beyond, through the trees, he could make out the distant light of a commercial estate. Walking on, he saw his hands reaching out to move the branches from his path, his feet repeatedly passing each other as they strode steadily onward toward the growing glow of the retail park. Reaching the wood's edge, he experienced a curious yet short lived blurring in his vision before stepping down the shallow kerb onto the tarmac and purposefully walking across the sea of speckled grey.

He reached into his trouser pocket and, pulling out a single fobbed key, he instinctively depressed the unlock-button of the plastic device. The pale, metallic, hatchback car directly in his path flashed its directional amber lights in response to the unseen command. He saw his arm reach out to open the driver's door and he stepped smoothly into the driver's seat. The engine stuttered into a rattling, diesel melody and, without any apparent conscious decisions, he drove the unfamiliar vehicle out of the car park and onto the broad, sodium lit lanes of the town's by-pass road. Whose car was this and why was he heading into town? He pondered the questions for a moment but then it didn't seem to matter. He smoothly descended the falling deceleration lane of the town centre junction and swung around the shadowed roundabout. The route became increasingly familiar and he soon recognised the layout of simple but attractive new build dwellings.

Without remembering the remainder of the journey he found himself staring aimlessly from a hillside vantage point, standing by the side of the parked car. Although some time after dawn, the sun was still rising and burned brightly in the clear morning sky behind him. He was on the far side of Hopefield holding pair of binoculars. Where the hell had they come from? He checked his watch. Didn't he have a leather strap? Eight twenty five. His hillside view overlooked the descending roofs of the town's suburban cul-de-sacs. He quickly recognised the layout of the homes beyond, in the flattened valley bottom, as that of his own small street of newly-built multi-storey town houses. He saw the familiar vehicles parked outside the neighbouring homes but could also see various other, unfamiliar cars spotted about the street and the approaching network of roads.

He could see that each had at least a driver and front seat passenger and that neither appeared intent on either leaving or moving the vehicles. Across to the left, out of sight of the small street, he noticed a large, police-liveried van. Several uniformed officers in heavy tactical gear were milling around the vehicle in a disorganised manner, apparently bored by some tedious delay. Over the houses, off in the distance, the tiny dot of the police helicopter was searching the industrial estates and the fields in the general direction of the shopping centre he had previously left.

He watched the scene for a while, each easily comprehensible image weaving an unfamiliar yet strangely recognisable picture of a surveillance operation centring on his home. He knew the police would be looking for him but this seemed somehow unexpected, as if he was seeing the house for the first time and was somehow surprised by the attending officers. He felt confused and the images blurred and swirled as if he was watching one moment and imagining the scene as described by someone else the next. Then he saw a woman approaching the house.

Even in his confused state, he recognised her immediately. Lucy approached the doorway and he noticed the milling tactical officers quickly file into the liveried van as if responding to some unheard order into a state of readiness. She stood at the door a while and, apparently getting no reply from the intercom panel, made a short mobile phone call. Then the door opened and Lucy briefly addressed someone inside, out of sight. The door closed and she walked away. As she did, he noticed a man and woman get out of the one of the unfamiliar cars and walk after her at a distance, as if not wanting to alert her to their attentions. Then he found himself starting the car and driving to a location ahead of her general direction.

He couldn't remember how he got there or what route he took but the next thing he saw was the car door leaving his hand as he threw it shut from his position, standing in an unfamiliar and deserted car park. He walked to an opening in the corner of the rough ground and, rounding the concrete-walled edge of the unkempt area, could see the approaching Lucy as she strode toward him. He went to call out to her but could not hear any words coming from his oddly uncontrolled body. Instead he turned in a reversing half-circle and backed up against the stone panels of the car park's perimeter wall. She passed the opening and continued along the road away from him.

Suddenly, his vision flashed, distorting like a video tape on fast forward. He found himself in another derelict factory with large floor to ceiling windows. It was dark again and he was staring down the barrel of a machine-rifle, the dark helmet and masked face of its owner barely focused amid the swirling haze of a stinging white cloud. He couldn't hear or smell anything and the dream-like image was slowed as if held back in time by some unseen hand. Worse still, he felt the cold steel of a pistol in his right hand and the soft warmth of Lucy's throat in his left as he held her in front of him as an unwilling shield. He pressed the muzzle of the pistol to her trembling temple. He felt a sudden heavy impact; a sharp pain in his head was followed by sudden darkness.

***

The dancing darts of light faded away, spinning downward to meet an imagined floor of darkest black. David's periphery view collapsed outward to reveal the star filled sky above the clearing he had retreated to in order to consider his dwindling options. It was dark. Had he had another seizure or had he just fallen asleep in the park?

A sudden sharpness leapt into his mind. He was still in the park. The events at the shopping centre and on the hillside hadn't yet happened. He tried to make sense of it. Was it a dream? No. He recalled the metallic taste in his mouth. Was it another seizure, a vision of the future perhaps? *'That's ridiculous,'* he thought to himself, but it seemed too detailed for a dream, well at first anyway. The house had been his; the girl had been Lucy.

He had seen the disjointed actions as if they were his own

but he now knew that they couldn't have been him. The rifleman though? Was the blackness that ended the vision *his* death, or rather that of his dream-self? Or, God forbid was Lucy the victim of some botched police assault?

He pondered the latter option. His mind was open to any explanation now, however bizarre. If it was the latter, if Lucy was to die from a gunshot to the head, then the previous week's peculiarities would begin to fall into place. Before this dream, this vision, he had touched Lucy's wrist at the hospital and then experienced a sudden pain in his right temple. Before he recalled seeing Murray's harshly-wired detention, his wrists had bled, right after she had encouraged him into the interview room by touching his elbow. Finally, there was the old lady. He had touched her hand to help her up to the bus platform only to suffer the agony of her breaking hip. Then later, in his hospital bed, he had recollected her fall on to the age-weakened joint, smashing it as *he* had mugged her.

In some unnatural way, he surmised, he was feeling the outcomes of crimes before they had happened and was later witnessing them as if he was somehow responsible. That said, how could he explain the surreal, physical manifestations of the victims' injuries? His mind skipped the logical impossibility of these inexplicable medical symptoms and he happily embraced his perceived clarity of the evolving hypothesis. It was the first, seemingly clear, string of an explanation he had come up with and he instantly convinced himself that it was the truth.

'*It's a complicated organ,*' the doctor had said. '*And some!*' thought David.

However, something was different. His racing exhilaration stalled for a moment as he fought to fathom the discrepancy. Then he had it. After the mugging, he had woken in hospital and had read about the crime in the local newspaper. It had already happened and only after reading about it did he begin to believe he was the mugger.

Then there was Murray. Again, he had woken in hospital. He had been having a dream, or so he thought at the time, about her kidnap, and had seen her demise on the silent television screens in the nearby store. It had happened, but again he only formed the full picture after the seizure.

This was different though. After the vision of Lucy's death, he had woken in the woods. Like before, he had suffered a seizure and seen a full detailed picture of the crime; but this time he had not been found, not been transported to the hospital. He hadn't seen or heard anything to suggest that it had actually happened. In fact, on the contrary, the vision had fast-forwarded into the sunlight of the following day and beyond. It was still dark. He was still in the woods. It had *not yet* happened and he knew exactly how it was going to happen. He could save Lucy.

He had to get back into town and warn the police *not* to open fire on the man they were yet to discover holding her hostage; *not* to potentially shoot her. Then he caught himself. As far as the police were concerned, *he* was the wanted man. *He* had killed Murray. *He* had mugged the old lady; yeah, they must have believed that too by now. He couldn't just walk into the police station and expect them to believe his newly formed theory of some supernatural ability to predict the future!

They would *definitely* throw away the key and then, with a *real* killer still out there, Lucy would be in real trouble. He had to think fast. He had to somehow prove his story to the police, to get them onside with his ridiculous version of the truth.

He decided that if the was to stop the killer he would have to do it himself. He considered his first move. He already had a lead; the pond and the car at the shopping centre. However, he didn't know where the pond was; it certainly wasn't in this clearing.

'*I never fished there as a kid,*' he thought. Never fished there as a kid? How did he know about Murray's killer fishing there? He dismissed the thought and decided to bypass this part of his vision and make straight for the car. The problem was his vision had no time table. In fact it had no stable time-line at all. The killer could be at the car already. He could have already left and be on his way to watch the house off Viscount Road, to see Lucy arrive and leave; and to follow her.

He chose not to imagine the unseen portion of his vision. David reached into his pocket to retrieve his phone. If he couldn't approach the police, he could at least call them and warn them of the premonition, to get them to the house to save Lucy before she left. Then again, could he trust that intervention to alter the images for the better? His mind was racing again.

'No,' he thought. The premonition involved the tactical officers getting to Lucy before he did and in the vision he knew they were already at the house, by their van, before the killer had even arrived.

Perhaps he could send them to the shopping centre before the killer even left in the hatchback car? Lucy wouldn't be there. If they came down hard on the killer there Lucy would be safe. He settled on the latter choice but he couldn't find his phone. He quickly patted down the pockets of his coat and pants.

'Of course,' he realised. The gang of youths who had mugged him the previous evening on his walk from the bus to the house had stolen it. The resultant seizure had attracted the attentions of the dog walker who, in turn, had called the ambulance. The problem was David had not been aware of his rescuer. He had not been aware of the loss of his phone, until now, when he bloody needed it!

Unable to call-in-the-cavalry he picked up the pace and before long found himself running toward the glowing, light-polluted horizon which marked the position of the retail park beyond the woods.

Chapter Fifteen

"Sergeant Backhouse." The young section officer gently nudged the senior detective from his sleep.

Backhouse lifted his brow in an effort to drag open his overtired eyelids. Eventually, the reluctant covers split apart and begrudgingly allowed the low-lit silhouette of the uniformed constable to enter Backhouse's vision. Although desperately tired, he did not snap at the officer, as the young man might have expected, and rightly so. He had been very specific in his instructions to the deployment centre that he should be awoken in the event of any incidents occurring that were considered out of the ordinary.

"What time is it?" he quietly asked, rubbing his face with the hand not supporting him in his newly propped-up position.

"About nine thirty," the officer replied.

"In the morning?"

"Afraid not Sarge, it's still Tuesday."

Backhouse let out an accepting sigh. He was beginning to think this day would never end. He yawned heavily.

"Come on then. What's the news?"

"There's been a car found burnt out in the Westgate Park."

"Hardly what I'd call *out of the ordinary*."

"Not normally, no. But we know you've been looking at the local drug users. This particular car had PNC markers all over it regarding drug dealing and, more interestingly..., it had two bodies in it."

"Well, that changes things, doesn't it?" Backhouse added, raising an eyebrow as he threw back the heavy coat he had being using as a makeshift blanket. He rolled his aching body from the low cot onto the carpet of his office and let out an exasperated "ooh" as his knees cracked while bringing himself to a standing position. Like an old, hunched over man he slowly turned to face the patient officer.

"Have we any ideas on the stiffs' IDs?"

"Maybe, yes. CSI are down there now. There's not much left to go on but what's of particular interest is the suggestion that both the bodies' throats were slashed prior to the car being torched. Intelligence suggests the car was used by a pair of brothers dealing heroin and crack cocaine out of Manchester."

"Not local then?"

"No, but regular to the area. The FIM thought you'd be interested that they both have violence and firearms markers on PNC. He thought that, if they were taken out by the same person, it must have been someone they had let into the car, someone they knew. Otherwise, they would have easily overpowered him before he had the chance to kill the both of them. He also thought, if we're looking at a druggie desperate enough to kill his own dealers, we may be talking about your Lewis guy."

Backhouse knew that the links between a burnt-out car and Lewis were a tenuous chain of suppositions but he couldn't argue with the logic of the FIM's train of thought.

"Fair enough. Who's the SIO*?"

"DCI Callander's been nominated but he's not here yet."

"Okay. Is DI Priest aware?"

"Yes. He's just getting a quick wash downstairs. He asked me to tell you to wait for him before going to the scene."

"Nice one. Cheers Tim. Let the control room know we'll be on our way in the next ten minutes or so. Oh, and get them to pull all the intell on the brothers and call me on my mobile with the details, will you?"

The young constable nodded his acknowledgement and left the office to complete the request before returning to his section duties. Backhouse leaned onto his desk. He squeezed the bridge of his nose, rubbing the sleep from the corners of his bloodshot eyes, and thought for a moment. Accepting the FIM's version of events for now, he pondered the possible reasons for the double murder.

The young constable had been right. No bag-head would do away with his own dealers unless he had no intention of getting his gear from them again. If that was the case, Lewis was about to jump ship and leave the area for good. Was Murray already dead or was Lewis about to transport her bound, and no doubt gagged, body somewhere else for whatever reason? Sadly, his experience of previous kidnap/murder cases suggested the former was more likely. Fleeing the scene of a murder or even moving a corpse for disposal elsewhere were far easier than risking transporting a live captive.

Either way, he knew that time was running out. If Lewis was bold enough to take out two violent dealers, he was close, very close, to making his next move. He wouldn't hang around to risk being swept up in the proverbial circus tent that was about to descend on the double murder scene at Westgate Park.

"Alright Steve?" the boss asked as he stepped through the open doorway to the Detective Sergeant's office. "Have you had the story yet?"

"Yeah, the brief details at least. Do you want to come down and take a look at the scene?"

"Certainly. Do you want a quick freshen-up or are you ready to go?"

"No, let's get down there before it turns into a sideshow."

"Probably a good idea," the Inspector agreed.

The two supervisors grabbed their radios and coats and made their way to the rear yard. They were soon on their way to the scene of the smouldering car, discussing the FIM's ideas en route. Despite wishing to favour the contrary, Priest had to share Backhouse's pessimism over the likely reasons behind Lewis's impending flight. The SIO, having been made aware of the possible link to Murray's abduction, had already thrown a cordon of road blocks around the town and had officers covering the train and bus stations. If Lewis hadn't already left Hopefield, he would have great difficulty in doing so now.

Where was he though? There were surveillance teams at the factory on Link One and at his house off Viscount Road, the address provided by his boss, Janet Seymour. However, there had been no movement at either location and, with the lack of a police record, Lewis had no listed intelligence to indicate any likely associate addresses for them to check. If it had been Lewis who had killed the fraternal dealers, the lack of any previous conviction record only added weight to the theory that he was dangerously desperate. That conclusion worried Priest and Backhouse even more.

***

The water was cold on his face but the cooling sensation was welcome on his swollen lips. He looked down into the settling ripples of the moonlit fishing pond and recognised the face of a tortured man. Self-tortured, by years of heroin abuse, his gaunt features had been easily bruised by the desperate attack of the escaping Murray. In addition, the cut to his forehead, caused when the snagged bag of that old bitch had unbalanced him into head-butting the High Street wall, was still weeping and was starting to show the tell-tale signs of infection. When he got hold of that bloody copper, he was definitely going to take his revenge on her face, he thought.

He took off his coat and discarded it on the bank. Then he tore the short cotton sleeve from his t-shirt and, dipping it in the cold pond, used it to wipe the spattered blood from his face. The blackened scab from his cut forehead painfully tore away and began to bleed again.

'Shit,' he thought, holding the wet compress against the wound in an effort to quickly stem the flow.

He knew that he would have to get out of town after the dealer-brothers' demise, and fast. However, first he wanted to find Murray and this David Lewis character from her notebook. He had read how Lewis had been seen by Murray at the police station and had given her directions straight to him at the factory. That's how he had back-tracked the detectives trail to find her car on the High Street.

The question was, how the hell did this Lewis bastard know so much about him? Was he a private dick or something?

No, that was crap. Who would hire a private dick to follow a druggie, even if he was mugging old dears? No, there was something weird about this Lewis guy. Whatever it was though, he couldn't risk him, or indeed the escaped Murray, finding him again; especially not now, after the murders in the park. He had to get rid of Lewis before he left and, thanks to that bitch-of-a-copper's notebook, he had the exact address to find him. All he needed was the car to get there, and that was still ahead of him at the shopping centre car park.

He finished wiping the brothers' blood from his face and hands and threw the soiled sleeve into the pond. He picked up the dealer's jacket from the grass and pulled it on to keep out the increasing cold of the night's dropping temperature. Then he set off toward the glowing lights of the distant retail park. As he noisily crunched through the undergrowth of the parkland woods, he thought of how he might get hold of the elusive DC Murray. Then it occurred to him that, once he had done away with Lewis, he might not have to bother with Murray at all. If her star witness was dead, she wouldn't have anything to go on, not even the written evidence in her notebook, now in his grubby trouser pocket.

She hadn't seen his face and her death wouldn't influence any forensic evidence he may have left at the factory. If that existed, he would soon enough be named, and killing her wouldn't help that. So, despite his desires to take revenge on the tiny woman who had, effectively, beaten the crap out of him, he concluded it would be better to just get rid of the peculiar witness, Lewis, and then get the hell-out-of-Dodge.

He reached the car park and paused for a moment a few metres from the edge of the tree-line. The score he'd easily convinced himself earlier as being necessary was a double hit from the dealer's batch and had wiped him out for longer than normal. It was just shy of midnight but the various shops at the centre included a twenty four hour superstore and the car park was surprisingly busy. He could see the hatchback he had left there earlier but decided to wait for a while; firstly to let the number of shoppers die down and secondly to check for any police attention around the abandoned car. He settled back into his impromptu observation post and watched the car park.

***

Across the tarmac, from the superstore's first floor restaurant, David sat and watched out over the car park and the woods beyond. Relying on his earlier vision as the truth, convinced that he had the ability to foresee the future, David knew that Murray's killer would be emerging from the tree-line. He also knew that the car involved was a metallic hatchback. However, amongst the fifty or more cars which were parked between the buildings and the woods, he wasn't sure which of the numerous metallic hatchbacks the killer would head for; hence the reason for elevating himself to this first floor vantage point.

From here he had an overview of the whole area, improving his chances of seeing the killer approach any particular car with enough time to call the police and get them to stop it before it reached his house; before the chance of a hostage situation, which he now believed would end in the death of Lucy.

***

"I guess we didn't quite beat the circus then!" Inspector Priest commented as he and Backhouse arrived at the Westgate Park ranger's hut. The small gravelled area was awash with fire engines, liveried police vehicles and the familiar dark estate cars used by the CSI team. The uniformed officers had finished erecting the four-unit halogen light stands and the accompanying generator was already pumping enough power into the self-contained system to turn the dark, tree-lined circle into an almost day-lit arena.

They were now busy rolling out the inflatable blue and white striped CSI tent in a line parallel to the nearside of the burnt-out hatchback. As Backhouse and Priest stepped from their vehicle, the tent blower sprang to life. The protective,

127

vinyl enclosure began to slowly rise, like some prehistoric creature stirring from its nest, and the changing shadows it threw from the halogen backlights engulfed the blackened vehicle and its cremated occupants as if the rising beast was closing its jaws about them.

The senior CSI officer, Dave Oxton, walked across to meet the approaching supervisors and, pulling the fibre face-mask from his mouth and pushing back the hood of his white, paper forensic suit, he eagerly greeted them.

"Alright Peter? Not much left I'm afraid."

"We can see that," Priest replied.

"Yes. Well, as I believe you're already aware, we've got two bodies, totally burnt. The likely cause of death would appear to be the gashes across the necks. Despite the fire, the flesh, albeit a bit *crisp*, has remained surprisingly intact so the neck wounds are fairly apparent. Obviously, the post mortem tomorrow will clarify whether they are the actual cause but I can't see anyone bothering to slice the pair open *after* death!" He was almost humorous in his observation and obviously not in the least bit phased by the gory nature of the scene before them.

"Any chance of forensics from the offender?"

"Not from the car really, no, but," he continued, leading the pair around the front of the vehicle, "there are signs of a struggle just into the tree-line; here, from the driver's door. Plenty of blood here to be tested. I imagine it'll belong to one of these two characters. Probably the driver but you never know."

"What about a time-line? Any ideas?"

"It's early days but I believe it was still well alight when the fire brigade arrived so certainly not that long ago. If we're talking about a single offender then I'd say they would have known him."

"How so?" Backhouse quizzed.

They'd already heard the FIM's theory on the same question but it always helped to have it confirmed by the professional scientist. The keenly eccentric CSI supervisor stepped excitedly around the car as he explained his conclusions, almost re-living each stage with over-acted gesticulations.

"Well, here's how I see it. The struggle is all over this side of the car, nothing on the nearside. I'm guessing the killer has lured them here, perhaps for a drugs buy, and has waited in the woods for them to arrive and park this close to the trees. You know about the drugs intelligence on the car, don't you?" The pair nodded. "Well, he, or she, has then entered the rear of the car and, for whatever reason, has reached over and killed the passenger first. The driver has fled the car and has got as far as the woods before the killer has managed to get out of the back of the car and catch him. Another slashing, killing or at least immobilising the driver in the trees and then he's dragged the body back into the car and dumped it in before burning the vehicle to destroy any forensic evidence. As it would have been dark, I'm guessing the killer didn't notice the trail of blood he left from the trees back to the car."

"Why do you think the driver wasn't slashed first and ran out of the car bleeding or died in the car and the passenger was the one killed in the woods?"

"Well, not that it makes much difference to the outcome but there's plenty of blood between the vehicle and the trees, so the driver was definitely bleeding while out of the car. If you take a look at the bodies, the driver's arm is on top of the passengers lap. If the driver was the first to go and the passenger was dumped into the car after the struggle then there would be blood on the nearside and the driver would most likely be underneath the passenger rather than vice-versa. There are, of course, possible permutations for the order of play but in my experience, with crimes of such frantic violence, the simplest explanation is usually the most likely."

"Fair enough," Priest accepted. "Any indicators of the killer's departure route?"

"Difficult to say in the dark, but if I'd just slaughtered two people and was on foot I'd head into the woods. There are no apparent signs of a fleeing vehicle. I'll check for disruption in the undergrowth once the sun's up. These lights are throwing more shadows in there than I can work around."

"Motives Dave?" Backhouse joked. After all, the intuitive investigator *had* already worked out plenty of detail in his short time at the scene.

"Come on gentlemen. The impossible I can do. Miracles take a little longer! Besides, isn't that your job?"

"Okay, thanks Dave. Keep us updated. You've got my mobile haven't you?" Backhouse asked.

"Yes. No problem."

With that the scientist, re-covering his head with the hood of his suit and pinching his face-mask's thin, metal nose-clip back into place, turned his attentions to the officers gathered either side of the now inflated tent and began waving his arms around as if directing the manoeuvres of some modern day zeppelin.

Backhouse and Priest walked back to their car and momentarily sat in silence, each assimilating the scene and considering their next course of action.

"What do you think then Steve?" the Inspector asked his subordinate, respectful of his years of experience.

"Well, we know the cars a dealer's but, albeit likely, there's no saying it was definitely being used by the dealers tonight. For now, with the lack of positive ID's, it could just as easily have been a jealous husband finding his wife *dogging* in the park."

Priest had not expected Backhouse to be so lateral thinking. He had assumed he would have leapt on the likely connection to Murray's kidnapper.

"I must say, you certainly like to keep an open mind!" he said. "Possibilities aside, Dave is right about the simplest explanation being the most likely. If Lewis is the killer then he's getting desperate. It's feasible, I suppose, that his recent bouts of epilepsy have had more of an effect on him than we imagined."

"Epilepsy boss?"

"Had I not mentioned that?"

"No."

"Sorry Steve. His supervisor, Seymour, was in the other night after you had left for the estate. She was telling me how

Lewis had been off work, and in hospital, from the afternoon of Mrs Nugent's robbery until the day he handed himself in at the station."

"That would explain the offences stopping after that then."

"My thoughts exactly. In addition, he's recently split up from his girlfriend and has been showing signs of depression over the last few weeks."

"So, apart from the unpredictability of his epilepsy, he's depressed, potentially armed and probably sexually frustrated. Explosive combination don't you think?" Backhouse offered.

"Well, the sexual aspect hadn't occurred to me but I suppose, on top of everything else, an overload of unfettered testosterone isn't going to help matters! What do you mean by potentially armed?"

"If the two rice crispies in that car are the Crabtree brothers then there had to be a weapon in there too. Intelligence was specific that they never travel without one. It might be early days but that isn't something Oxo would have overlooked. If there's no gun in the car now then we have to assume that Lewis has it." Backhouse shook his head. "We're running out of time," he concluded.

"Indeed we are. Suggestions?"

"The town's exit routes are covered but it's still a big area, too big to search it all effectively. Dave said that he would have gone into the woods and, if Lewis is as desperate as we suspect, it makes sense that he wouldn't head for either his house or the factory, which corroborates Oxo's theory. I think it would be a start to move west from here. There's not that much between here and Little Dunsford, apart from the Westgate shopping centre and the new housing estate built around it, so it might be an idea to get the chopper up again to do a thermal search of the open fields so that we're just left with the shops and the estate."

"Short of anything else, it sounds like a plan."

"It's a start but I still want to head up tomorrow's obs on Lewis's house. He might get a little braver once the town is up and about and go take-a-looksy at home before he leaves. It's a long shot but we've little else at the moment."

"Fair enough, but I want you to get back to the office and get at least six hours of proper rest. Otherwise, you'll be falling asleep instead of observing anything. Plus, if things start to happen, I want you to be sharp. We're talking about a kidnap and double murder here." He paused. "If not a triple murder," he reluctantly added, aware of what the supposition was suggesting. "I don't want him slipping the net, before *or* after arrest, because of a mistake caused by tiredness."

"Understood boss."

Backhouse knew the Inspector was right and had no intention of adding another fatigue-induced error to his résumé. He started the car and the pair returned to the station. DCI Callander had arrived by the time they got to the first floor offices and another major incident room was already in the making. Backhouse returned to his office and closed the door behind him.

The mêlée outside in the corridor had little effect on his efforts to fall back to sleep on the low, olive-green cot waiting dutifully behind his desk. He had barely pulled his coat over his head before his heavy eyelids converted the dimly lit room to total darkness and he fell into a deep, restful sleep.

Chapter Sixteen

'That's long enough,' he thought to himself.

There had been no activity around Murray's car for hours and, as it approached dawn, the number of shoppers milling about the car park had dwindled to a mere trickle. This had to be as good as it was going to get before the new morning's visitors started to arrive. He lurched forward and levered himself upright. He stood a while, shaking off the cramps from his legs, before approaching the edge of the fresh, black tarmac of the recently laid car park.

He checked his newly acquired jacket was still covering the weapon concealed in the back of his belt and casually brushed down his arms and pants to flick away any leaves that may have attached themselves to him during his long, wood-line vigil. He didn't want to attract any unnecessary attention. He quickly scanned the cars nearest to the trees and, noticing no movement, nonchalantly strode out toward the parked hatchback. He reached into his trouser pocket and pulled out the car's single fobbed key. His head was still but, as he got closer to the car, his eyes flitted between the shoppers, checking their respective attention levels as he approached the bulk of the parked vehicles.

Despite the various splatters of blood on his shirt and trousers, the combination of the stolen jacket and the darkness of the hour covered the signs of guilt literally written all over him. This meant that no-one showed him any interest and he waited to the last moment to remotely unlock the car's doors so that he could slip quickly into the driver's seat before the beep and flash of the deactivating alarm drew him any unwanted glances.

He dropped into the seat but, with the unfamiliar sharpness

of the pistol reminding him of its existence, caught himself before allowing his full weight to fall on the weapon. Carefully drawing the gun from behind his back, he placed it onto the passenger seat. He inserted the key into the ignition and turned it to bring the car's electronics into life. He paused a moment and decided the pistol's new perch was too open to the view of any passing shoppers. Taking his ex-dealer's lead, he reached over and tucked the weapon under the passenger seat. Now happy with its concealment, he returned his attentions to the key and further twisted it to start the car's rattling, diesel engine.

***

"Can I help you with anything, Sir?"

David's attention was snapped away from the glazed wall as he reacted to the voice. His heart leapt as the first impression of a blue, epaulette-crowned jersey and peaked cap came into view against the strong, halogen backlights of the restaurant.

"Sorry?" he spluttered a he swiftly realised the man was, in fact, one of centre's security staff and not the police officer he had initially thought him to be.

"I was just wondering if everything was alright, Sir," the polite official repeated. "The restaurant staff were concerned that you've been here for quite some time and appear to have long finished your drink."

It was instantly obvious to David that the polite approach was a shallow attempt to cover up a request to vacate his position at the table overlooking the car park. He quickly concocted a reason for his extended stay.

"Sorry. I'm actually waiting for someone to pick me up but they've not shown yet. They should have been here ages ago."

There was a pregnant pause as David anxiously waited for the security officer to decide whether or not the explanation was going to buy him any more time at his vantage point.

"Okay," the guard acknowledged. "The staff were just a little worried. The time of night and all; you understand?"

"Yeah, no problem," David answered, trying to conceal his relief, so as not to alert the guard to his deception.

The security officer moved away and David returned his attentions to the car park. As he did, he caught sight of someone walking across from the far side of the expansive tarmac. His heart leapt again, barely recovered from the shock of the guard's uniform, and adrenalin began to surge through his body in anxious trepidation of what his next move should be. Was it the guy he was looking for; had he just left the trees or not? He couldn't be sure. Damn that guard.

The person moved swiftly across the car park in a direct line for a small group of cars close to the service yard access gates. The indicator lights flashed on one of the vehicles, a hatchback. Too far from David's vantage point to identify, the figure slipped quickly into the car. It matched the car from his vision. David had to assume this was the guy. There was a short pause and then the car began to move. There was no way that David could reach it before it was gone.

The logic behind his choice of vantage point suddenly felt less sound. That said, David had, at least, chosen somewhere near a phone. The loss of his mobile two evenings before had made him consider at least that much. Plus, he knew where the vehicle was going, the hilltop view overlooking the town. He moved swiftly to the phone, passing the retreating guard and giving him cause to take a second look at the curious customer.

He snatched the payphone from its hook and quickly dialled 999. He paused, waiting for the familiar ringing tone, but it never came. He tapped the receiver with his free hand and tried again. Nothing happened. The phone was dead.

'Damn it,' he thought. He glanced around for a second kiosk but none were in sight. He strode to the restaurant counter and called the cashier over from her cleaning duties just beyond the kitchen door. The girl came over and he hurriedly asked for the use of the shop phone. The young girl, obviously in no position of authority, looked perplexed and unsure of how to deal with the request.

"Come on, please, it's important," David urged the girl in

an excitedly elevated voice. She stepped backward toward the safety of kitchen door.

"Is everything okay, Cheryl?" the security guard quizzed in a manner authoritative enough to let David know he considered his *demands* on the cashier to be unwelcome.

The cashier hesitated and stuttered to respond. Her uncertainty was enough for the large guard and he took hold of David's arm to guide him away.

"Come on lad. I think your *friend's* not coming. I'll have to ask you to leave."

David recognised that the guard was not going to reason with him and, by his sarcastic tone, that he no longer believed his earlier diversion.

"Okay, no problem. No offence meant."

With that, he quickly made his way to the nearby stairwell. He leapt the stairs in one to the landing turn and completed the second descent with equally acrobatic flare. Running to the exit, he twisted to narrow his passage as the automatic doors failed to open fast enough in response to his hasty approach. Once outside, he quickly re-oriented himself to his previous viewpoint and could see the car had reached the centre's exit barriers. He began to run after it but the barrier rose and he realised the futility of his actions.

He reached the descending gate and allowed his pace to break into an untidy walk. Then, out of breath, he came to a gasping halt and leaned heavily onto his knees. He looked up and watched, uselessly, as the car drove away toward the town and the hillside viewpoint beyond. He hadn't even seen the registration number. As he gasped in great gulps of air, a small sports car swung in from the main road and came to a halt at the adjacent entrance barrier. The car was so low to the ground that the driver couldn't reach the dispenser. Instead, he released his seatbelt and, pushing the door ajar, stepped one foot out and leaned over the tiny, open door-panel to retrieve his ticket. David, desperate and beyond reasoning, grabbed the man's arm.

"Get out, NOW."

"What the f..?"

The startled driver, with no time to respond, found himself being dragged from the open door. David, strengthened by the hormones rushing through his veins, wrestled the staggered driver into an untidy heap at the base of the ticket machine. Several of the security staff, who had been monitoring David from their camera office since his hasty exit from the restaurant, were already running in his direction from the enormous building.

David leaned down to the sports car driver, who was cowering defensively after the madman's assault, and calmly announced,

"No time to explain but I'll bring it back, honestly. Sorry mate."

He jumped into the low bucket seat, glanced at the gear stick to ascertain the position of reverse and roared the small vehicle away from the gate. The screeching tyres flared into plumes of blue, acrid smoke and, after a short pause to change into first gear, he revved the powerful engine into an equally dramatic departure and sped forward after his quarry.

***

"Morning boss," Backhouse said, introducing himself to the Detective Chief Inspector who was leaning intently over a large, blown-up map of the Westgate Park crime scene.

DCI Callander looked up from his conversation with the search team Inspector.

"Ah, morning Steve. Get some sleep?" the supervisor asked.

"Thanks, yes. Any progress on the murders?"

Although it was not really Backhouse's place to be questioning the experienced SIO's investigation, Callander knew that Backhouse had a vested interest in his progress. He knew that the double murder had the potential of being linked to the kidnap of DC Murray and was only too aware, by the fact that Backhouse had spent an uncomfortable night behind his desk, that her welfare was at the forefront of the old Sergeant's mind.

Backhouse was looking for leads, for some direction to the forthcoming day's efforts to bring the young detective back into the fold. It was still before dawn and Backhouse had been up for an hour or so. He had already visited his own silver command for the kidnap and knew that the ongoing search had, so far, been fruitless. He was about to head up the team to take over the surveillance at David Lewis's house. He had been into the divisional control room and checked on every incident even remotely connected to the area.

He had read the long list of calls made following the television broadcast of the kidnap. Despite the closed-circuit picture of Lewis being of poor quality, there had been dozens of calls identifying the young suspect. Sadly, all the intelligence was historic: plenty of people had named him; plenty of people knew where he lived; plenty of people even knew where he worked. No-one, however, knew where he *was*. Backhouse was becoming increasingly frustrated but he knew he had to keep his head. Physically, he was rested, to a point, but mentally he was exhausted.

The DCI sensed the Detective Sergeant's concern and, although he had little to offer, he tried to be as reassuring as he could.

"Well, as you know, CSI Oxton has been on site for most of the night. He's recovered a number of forensic exhibits and the samples are already en route the lab. The intelligence suggests we're looking at the Crabtree brothers from Moston in Manchester. The post mortem's due for nine o'clock and, now that the sun's coming up, the forensic search of the wood-line near to the car can begin in earnest."

"Have we anything on the suggestion from CSI that the killer had headed west toward Little Dunsford?"

"Actually, yes. I had a dog handler circumnavigate the scene this morning and I've just this minute been told he's picked up a trail in the direction CSI Oxton had indicated. He's currently tracking further into the woods."

Backhouse's mood lifted immediately.

"That's fantastic. Which handler is it?"

The DCI checked the printout passed to him seconds before the DS had entered the room.

"Let me see….. Lima Golf Two Six"

"That's John Evans and Satan. He's a good man," Backhouse commended.

"Well, that seems evident. Andy," he called over to the room's communications officer, "can you turn up that loudspeaker while PC Evans is tracking please?"

"Sir," the rather rotund comms officer responded.

"Request an update, will you?"

"Sir. Echo Charlie, Lima Golf Two Six."

"Two Six, go ahead."

"From DCI Callander", the operator cryptically introduced the request to ensure the dog handler made his response concise and suitably levelled at the ranking officer, "can you provide an update on your progress, please?"

"Roger that", Evans responded, acknowledging the clue. *"The dog picked up a strong trail as soon as I reached the location directed by CSI. I've gone about four hundred yards,"* the imperial reference betraying his length of service. *"I'm still on a west track paralleling the Midland Road by-pass. If I remember rightly, there's a small fishing lake a little further ahead. It looks like we're heading in that direction."*

The DCI, listening intently, raised his arm and clicked his fingers in a directive gesture to another computer operator. The far wall of the room had an overview map of the western side of the town projected onto a pull down screen. The operator tapped away at his computer mouse and the image scrolled quickly westward to centre over a small sky-blue shape. The image grew as the operator zoomed in on the modest fishing spot. Another few clicks and the picture showed a diagrammatic overlay of pathways that meandered through the suburban green belt. A name also appeared, hovering over the smooth oasis in the otherwise hatch marked woods; 'Friery Tarn'.

The image stopped and the operator turned to his superior like a dog seeking approval after completing some trained feat. Callander nodded in acknowledgement, not wanting to speak over the radio loudspeaker.

"What's the next area west of that, please?" Backhouse asked the operator. Without further conversation the map scrolled again, further westward, beyond the tarn. The green of the map's wooded legend gave way to the white representation of open land and the regular, beige blocks of a large, octagonal building.

The fast scroll over-rode the site and the screen cursor could be seen flicking to the peripheral column of map controls to locate the centring icon. The cursor flicked back to the octagonal building, the map quickly reversed its movement and the title of 'Westgate Retail Park' joined the locations identified along the dog handler's course.

"How far is the nearest patrol to that location, please?" the DCI asked.

"There's a traffic car further out on the Little Dunsford junction, about ten minutes away, five at speed."

Callander glanced over at Backhouse. "Thoughts?" He knew Backhouse was an extremely competent detective and valued his input. Besides, he was concerned by the fact that the Sergeant had taken a step back at the suggestion of a traffic car being the closest patrol; a distinctly non-verbal protest.

"Do you think a marked car would give us anything of value? We don't know Murray's situation and it's been over ten hours since the fire was reported at the park. If Lewis is at the shopping centre, a marked car will simply drive him into hiding. Worst still if he has Lizzy with him he might be forced into something stupid. I'd rather acquire him covertly and, if he's alone, follow him back to wherever Lizzy is being held."

There was a short pause while the silver commander considered the logic of Backhouse's thoughts as well as the potential ramifications of a poor decision. He couldn't fault the more experienced officer but, without wanting to distance the older man with a flippant remark, he knew his priorities lay with catching a murderer, not a kidnapper.

"Agreed," he concluded, seeing that the idea would serve both investigations just as well. "Get me a plain car up there. Steve, are your team ready to take over the surveillance at Lewis's home address?"

"They're due in any time now, Sir. I can have them on plot for seven thirty."

"See to it, Steve. Andy, contact DS Green on the home address team and tell him his staff will be released from there at seven thirty. But tell him I want four of his team to break off immediately and get to the area of the Westgate Retail Park as soon as possible. If that plain car spots anything, I want the DSU* on plot to pick up the obs until the rest of their team are relieved. Once DS Backhouse is on plot, I want the remainder of DS Green's team to move up to the shopping centre. Let him know I appreciate it'll put them over hours but I'm sure under the circumstances he won't be at all concerned."

"Roger that, Sir."

With that Backhouse, recognising the apparent shift in manpower for what it was worth, walked briskly from the room. As the spring-controlled door closed slowly behind him, DCI Callander could sense the old Sergeant's determination to bring the *Murray* portion of this disaster to a swift close.

"Good hunting Steve," he called after him.

"Boss," Backhouse acknowledged in a resolute, but distinctly dismissive tone.

Chapter Seventeen

Driving into the town, he found it strange that there weren't more police cars in sight. The helicopter was still hovering over the countryside between the industrial estate and the shopping centre he had left some fifteen minutes before but he was curious as to where all the ground units were.

He scanned across the cheap, standard interior of the plain police vehicle he had recovered from the outlying car park. He glanced down and noticed a short, stubby aerial sticking up from the passenger door pocket. Briefly re-checking the empty road ahead, he leaned over to reach the device. However, it was a little too far away and before he had even touched the abandoned radio he felt the sudden vibration of the lane-edge vibra-line telling him he was swerving off course toward the kerb. He bolted back upright and snatched at the wheel to correct the wayward vehicle.

David could see the hatchback's rear lights in the distance. He had quickly caught the slower vehicle in his hijacked sports car and had been tracking it at around a quarter of a mile distance for several minutes. Suddenly, he saw the car swerve toward the kerb before untidily correcting itself to return to the running lane. His mind quizzed the peculiar detour. Was Murray still alive, still in the car? Had she tried to escape her captor and caused the car to swerve? If she was with the real mugger in the car just ahead of him then David could be cleared of all suspicion *and* save Lucy in one fell swoop.

He decided he had to know if Murray was alive or not. If he overtook the car he could get a look inside. Accelerating the powerful two-seater, he caught the larger, slower vehicle in a matter of seconds. Pulling alongside the hatchback, he looked across to see the occupants. The driver was a white lad, about his age and with the same dark hair. However, he was drawn, with gaunt features and the hair was greasy. His stubbly face and dark, dirty skin portrayed a distinct lack of grooming and his clothes were dull and on the vagrant side of casual. Even the open-minded David immediately suspected he was a druggie. However, his opinion of the decidedly unpleasant looking driver aside, he had more important concerns; where was Murray?

From his almost horizontal position in the low-lying sports car, he couldn't get a clear view of the higher hatchback's passenger side. He arched upward to elevate his line of sight but the other driver suddenly noticed the hovering car and turned to look at David. He snapped his head forward and accelerated away.

'*Damn,*' he thought.

The manoeuvre had achieved nothing except putting him on the wrong side of the very person he was supposed to be following. What was worse was that, in his efforts to take a peek into the other car, he had overshot the deceleration lane which the evasive hatchback was now descending toward the town centre.

"Ah, bollocks," he cursed out loud. He pressed the accelerator hard to the floor and the lightweight vehicle shot forward toward the next exit, an infuriating five miles further down the road.

***

He frowned at the strange driving of the tosser in the silver Lotus.

'*What the hell was that all about?*' he thought momentarily, but he had other concerns and returned his attention to the road ahead. Pulling away from the junction roundabout, he spotted a lay-by and quickly pulled over to allow him to get at that elusive radio. He ignorantly tested each button until the device sprang into life.

***

"Morning everyone," Backhouse announced himself as he re-entered the somewhat less grandiose command room which had been set up in response to Murray's disappearance.

There was no overhead projector shining flashy, interactive maps onto *this* room's walls. There were only about half the staff sat over command and control stations as were being utilised in the adjacent double-murder's incident room and, although the Divisional Superintendent had been present at the briefing, the most senior officer still involved in *this* investigation was now DI Priest. Backhouse was somewhat dismayed at the fact that this search, of a serving police officer, had somehow become second fiddle to the murder of two drug-dealing *scum-bags*.

Still, after his length of service he'd become accustomed to the welfare of officers taking a back seat to the rights of the low-lives which had plagued his whole career. He dismissed the thought knowing that, at least in here, in *his* incident room, the needs of Lizzy far outweighed those of any potential offenders.

The room's attention was once more drawn to the ageing DS's voice. It was more than that though. The intensity of that attention was far greater than the sleep deprived officers had been offering for the latter days of Operation Cassandra. They pulled up their chairs and the Sergeant had silence. Even the pleasantry of a reply to his greeting was muted by their need to get back out on the street in the search for their lost colleague. Backhouse instantly felt the electricity in their drive and got straight to the point.

"As some of you might already be aware from the somewhat over-the-top contingent next door there's been a double murder during the night. Two males from Manchester, believed to be the Crabtree brothers, were torched in their vehicle in Westgate Park after having had their throats slit open by who we suspect to have been a user in the back seat. Now, it's my suspicion that the killer was David Lewis and that, because of the Crabtree's warning signals and intelligence, he may very well now be armed."

"So why have there been two incident rooms set up? Is

Callander not linking the two jobs?" Wazzer interrupted, instantly recognising the manpower discrepancy from the previous night's search efforts.

"For now, no; and to be honest I prefer it that way. The need to find Lizzy would be lost on the search for the murderer and, even if they are the same person, I want us to concentrate on the fact that Lizzy is still alive. If we turn this into a reactive investigation it'll become too cumbersome and we may not find her in time. With the Super's approval DI Priest has been made SIO for this matter and we're heading up the search to find Lizzy safe and well. I want to keep it proactive and dynamic."

There were approving nods from around the room.

"We intend to run the search in parallel with that for the Crabtree murderer. We'll take on any leads they get while staying separate enough to not get bogged down with any red herrings. For starters, within the last half hour there's been a development on the double murder in that John Evans has picked up a track from the park scene toward the Westgate Retail Park. DCI Callander is intent on getting the DSU up there as soon as possible so we need to replace that unit down at the Lewis OPs straight away. I've promised a change-over for seven thirty which gives us under ten minutes to be on plot. As such let's go and I'll brief you on the day's surveillance over the air en route. Same channel as Cassandra. Let's leave the monitored channel for the DCI's team. Atticker, keep a spare set tuned into that channel though, so we don't miss anything that the boss *forgets* to tell us about!"

Atticker nodded his acknowledgement. The rest of the team rose to their feet and quickly grabbed the assembled kit they'd prepared while waiting for their leader's arrival. Within a minute the door was quietly closing behind them, leaving Atticker to take up his place at the comms station he had been using throughout the previous week's observations. As he reached over the desk to retrieve his headset, he noticed the small flash of the 'received transmission' light from his airwave terminal. It flickered off and, pulling the headset over his head and positioning the earpieces into place, he heard the faint *click* as the call disconnected.

"Last caller, say again," he beckoned.

There was no reply. He dismissed the anomaly, believing that one of the team must have simply snagged their push-to-talk button on something or other in their haste to leave the building. Little did he know that the recipient of his call was now satisfied that he had, by childish experimentation, finally mastered the controls of his newly acquired police radio.

***

He carefully placed the half rounded, half flat profile of the radio face down on the hatchback's dashboard so that it wouldn't roll out of reach and, glancing over his right shoulder, accelerated harshly away from the lay-by. He had already re-checked the address details of the *witness* Lewis and was heading directly for it.

"Okay, now that everyone's mobile," the radio chirped up once again, *"let's go over what I want to happen. You've all seen the plan of the OPs. Wazzer and Thomo, I want you to take over plot three. That'll keep you far enough away to pick up any vehicles leaving the site without you being blown out. Tracey and Dave, I want you two to take up plot two. If we get any visitors to the address, I want you to be in a position to pick up a foot follow until Atticker can direct the other teams ahead of you. Barnes and I will take up plot one with the eyeball on the actual address. The rest of you take up periphery positions to allow for swap-overs. I don't want this Lewis character getting wise to our presence so let's keep it fluid."*

Lewis? The name sent a sudden doubt racing through his drug tortured mind. Why were they watching Lewis? Had the missing Murray been looking for Lewis all along? *David* Lewis? She had used the name David back at the factor, but that was *his* name too.

'Shit,' he thought. He'd taken her using it, as she had, to confirm his suspicion that she was after *him*, that this David Lewis character had led her straight to him.

"Shiiiiiit," he protractedly exclaimed at the realisation of what he now believed to be the actual situation. She hadn't been after him at all. She had been after Lewis. Just like the coppers on the radio were after Lewis. He had misunderstood her using his name and, because of that mistake, he was now a double murderer, with a gun in his car and, no doubt, a whole posse of coppers breathing down his neck. Still, Lewis knew all about him. If the police got hold of Lewis he could still lead them to him. Who the hell was this David Lewis?

He saw a junction up ahead which he knew led away from the trap he was driving straight into. He swerved the stolen police car into the side street and sped along the ever-narrowing country road that led up to a hillside lay-by he knew overlooked the town. He had to find out what the hell was going on. He still had to get rid of Lewis.

***

David, David Lewis, stamped down hard on the brake pedal of the Lotus Elise he had stolen from the Westgate shopping centre earlier that day. Its anti-lock braking system shuddered the car's lightweight frame to a frighteningly harsh stop. It was still early, within the first hour of daylight, and the road was thankfully empty. Fortunate too, as he had totally misjudged his extreme speed in the unfamiliar vehicle and had overshot the descending junction by at least a car's length, stalling it in the middle of the roundabout.

His fury over losing the hatchback had completely dissolved his sense of self preservation. He had to get a grip, to concentrate on what he was going to do next. Killing himself in the process was not going to help Lucy.

He fumbled with the gear stick and ignition keys and the throaty exhaust roared back to life. More gently now, he reversed the low-lying car away from its nose-to-kerb position and traversed the roundabout before heading off toward the town centre. As he joined the main road from the junction, he passed a lay-by and noticed two deep, parallel tyre troughs leaving the short parking area back out onto the road. The mud still left on the road gave the distinct impression that the vehicle leaving was doing so in a big hurry.

Initially tempted to dismiss them as a coincidence, David

couldn't help but think it could have been the hatchback. Did the mugger have to stop to re-secure the fidgeting DC Murray? It fitted the circumstances he wanted to believe, that Murray was alive. His confidence, his belief that he was heading in the right direction, grew by the second.

He thought back to the vision he'd had about Lucy. The police had been at the house, he was sure of that, so he knew he couldn't go straight there. He couldn't give himself up and expect them to believe his story of premonitions. He concentrated harder to recall the details of the forewarning. It was like a dream, more and more difficult to remember over time. He had seen his house from an elevated viewpoint, a hillside, and the direction meant it could be only one place of which he was aware.

***

"... was that great eighties release from Phil Collins. Coming up after the news is the new number one but now it's almost eight o'clock so I'll hand you over the Mark in the news room."

Lucy's alarm clock/radio chirped into life and she woke from her deep dreamless sleep. For a moment, the reality of the previous day, as unfocused as her bleary eyes, seemed as though it could have been the dream she had gone without. Sadly she came, only too quickly, to realize the truth of the matter.

Fully awake, she threw back her sheets, sprang from her bed and strode through to the bathroom. She quickly tied back her thick, black hair in a style-forgiving clip and washed herself. There was no time to waste putting on her make-up so, instead, she quickly cupped the still-warming water and rinsed the soap from her face and neck. Towelling herself dry whilst walking back into her bedroom, she hastily grabbed the first casual clothes to hand.

Her slender legs slipped easily into the pale tracksuit bottoms and she tucked in the simple white t-shirt which she had pulled from her bedside drawers. Dropping to her knees, she reached under the bed to retrieve a pair of clean, white running shoes. Then she discarded them by her feet while simultaneously bouncing down to sit on the bed and slide on the short socks which were kept in a neat roll in one of the trainers.

She pulled on the footwear, tucking the laces down the sides, and jumped up toward the lounge and her apartment door beyond. Stalling in the bedroom doorway, she leapt back to recover her mobile phone from the bedside cabinet before continuing out toward the hallway. She grabbed her white tracksuit jacket from a peg by the exit and, as she opened the door, shook the jacket to check for the jingle of her house keys. Confirming their presence, she pulled the door closed behind her and walked out toward the nearest bus stop.

***

"All patrols, no change, no change," Barnes announced over the back-to-back radio channel.

It was eight-thirty, Wednesday morning and the team had arrived on plot as promised to the Detective Chief Inspector by Backhouse. The DSU were long gone and, besides the presence of the uniformed operational support unit out of sight nearby, the surveillance of Lewis's modest bedsit had fallen solely to Murray's closest colleagues.

It had been a long week and the stillness of the observations gave Backhouse the opportunity, once again, to go over the massive shift in role from robbery DS to surveillance team leader. He was desperate to recover Lizzy, an experienced officer maybe, but still just a slip of a girl who he may well have driven into the unlawful custody of a crazed killer. It was not the career-ending highlight he had foreseen for himself.

The traffic had been building up for half an hour or so as the rush hour had gotten into full swing. There was plenty of movement, just none from the narrow-fronted, new-build apartment block occupied by the absent David Lewis. The cars previously parked about the suburban street were thinning out as the residents left on their respective commutes to the various workplaces dotted around the town. Backhouse was becoming increasingly concerned that the vehicles they were using as impromptu observation posts were beginning to stand out in the ever-decreasing crowd.

"Barnes, get Tracey and Dave to move up to this plot and we'll take a back seat for a while. We're starting to draw a few sideways looks from the locals."

"Will do, Sarge. Jem to Tracey, from the Sarge can you and Dave swap with us on plot one please and takeover the eyeball."

"Roger that." The obedient duo left their plot and began the short drive to relieve Backhouse and Barnes outside the quiet address. As they approached the location, Tracey called up once again.

"Standby. We've got a dark haired female in a white tracksuit jacket and light pants approaching plot one on foot."

"Roger that," Backhouse replied snatching the radio from Barnes. "Back off and return to plot two until we've seen what she's up to."

"Roger Sarge," the young detective responded. Their car passed in front of Backhouse and Barnes' position momentarily blocking their view of the attractive young woman now in sight.

She briskly climbed the short flight of entrance steps to the communal front door of the apartment block and pressed the bell to David's apartment. There was, of course, no reply. She tried again, and again she waited pointlessly for a reply. Reaching into her pocket, she flipped open her mobile phone.

"Female one uses mobile phone with right hand," Barnes relayed to the observation loggist, Atticker.

"Roger, female uses phone with right hand."

Lucy got the same 'switched off' message from David's phone and once again pressed the doorbell to his apartment. As she did, the landlady, who had noticed her loitering on the doorstep from her ground floor bay window, opened the door to greet the momentarily excited young woman.

"Can I help you dear?" she asked Lucy.

"I'm looking for David Lewis, he lives in the first floor flat."

"Yes, he lives here, dear. Oh, but I haven't seen him for a week or so now. Are you a friend of his?" she asked inquisitively.

"Yes, I am," Lucy replied, unaware of the old woman's status within the building and curious of her interest.

And it was interest indeed. The old landlady had seen the television appeal for information on David Lewis's whereabouts. In fact, being the general busy-body that she was, she had been one of the earlier callers to inform the police of the details which they had already obtained from David's employer. Had she not been out shopping that Monday, she would have known that David had been to the apartment to shower and change after his first release from the hospital.

"Would you like to leave a message? What's your name, dear?"

Lucy suddenly felt uneasy at the intrusive nature of the woman's interest and excused herself as politely as she felt necessary.

"Err, no it's okay. I'll catch him another time." With that, she left the building and walked away back toward the bus stop for town.

"Female two returns inside building and female one leaves heading across road to the town-bound bus stop," Barnes updated Atticker with the visitor's progress.

"Female one waiting at bus stop checking timetable poster; female one checking watch, left wrist; female one leaving bus stop and walking toward town centre."

"Tracey, Dave, pick up a foot follow on that female, please," Backhouse directed after once more snatching Barnes radio from his hand.

"Wazzer, Thomo, take up a position ahead of them and relieve as required. Phil, Tina come and take up our position at post one, will you?"

"Girlfriend?" Barnes intuitively asked his supervisor.

"Ex I think, yeah."

"Doesn't look like she knows where he is though."

"Nope," Backhouse agreed with the young detective. "But if thirty years in this job has taught me anything it's that a woman wanting to find her man, ex or otherwise, will *always* find him. It's like they've got radar, especially if she thinks he's up to no good."

Barnes considered the sexist undertone in the Sergeant's comment but, since his initial outing to the hospital to visit Mrs Nugent, Barnes had begun to warm to the older detective's idiosyncrasies. Backhouse's stopping at the station, like a concerned father, since Murray's disappearance had raised Barnes' respect for the old bigot. As far as political correctness went, Backhouse was still a dinosaur but his uncharacteristic concern over his team gave Barnes cause to reflect before criticising the DS as quickly as he previously might have. Besides, Barnes actually found the comment had some merit. The old adage *'Hell hath no fury...'* came to the forefront of his mind.

"Plus, from the initial house-to-house in this area Lewis hasn't been here in over a week. That takes us back to the Squadron Leader's attack. I think that girl has just become our best lead."

"Fair enough," Barnes tritely concurred.

Backhouse was tempted to give the younger man a sarcastically sideways look at what he would normally have taken as an unnecessarily condescending remark. However, he detected a novel, relaxed tone in the new detective's voice and decided to let the over-familiarity pass without reacting.

"Here are Phil and Tina. Let's go."

***

In the glove box of the stolen hatchback he had found a small pair of rubber-encased binoculars. As he held them to his face, he could see the distant show play out as he suspected a surveillance operation would. The cars dotted about with two occupants in each were a dead giveaway and a short distance away, out of sight of the address, a liveried police support van was parked with its sliding side door open. The heavily armour-clad officers were milling around aimlessly and he surmised that they were waiting for something to happen.

Then he noticed a young, slim girl with flowing, dark hair

walking toward the address he had read about in Murray's notebook. He was familiar with the block of newly built apartments having cased the location as a potential burglary target just after it had been completed a year or so ago. Fortunately for him, the new build, subject of ever-stricter planning regulations, had large block numbers at each entrance door, placed in obvious view of the roadway for the use of emergency services answering calls to the area.

With his newly acquired optics, he easily distinguished the correct address from the various apartment blocks along the road. The young brunette climbed the few steps to the front door and, looking back at the liveried police vehicle he noticed the support unit officers scrambling for their places in the van.

'Well, who are you then?' he thought to himself. The attractive young woman was certainly of some interest to the onlooking police. He swept the binoculars back to the female at the door. She was talking on a mobile phone and hadn't gone inside.

'You're looking for someone who isn't home,' he narrated the scene to himself.

An older woman joined her at the doorstep from inside the building.

"Hello deary, looking for David 'bloody' Lewis," he spoke out loud, filling in the inaudible conversation. "Yes thanks, he's my lover-boy," the voice-over continued.

His sarcastic wit had struck a chord of truth closer to reality than he could have otherwise imagined.

'I'll bet that's exactly what you are, aren't you, deary,' he thought, forming an insipid plan to secure the elusive David Lewis.

He watched her leave to get her direction of travel. She stopped at the opposite bus stop. He tried to make out the shelter's route sign but the compact lenses weren't *that* powerful. In any event, she was now leaving, on foot, toward the town centre.

'Bus too long of a wait lover girl?' he considered. If she was confident enough to take on the walk into town, rather than waiting, he deduced she must have been local. Furthermore, if she was, he knew exactly what route she was likely to take. He dropped the binoculars to his side but continued looking at the, now miniscule, scene unfolding before him.

Confident in his assumptions, he was about to head back to the car parked nearby. However, at the last moment, just as the woman walked out of view in his predicted direction, he saw a man and woman step from another hatchback car, equally as bland as the one behind him. They walked after the attractive woman in white and were instantly recognisable to him as plain-clothed police.

'*Shit,*' he thought at the complication to his plan.

He returned to the car and, casually discarding the useful optics onto the passenger seat, revved the rattling diesel engine to life and sped away to the location along the woman's route at which he intended to intercept her.

Chapter Eighteen

David threaded the tiny roadster through the bends, up to the hillside viewpoint, with an almost race-like professionalism. He was calmer now, thinking more clearly and, besides, he was becoming more accustomed to the tight chassis' handling characteristics. He almost regretted making the promise to take it back.

He rounded the final bend and made a more controlled, far quieter stop a hundred or so metres short of the location. Quickly, he extricated himself from the low-slung seat and, leaving the door slightly ajar to make as little noise as possible, left the vehicle and set off around the shallow bend.

He reached the empty lay-by, instantly abandoning all effort to remain quiet. The hatchback wasn't there. Was he early or late? He quickly paced about the small area, scouring for clues. There they were, two tell-tale troughs in the mud of the grassy verge trailing out onto the rough gravel of the hillside lane. They were just like the ones he had seen at the lay-by near to the dual-carriageway. He was late. He cursed at this second consequence of his earlier mistake on the fast, by-pass road.

He checked further into the lay-by and stared intently over the expanse of buildings set out beneath him. In the far distance, beyond the town toward the shopping centre, he could make out the hovering dot that he knew was the police helicopter. Even now, without its searchlight illuminated, its changing profile gave away the circular nature of its flight pattern.

He looked closer and finally made out his apartment nestled within the sprawl of new-build premises to the north of the town centre. He thought for a moment, recounting again the steps of the premonition which had led him this far. He strained his eyes to locate the police van. It was there but the door was closed. No-one was milling around it as he had foreseen. He checked back at the house, squinting for detail, but without the binoculars from his vision he failed to achieve it.

Some of the unfamiliar cars were there but something felt wrong. The lack of police around the van meant he hadn't seen the image this way. Was this the scene before the *start* of the vision, *before* Lucy had arrived or was it *after* she had left? Suddenly, he realised that if he'd seen his visions the through the eyes of the mugger then he was in the wrong place. Murray's kidnapper had already been here and gone; the wheel tread debris had told him that much, and if that was the case then he was losing ground.

He hadn't seen the route to the car park and pathway where Lucy had next appeared. He hadn't recognised the scenery around it. He was at the end of his trail of clues. All he knew was that Lucy was being followed by a man and a woman by whom the mugger didn't want to be seen. He concluded that they were the police who had followed her from the house in his vision.

Finally, and most worryingly, the time line of his premonition, dubious at best before the empty car park, was totally lost after that point. He had no way to judge if the time between the car park and the firearm appearing in his face was an hour, a day or even a year. He decided to work on the rate of things so far, on the worst case scenario.

He had no option but to call Backhouse and put his trust in the detective. He took a moment to reconsider the option. His previous encounter with the Sergeant was far from productive but he had no choice. Having lost his quarry, the only person he knew who had any chance of finding him was Backhouse. He would know where the man and woman following Lucy were. He ran to the Lotus and raced back down the hill toward the nearest house.

***

It had gone nine o'clock. The Benefit Office would be open. Lucy flipped open her mobile phone once again. Pressing the recall, she searched the device's memory for the number belonging to Lisa Turner, David's work colleague.

'Oh, bugger,' she innocently thought to herself, realising her error.

She hadn't used her mobile the night before and had called the party organiser from her house phone. As a result, of course, the number wasn't saved to the last-dialled list on her mobile. She continued on her route into the town to visit the potential source of information on David's whereabouts in person. Knowing the area well, she used as many shortcuts as she could to reach the town centre and the promise of help from his workmate. She ducked down alleyways and through cul-de-sacs which had thoroughfare pathways between them and their adjoining roads.

Tracey and Dave followed at a discreet distance but Lucy was an easy subject. Oblivious in her thoughts to everything around her, she had no sense of anti-surveillance and they easily relayed the directions to Atticker who was maintaining an accurate record of each twist and turn. There had been no need for Wazzer, Thomo, Barnes or Backhouse to take over the surveillance but they kept skipping ahead to potential swap-points, should the need arise.

"Left, left, left into Achilles Way," Tracey transmitted to Atticker.

"Roger that, left into Achilles Way," Atticker relayed, in case the other patrols didn't hear the back-to-back message.

"Backhouse, permission."

Atticker recognised the Sergeant's request to interrupt.

"Go ahead Sarge," came the reply.

"Any indication on her destination?"

"She's been making a bee-line for the town centre, and she knows her streets. Her route has been about as direct as it could have been."

Backhouse knew that Atticker couldn't offer any more. Lewis had no previous record. There was no information or associated addresses for the intelligence officer to search on which could suggest where she might be heading. She could have been going to work for all they knew.

The only reference to the town centre was Lewis's place of work, the Benefit Office. That said, Lewis wasn't in work, he hadn't been in over a week. Surely his girlfriend, even his ex as she was, would know that? She must have had information or at least knew someone at his place of work who had it. Why else would she be making such a direct march for the place?

As usual Backhouse's chain of thought, the links of which were tenuous at best, was strewn with suppositions. However, as his reputation resoundingly supported, his hunches regularly bore more fruit than hours of the investigative elimination technique that many other detectives used, meticulously ruling out every alternative until only the truth could remain. He was a risk taker and, up until the untimely disappearance of Lizzy, his luck in successfully pulling off some hair-raising enquiries had spanned decades.

In his haste to progress his latest *gem,* he by-passed the normal protocol for interrupting the radio traffic.

"Atticker, get me the number for Janet Seymour, Lewis's boss at the Benefit Office. DI Priest has it."

"Roger that," the reply came.

"Penny for them?" Barnes quizzed.

"She's heading for the Job Centre, where Lewis worked. I'll bet a pound to a pinch of shit she's got a source in there, a friend of Lewis or something, and I want the head's up on it."

***

As he swung the non-descript hatchback around the open space the loose gravel crunched beneath its wheels. Stopping the vehicle close to a concrete-panelled wall, which stretched the length of the car park's northern edge, he walked alongside the grey, pebble-stippled barrier until he was standing just short of an opening between it and the unkempt, adjoining hedgerow. Briefly, he leaned out through the opening to view the pathway and road beyond.

Immediately, he recognised the light, casual tracksuit and

long, black hair of the young woman from Lewis's house. She was confidently striding toward him and he knew it would have been the easiest thing in the world to snatch her from the pathway and out of view into the hidden area of the secluded car park. However, the attractive female was not the only person his quick glance had spotted. The man and woman who he had seen leaving after her from Lewis's house were still on her tail.

Despite their obviously police-like gait, the fact they were still following her confirmed to him who they were and that this was no place for a struggle. Before he was spotted, he swung back against the concrete panelling in a smooth half circle, the gravel crackling beneath the twisting ball of his foot. He thought for a moment. Then, in the bushes just to his left, he spotted an old, abandoned pram. It was the collapsible, folding type with the thin, cloth seat torn down the middle but, abandoned by its original owner, it served his purpose.

He watched, tucked safely out of view, until the brunette walked past the opening. The following couple were about a hundred and fifty yards behind her. She turned another corner out of sight and he felt the forthcoming success of his plan welling inside him. Right on cue, a car came into sight and drove between the lines of parked cars toward the opening. Firmly gripping the unfolded pram's handles, he rocked backward and forward as if he was the brake man of a bobsled team building up momentum before a run.

Checking and re-checking the vehicle's approach, he timed his thrust perfectly. The pram shot out from the opening and slotted neatly between two parked cars. Emerging at exactly the right moment, it came into the view of the driver with only feet to spare. Assuming the worst, that the wayward buggy had a child in it, she instinctively swerved away from its path. In the narrow, double-parked street there was simply no space for manoeuvre and what seemed like a reasonable speed of thirty miles an hour was suddenly brought, in the space of a bonnet, to a bone-crushing halt. The cacophony of shattering glass and twisting metal was surprisingly short lived; so much so that the barely absent Lucy wasn't even diverted from the intensity of her thoughts.

For Dave and Tracey, though, it was a completely different matter. There was no way, as police officers with a sworn duty to protect life and property, that they could carry on past the crash to continue their pursuit of the only lead left open to their supervisor. They ran over to the oddly silent wreck to find the driver slumped, unconscious across the wheel.

"Tracey to Atticker, urgent."

"Go ahead," Atticker acknowledged, spitting out a chocolate biscuit and nearly falling off his chair from his relaxed, feet-on-desk position.

"We need an ambulance and uniformed assistance to Achilles Way. One vehicle TA'd* into parked cars and a child's buggy knocked down in the street."

She leaned through the smashed driver's window and gently slipped her fingers beneath the woman's scarf to check for a pulse.

"One adult, female driver, breathing but unconscious. We're going to need fire brigade too," she added, noticing the collapsed position off the steering column set deep into the driver's lap.

"Dave?" Tracey quizzed to her colleague who had scrambled over the concertinaed vehicles in search of the errant pushchair thrown there by the collision.

Dave popped up into her view, his hands raised in frustrated negativity.

"I can't find it. The pram's here but no baby," he announced.

Neither of them had considered in their panic to even look in the direction of the pushchair's origin, of its owner.

He was long gone, racing across the car park out of sight to the waiting car.

"Shit," Backhouse proclaimed loudly, banging his palms down on the wheel of his vehicle.

He and Barnes were way out of position to pick up the eyeball. They had headed off toward the Benefit Office in advance of Atticker's information on the number of Lewis's supervisor.

"Wazzer, Thomo, where the hell are you?"

"Making ground Sarge but we were stuck behind a bin lorry for a while there and we're still a mile or so away."

"Make ground, make ground," he loudly snapped at the pair.

Racing in what was now the wrong direction, he characteristically threw caution to the wind and slewed the car across the busy town centre roadway in a dramatically huge and equally screeching hand-brake turn. He pointlessly wheel-span the car which eventually responded by gripping the superheated tarmac and lurching forward toward their quarry's last known position.

Barnes' head bounced off the passenger-side window at the unexpected manoeuvre and, although he stayed indignantly silent, he could almost picture the control room switchboard lighting up with calls about a 'mad driver in a stolen car'.

Their 'easy subject' was being suddenly, albeit unintentionally, evasive.

***

David thanked the elderly couple as he ran back to his hijacked car and sped away toward the town. He had been unable to get through to speak to Backhouse in person. He was 'out' and unavailable and, despite David's protestations, the civilian operator had only offered to either pass a message or put him through to voicemail.

After opting for the former, and leaving a message for the robbery squad DS, he wanted to get closer to the town centre before trying to contact him again. Although he hadn't recognised the car park from which he had envisioned Lucy, he had recalled enough detail of the image to know it wasn't out here in the hills of the countryside surrounding the valley-bottom town.

***

"Atticker to Backhouse."

"Stand by, stand by," the occupied Sergeant shouted into

the radio as he weaved, one handed, through the busy morning traffic.

"Sarge, you're going to want to hear this. I've just had the control room on the line. They say David Lewis was on the phone wanting to speak to you."

"What the hell?" Backhouse exclaimed. "What did he want?" he asked the equally astonished Atticker.

"That's the bit you won't want to hear. They didn't ask him and the operator didn't realise who he was until he commented on the guy's agitated state to his supervisor who practically choked on his tea and toast."

"Bloody civvies," the furious Backhouse cursed at Barnes, again punishing the car's hard-done-by steering wheel.

"Did we get a location, a number, any damn thing?"

"Just a number Sarge. But they've already called that and it belongs to an old couple out in the country east of town. They said a 'polite young man' had stopped to use their phone and had left in a big hurry toward town in a sports car."

"Get Phil and Tina up there anyway to speak with the old dears and let DCI Callander's lot know about the car. Perhaps one of his road blocks will spot it. Any make or VRM on the car?"

"Old people Sarge, it was silver!"

"Fair enough," Backhouse acknowledged, not having expected much more.

"Sarge, I've just been told that the DCI already knows about a silver sports car. Apparently, a silver Lotus Elise was hi-jacked from Westgate shopping centre this morning. The road blocks are already watching for it but there's been no sign of it leaving town. Uniform haven't attended yet for the full details to keep the area clear for the DSU but the initial report description does sort of fit Lewis."

"That's got to be him. Ask the DCI, from me, to release one of the DSU to speak to the owner. It's too much of a coincidence to ignore."

"Will do Sarge."

It tallied with the theory that Lewis was responsible for the double murder; the fact he had left in the direction of the retail park. That said, why had Lewis driven right across town to use an old couple's phone, only to head back into town? Why wasn't he fleeing away from Hopefield altogether? The old detective pondered the thought but his usual thought process of leap-and-bound was interrupted by the need to avoid the school run traffic, awash with four-by-fours and MPV's. In any event, as long as Lewis was heading toward him and not away, he was happy for now.

Chapter Nineteen

Another one of the bank of incoming call lights flashed in the Hopefield control room.

"Good morning, Hopefield Police. How can I help you?" the pleasantly polished voice of the operator asked the new caller.

"Hello. Is DS Backhouse there yet, please? This is David Lewis. It's urgent."

After the furore which had followed the previous mistake, every operator in the room now knew exactly what to do with *this* call. The operator swung around in her chair to face the elevated desk of the duty Sergeant and, holding the microphone away from her mouth, called out,

"Sarge, Lewis, line eight."

The supervisor, acknowledging the alert, clicked on his microphone, depressed the relevant switch and spoke confidently and clearly.

"Mr Lewis, my name is Sergeant Carter. I'm here to help you."

"Put me through to DS Backhouse. It's urgent."

"Can you tell me where you are?"

"Listen. Don't waste my time trying to get to me. I'm not calling to hand myself in this time. Just put me through to DS Backhouse, NOW," David shouted, losing patience with the polite but inquisitive Sergeant.

"Very well Mr Lewis. Please stay on the line."

Carter pressed a few buttons on the expansive control panel laid out before him and, carefully dialling the current number for Backhouse from his internal phone directory, he contacted the senior detective and addressed his peer.

"Steve, it's John Carter in the control room."

"Go ahead John, and please make it good news!"

"I've got Lewis on hold for you. Any instructions?"

"Have we got a trace?"

"He's calling from a TK* on Bank Street, opposite the Benefit Office."

"I knew it," Backhouse exclaimed. "She's heading straight for him. John put him through to me."

"Will do. Do you want me to get a patrol to him?"

"No. We're a couple of minutes away and I don't want him spooked. I somehow doubt he's got Murray with him. Let's hear what he's got to say before we send in the cavalry. Move them up but keep them quiet. No blues-and-twos. Understood?" The sternness of his final word left Carter in no doubt about Backhouse's current disregard for the control room Sergeant's staff.

"Completely," the station Sergeant acknowledged. *"Good luck."*

"Cheers." There was a short silence and then,

"Is that DS Backhouse?"

"Yes, David it is. Tell me about DC Murray. Is she alright?"

"She's not dead then?" David asked in a relieved tone.

"What?" Backhouse replied, surprised at both the tone and content of David's question.

"Thank God. I saw the television news and thought she was dead."

"Lewis," Backhouse's tone was less friendly. "Are you trying to tell me you don't know how she is? Where did you leave her?"

"You have to believe me Sergeant. I haven't seen or heard from DC Murray since I left the police station on Monday."

"Don't mess with me lad. Where is she?"

"Come on Backhouse," David affirmed, equally as annoyed at the detective's tone. *"Do you really think I would be phoning you if I had actually hurt her? I'm phoning because my friend Lucy is in danger, and I mean now. Are your people still following her?"*

Backhouse was perplexed. If Lewis had nothing to do with Lizzy's disappearance, how did he know about the surveillance? Had the girl spotted her observers and called him? No. If she had, why would Lewis be calling him for help? The girl could have done that herself if she was in danger. Putting his concerns for Lizzy to one side for a moment to try and make sense of Lewis's opening gambit, he quizzed the young lad once again.

"Where is Lucy now?" he asked.

"What, you mean you don't know? I saw your people following her but I don't know where they went after the car park."

There was an edge of panic in David's voice and Backhouse's years of investigative experience spotted it instantly. So, what the hell was he on about? What car park? Backhouse's mind was struggling for an explanation but every question he asked only seemed to create another two.

"Where did you see them David?" he asked, more calmly now, trying to peel back the obstructive skin of David's tale.

David was quiet for a moment. He considered his next answer carefully, knowing that Backhouse was short on patience and was not likely to take a story of premonitions and pre-offence injuries very well.

"Can you please just accept that I know? I know the old lady broke her hip. I know that Murray was taken to a factory and then somewhere dark and I KNOW that Lucy is going to be kidnapped and possibly shot."

Backhouse was now more confused than ever. Was Lewis trying to ask for help or make a confession? And that latter claim; was he telling the detective what he was going to do next? Was he actually taunting them?

"Now wait just a bloody minute. You said you last saw DC Murray at the station and now you're telling me you saw her at the factory and again after that. What the hell is going on Lewis?"

"I saw her in person at the station and then saw her taken from the factory, but it wasn't me that took her. Believe me, I've never been there."

This was getting ridiculous. Backhouse was quickly losing his temper. However, he was also quickly getting to the area of Bank Street and he knew that, even if he couldn't talk some sense out of Lewis, he would very soon be able to *beat* it out of him.

"Do you know where Lucy is or not?" David insisted.

Backhouse was curious but so close to Lewis now that he felt it safe to test the young man's resolve.

"Well, I think she's coming to see you David," he said solemnly.

Initially David didn't realise the hidden meaning that Backhouse was closing him down. In his naivety, he actually thought the detective was being genuinely helpful. He instinctively looked up from his feet to check the street outside through the scratched perspex of the telephone box's panes.

Across the road, at that very moment, the beautiful Lucy entered his line of sight from a side road a short distance away.

"*Cheers,*" David thanked Backhouse and hung up the phone to run and greet her.

"Hello... David. Shit. Get out of the way you arsehole," he shouted at the painfully slow morning shoppers.

***

He spotted the young and now alone woman and slowed the car as he drew alongside her. Her face seemed worried and her thoughts distant. She was totally oblivious of him as he smoothly and calmly pulled across the road to park his stolen hatchback, driver's side to the kerb, just short of her approach. Gently releasing the door, he slowly opened it, timing his exit from the car with her arrival on the vehicle's front, offside quarter.

Suddenly, she stopped, distracted somehow by something or someone across the road. Her expression changed to one of shocked relief and she quickly raised her hand to wave at some unseen friend. He had to act now. Leaping from the vehicle and grabbing her right arm, he punched her hard and square in the face.

She was instantly knocked unconscious and slumped toward the ground, twisting about the support of his tightening grip. Reaching around her waist he caught her light frame and, opening the rear door of the car, bundled her inside. He slammed the door closed and jumped back into the driver's seat. Jamming the vehicle into gear, he was totally unaware of the man rushing from across the street to the pavement beside him.

David couldn't believe what he had seen. Anger surged through his body and, reaching the driver's side of the car as it began to pull away from the kerb, he swung at the glass panel with all his fury. The glass shattered under the blow and a thousand nuggets of silica rained down on the startled driver.

Reactively jerking away from the downpour, he snatched at the wheel and the accelerating vehicle wallowed violently on its suspension before colliding with the car which had been parked directly in front of it at the kerbside. Unbelted, his body slammed against the steering wheel. Unfortunately for David, the impact was insufficient to incapacitate the offensive man. He quickly recovered some composure and hastily selected reverse gear. Two feet rearward was all he needed to clear the shunted obstacle and he was quickly reselecting first.

However, two feet was also all David needed to be close enough to reach the door handle to rescue the unconscious Lucy from the rear of the car. Defiantly, it was locked. In the mêlée the driver had knocked his elbow against the internal door lock and had activated the central locking. David reached in through the smashed windowframe and grabbed the driver around the neck.

With the skin-to-skin contact, a crushing blow exploded in David's groin. Every muscle in his body contracted and, involuntarily releasing his grip on the sweaty offender's throat, he collapsed in a crumpled heap onto the floor and rolled, uncontrollably, into the gutter.

The car sped away and, as David helplessly arched his neck to watch after the fleeing vehicle, the distinct taste of tin once again washed over his tongue. The shrinking, blue hatchback was the last visible motion David saw as his peripheral vision once again blackened and narrowed like the shutter of a camera.

***

"There's the Lotus Sarge," Barnes exclaimed pointing at the abandoned sports car.

"And the TK, look," Backhouse added as he screechingly brought the unmarked police car to rest at an angle across the bonnet of the stolen two-seater.

Wazzer and Thomo, arriving from the opposite direction, blocked their approach with equally theatrical gusto and all four officers simultaneously exited their respective doors. The kiosk was empty and Backhouse frantically span around, searching the scene for clues. It hadn't been more than sixty seconds since Lewis had abruptly ended their call.

"Sarge, over here," Thomo shouted from the far side of the skewed crime car.

The supervisor ran across to meet his subordinate and was confronted with the sight of a collapsed David Lewis, curled up like a sleeping cat in the gutter. He kicked the unconscious Lewis in the backside, more than firmly. David did not stir and Barnes looked at his superior in surprised disbelief at the apparent assault.

"What?" Backhouse questioned the younger detective's look. "Just testing!"

***

He had almost crashed into the approaching police saloon as he sped from the area. He had recognised the vehicle as a crime car. It may have been unmarked but in their rush to get to the very location he had just left they had been using their grill-mounted strobe lights. Contrarily, they hadn't recognised his car, his stolen, plain police car. He was curious as to why. They had been in a real rush to get there but it couldn't possibly have been in response to his latest abduction.

That was only seconds old and, even if anyone had witnessed it, they wouldn't have even managed to telephone the police yet. Nor could anyone have reported the stolen hatchback as being in the area. He had only arrived moments before bundling the brunette into the car's rear seat. No, the saloon was arriving for something else.

He saw the powerful car screech to a smoky halt across the road in his rear view mirror. However, he wasn't going to hang around to find out what they were after. He turned out of any potential view into a side road and slowed to a more inconspicuous speed in order to attract no further attention.

Then the penny dropped. They were after Lewis and he had Lewis's girlfriend. The guy who had punched out the window had to have been Lewis. He momentarily cursed himself for not taking the opportunity to do away with the curiously knowledgeable witness right there, but quickly recognised the blessing in disguise for what it was worth. As it was, he was leaving the area with no police following him. With the earlier radio transmission, which he had overheard, he now doubted they even knew he existed. They were after Lewis and if he had shot the bastard there and then he would have instantly been under a piled heap of police.

No, he had been handed a lucky escape. He let out a self-satisfied chuckle at the unintended good fortune before glancing over the seat back to check on his latest acquisition. The girl was still unconscious and her head, its nose bleeding steadily from his immobilising blow, gently rocked in response to the car's movements. He returned his gaze to the road ahead and considered his next move. He had gotten the girl to get to Lewis but the police had Lewis now.

It was a frustration to his plans but at least he knew that he now had time to think. Lewis would be transported back to the Hopefield nick and processing a prisoner took hours; he knew that much only too well. Everything the police did took ages. Still, that suited him. What was even better was that now they had Lewis the chances were that the search would be called off.

That said, what if Lewis talked; told them about him? His earlier concern returned. Lewis knew too much about him. Murray had found him off the back of what Lewis had told her. Wait a minute, though. He was confusing himself now. His earlier conclusion, after the radio conversation, was that Murray had gone to the factory to find Lewis. Hadn't she? Why would he have led her there? He knew that Lewis had; he had read the notes himself, but he'd failed to recognise the contradiction earlier.

Something wasn't right. He pondered the opposing facts

for a moment. Lewis had directed Murray to him but the detective had thought he was Lewis. No, wait. She only thought he was Lewis *after* hearing his voice and had sounded surprised that the person she thought was Lewis was there at all. She *had* been looking for someone other than Lewis, for him. Lewis *had* led her there and it was only down to a misunderstanding that she had mistaken him for Lewis. Her informant was still a danger to him. No, hang on, if that was the case why were the coppers after Lewis and not him? If Murray had gone to the factory looking for him then surely they would have been after him too?

Then he remembered her arrival at the factory. No cars, no mates. She had been all alone and had surprised him. No-one had even known she was there; not very smart when you were looking for a mugger. Then it finally dawned on him. She hadn't been looking for anyone. She had been after some *thing*. Lewis had directed her there to find something tangible, some evidence. She hadn't seen his face; she'd thought he was Lewis. She'd escaped at the railway tunnel and had gone back to her bosses to report that Lewis had abducted her and that's why they had been after Lewis. Yeah, that was it.

The thing now was could Lewis explain his way out of it? He certainly knew about something at the factory. Was it even connected to *him* though? The thought that the events set in motion were the result of a huge misunderstanding sent a chill down his spine. No, he couldn't accept that, he didn't *want* to accept that. He had to cover his back and continue the course of action to which he had committed himself with the kidnap of the brunette behind him. He would use her to get to Lewis and then get rid of him. Misunderstanding or not, that would eliminate any doubts once and for all. It was settled then. He dismissed any further argument either way.

For now though, until Lewis had been processed and had been given any opportunity to explain things to Murray and her mates, no-one was looking for him. He allowed himself another short laugh at the irony.

"Sweet," he quipped to himself. Lewis was the perfect patsy to cover his escape, an escape from a situation created *by*

Lewis. He could easily slip out of town. He had money. He had some gear. All he needed now was a change of vehicle. He may not have been *hot* but his car certainly was. Murray would have certainly told them about the car, wouldn't she?

He drove on, content in his convoluted conclusion of the facts and, adjusting the internal mirror to monitor his captive, he considered his next move.

***

The mag-lock clicked open in response to the swipe of Backhouse's pass-card and Barnes tugged at the heavy staff-entrance door to Hopefield police station. He held it open, still respectful of his supervisor's position. However, he'd been uncharacteristically quiet on the way back from the Job Centre and Backhouse knew it was a silent protest over his earlier actions.

"Okay, so he wasn't faking it," Backhouse offered the disapproving detective, feigning some concern over the incident in order to placate the young officer.

Backhouse needed everyone on board and fully focused for the impending interrogation of Lewis and he could do without Barnes' namby-pamby issues with his methods. However, Barnes confirmed his continued protest and remained silent.

'Bollocks to you then,' Backhouse thought. He had offered all he was about to and walked on ahead of the rigid-minded Barnes without further ado.

As a result of the seizure, brought about by his contact with her assailant, Lewis had remained unconscious at the roadside after the kidnap of Lucy. Despite Backhouse's frustrations, he had not stirred in response to the older man's *test*. As a consequence, although being technically arrested on suspicion of the kidnap of DC Lizzie Murray, the police cells were no place for the cataleptic offender. Instead, an ambulance had been called to the scene and Lewis, accompanied at Backhouse's direction by Wazzer and Thomo, had been transferred to the hospital for treatment.

Content, in the fact that the two detectives at the hospital would contact him as soon as Lewis stirred, Backhouse grabbed the black, plastic handrail and started up the stairway to the first floor incident room. Barnes followed quietly, no doubt waiting for an opportune moment to make notes of his Sergeant's actions at the Job Centre in his pocket book.

Now that the errant Lewis was in custody, albeit away from the station, Backhouse wanted to collate the circumstances of all the street robberies as well as the abduction of his subordinate. Despite the latter being his strict priority, he fully intended to throw the book at Lewis and put the little bastard away for good.

Although potentially linked to the murders in the park, there was no direct evidence to suggest Lewis's connection to the Crabtree brothers' demise so, until forensic testing changed that fact, Backhouse's investigation took primacy with regards to the processing of their unconscious prisoner.

"Milk, two sugars," he flippantly tasked Barnes as he turned off the main corridor into the Detective Inspector's office. Barnes continued on into the team's office to complete the requisite order.

"Fancy a brew Atticker?" he asked his desk-bound colleague as he reached down and picked up the office kettle.

"Cheers," Atticker replied. "Coffee, no sugar thanks."

Barnes set about the task while deciding that his pocket book could wait until later. In any event, he felt a peculiar twinge of guilt over trying to make Backhouse feel uneasy about kicking Lewis earlier. While he did not agree with, or condone, the Sergeant's actions, he had to, at least, concede an understanding of the senior detective's frustrations over Murray's disappearance.

His time with the older officer over the previous week had begun to fuzz the edges of Barnes' strict adherence to the rules. Maybe there was something to learn from Backhouse that he could mould into a lawful version of policing at some midway point between their respective methodologies?

***

"We have him then?" DI Priest asked the arriving Sergeant.

"Not quite. He's at the hospital with Holliwell and Thompson."

"Any news on Lizzie?" the senior officer asked optimistically.

"No such luck. The little tosser's still comatose and not exactly what you'd call chatty."

Backhouse's frustration was exacerbating his sarcastic vocabulary to a point where Priest would have normally felt the need to interject with some supervisory advice. However, with the events of the last few days, it washed, unnoticed, over the Inspector's head. Although not as tired as Backhouse, his senses had been numbed by the protracted search for the missing officer.

"How do you want to handle the interview? Are you going in with Barnes?"

Backhouse was perturbed, almost insulted, by the comment.

'With Barnes?' he thought. If anyone was going to be doing any 'withing' it would be *them* going in with *him*. Besides, what was so special about Barnes that he should be part of the interview team at all? If anything, he thought, the DI would be second seat to *his* lead. Backhouse decided to be vague in his response to give him time to consider the matter further.

"Not decided yet boss," he said. "But we've got to consider the guy as a suspect for the robberies as well as Lizzie's abduction."

"Fair enough, but the priority is…" He caught himself short, a sudden sense of being patronising slapping him in the face. He knew that Backhouse was fully aware of the priority.

"Well, you know…Good luck," he half apologised.

Backhouse turned and left the office to head for the incident room run by DCI Callander. He wanted to surreptitiously check if the murder enquiry had made any progress. A positive forensic result would altogether change the interview of Lewis and he didn't want to lose his chance to get the location of Lizzy out of *his* prisoner before it was overhauled by the larger investigation.

174

Fortunately, for him, there had been no developments but he knew he most likely had precious little time to get what he wanted from Lewis.

'*Bloody protocol,*' he thought. He wanted to beat the truth out of Lewis, 'Old-School' style.

'*Maybe later.*'

Chapter Twenty

"Any update on the consequential paradox yet?"

"No, not yet, Director. I'm picking up intermittent signals but it's unclear whether or not the memory engrams have been affected by the transfer. The degree of stammer is reducing so I imagine the solution of nanites is starting to improve matters. Once the balance of recall-rate tips the implant's processor I believe it'll re-boot and we'll regain a full picture of what's going on."

"Bloody rehabilitation, I knew this crap wasn't going to work. Why don't we just put them down like we used to and have done with it?"

***

From beneath the darkness of his blindfold David was conscious of a short-lived, red glow. His body rocked gently, its momentum stalled by the halting of the surface beneath him. He could feel an intense burning in his wrists and felt uncomfortably confined. As his senses returned he realised he was horizontal, lying in a foetal position on his left side. His hands were bound by something immensely painful and he felt that his mouth was as covered as his eyes. He moved his legs to stretch out but was immediately restricted by an awkwardly shaped surface beneath his feet.

The low, rattling noise about him fell silent and, following a mechanical click, the compartment confining him shook gently. Another click, a piston-like whoosh of gas and he felt the coolness of the night's air rush in around him.

"Out," a strangely familiar voice said.

Unable to raise anything more than his legs, he felt the stranger grip his upper arms and begin to pull him from his confinement. The stinging binds about his wrists dug in and he winced at the agony. However, the voice's owner continued to wrench him from his enclosure. He was lifted over a small ledge and fell in a heap onto the ground.

The stranger dragged him to his feet and he considered that he was about to get a good beating from the colleagues of the absent DC Murray. Then again, there was that metallic taste in his mouth once more and the reason for his being wherever he was felt considerably more dangerous.

The action of dragging him, from what he had by now concluded was the boot of a car, had dislodged the coverings over his eyes. He went to look up at his assailant but his head did not move. He wasn't in control of his actions. A dizzy blurring of reality phased through him and it suddenly occurred to him, with a bizarre sense of clarity, that he was having another seizure, another vision.

Now this was definitely new. He was conscious of the fact he was fitting *while* it was actually happening. He had detached himself from the confusion of his previous premonitions and was a spectator to what was happening around him. So, was it the future, or the past? The evolution of his condition sent a wave of childish giddiness through his body, or at least what he was sensing to be his body. He decided to try to relax and let the events play out before him.

He walked on and felt himself trip, almost theatrically, over what appeared to be a railway track line. The ballast between the sleepers crunched beneath his feet and he could sense the person he now considered to be an abductor tugging him forward by his clothing. He sensed an urgent feeling of fear and impending doom, curtailed only by a determination to survive and escape the situation.

The crunching ground underfoot began to echo and he realised he was entering a tunnel. The determination welled up inside him and, as the adrenalin began to peak, his sense of control over the images began to waiver. The dizziness returned and the confusion re-entered his mind. *He* was there, in the tunnel. *He* had to escape and the only weapons available to him were his free legs.

The stranger was ahead of him, facing away. Intentionally stumbling, he dropped to one knee and broke free of the grip on his clothes. Then he rolled backward onto the sharp granite ballast. In reaction, the kidnapper span around to regain control and stepped quickly toward him, straddling his feet in order to bend down and make a grab for his upper arms. With all his strength, he coiled his right leg high into his chest and drove his sole deep into the man's groin. There was a sudden expelling of air and the stranger crumpled slowly over to one side. Failing to support his torso as he fell, his head hit the far rail with a thud.

In his moment of triumph he gymnastically threw his legs over his own head into a swift backward roll and brought himself into a crouched, kneeling position. He pushed up forward and was quickly standing over the sprawled, groaning heap of a man. This guy had been trying to kill him. He was angry and needed time to escape. Holding his head back in an unnatural arch to partially see the face-down male's head, he kicked and kicked until the groaning stopped. Then he turned and ran.

He stumbled on toward where he thought the car might be. His heart was racing, he was dizzy and the metallic taste in his mouth was bitter to the point of vomit-inducing.

'Where's that car? Must be close,' he thought. Wary that his attacker could be recovering, he turned sharply to get off the line and out of sight.

There was a sudden sharpness across his thighs and he tumbled forward. Unable to stop himself, with his hands still tied, he rolled on to the cold iron girder and, briefly feeling the large mushroom-headed rivets against his stomach, he continued over the parapet and into a silent nothingness. A rush of air, a gut-churning weightlessness and the silence of his descent was shattered by a breathtakingly cold immersion into the river below.

Already starved of oxygen, his lungs, afire with the effort of his escape, were crushed inward by the shock of the cold water sending what little precious air was left rushing from his body. Had his mouth not been gagged, he would have surely swallowed a fatal volume of water but, as it was, he simply halted in the murky silence of his underwater milieu.

As the transition from descent to ascent became apparent to his disoriented senses, he began to frantically kick his legs. His face broke the surface, the impact of the fall having now totally dislodged the blindfold. The roar of the fast moving water was rapture to his ears and he sucked in a huge breath of air through the now-loosening gag while trying to get a sense of his surroundings through his water-blurred eyes.

Still kicking in the deep water, he bobbed up and down, pushed and pulled by the strong current around him. It was pitch black and the noise of the river was speckled with short silences as his head dropped back beneath the surface between kicks. With his hands tied, his chances of survival were in serious jeopardy. He had to reach the shore, and he had to do it quickly.

He kicked again, twisting the effort this time to turn his body in the rushing water. Immediately he came face-to-face with the concrete base of the bridge support. Unable to halt his movement in the rapid current, and with only enough time to reactively duck his head, he struck the stanchion; he struck it hard. The blow sent a shockwave through his skull and his head felt as though it would explode. He pressed his eyes tightly closed in response to the agony and his body, pushed by the water crashing against the upright, rolled along the stone surface toward one corner.

Opening his eyes just in time to see the edge of his harsh saviour, and the open water beyond, he knew that if he got washed away from the relative safety of this pillar he would most definitely drown in the cascading water of the river beyond. He ignored the pain beginning to throb in his head and kicked frantically at the sub-surface concrete trying to catch a foothold.

The weight of water pushed him closer and closer to the precipice. Reaching the very brink of the stanchion's vertical edge, he lifted and bent his trailing leg in an effort to hook it against the upstream face of the foundation block. The water rolled him around the corner and, successfully gripping the calf of his raised leg against the stonework, his unprotected face and chest once again smashed against the side of roughly-hewn concrete.

The rushing water crashed against his torso and he knew he had precious little time to maintain his hold on the pillar. Turning his face away from the breathtakingly cold water to search downstream in the hope of sighting the shore, he immediately found himself looking at a set of iron steps rising out of the water, which were attached to the stanchion as a service access.

About six feet away, reaching them was going to be tricky. Once he let go with his flexed, lower leg he was committed to either catching the ladder, which only stood proud of the stone face by about six inches, or missing it altogether and drowning in the churning blackness beyond. He reached out tentatively with his free leg but, realising it fell far short of reaching the upright, decided he had little choice but to release his rapidly numbing grip and hope for the best.

Considering it could be his last, he took a deep breath and began to straighten his left leg. The water recovered its hold on his battered frame and his calf scraped harshly along the corner of the stone beneath the waterline. Momentarily halted by his heel snagging on the roughly eroded edge, his body slid closer and closer to the steps. The moment of truth had arrived. Still about three feet away, the rusted ladder silently mocked him.

Without time for further deliberation, the rushing water decided his fate. The pathetic hold he had with the heel of his left foot gave way. Within a second, his right leg, skidding helplessly along the side of the bridge support, jammed between the hard flat surface and the jagged upright. Still bound and unable to take a hold of the ladder, he drew his trailing, and now bleeding, leg up to meet the trapped limb. However, with facing the stanchion and unable to contort himself into remaining flush to the stone, his efforts caused his body to move out slightly into the raging flow.

Suddenly the weight of water regained the upper hand. Unable to counter its force, he was rotated around away from the ladder. Unheard below the roar of the river, his trapped leg cracked across the tibia and fibula. He screamed in response to the twisting limb, sinews tearing and muscle splitting in response to the overpowering waterway. His body slammed backward into the stepladder and his bound hands found themselves gripping a sub-surface rung. Holding tightly, he roared in agony at the pain of the trapped limb, now folded completely back on itself behind him. Thrashing with his free leg to gain a foothold, he quickly found a lower rung and instinctively pushed upward in some vain attempt to relieve the pressure on the shattered calf.

He raised his torso to the surface of the water and jerked his bound hands to the next upward rung. Leaning as far as he dared to the upstream side of the ladder to release the hanging limb, he repeated the action to lift himself clear of the water. Shifting his weight from foot to hands, to buttocks, he snatched his way from rung to rung. He knew that a careless reach would send him crashing back into the water and ultimately to his death, but exhaustion was approaching fast and, if he hadn't reached the flat top of the foundation block before it overtook him, the outcome would be the same.

Some ten feet later his thighs finally fell rearward onto the plateau of the stanchion. He dragged himself away from the edge and collapsed down onto his back. His broken leg, twisted and trailing behind him was already numb and lifeless. His left leg was bleeding and his head was banging from its collisions with the concrete. He looked upward toward the bridge crossing some hundred or so feet above him. The noise of the violent river, a dozen or so feet below, was more subdued than before and he considered how calm it sounded from his perch atop the concrete block.

Then the vertical supports near to his head began to rumble. Louder and louder the structure reverberated and the vibration shuddered through his body. Staring skyward, he could see the growing glow of a locomotive's headlight passing above him and, as it thundered across the huge steel structure,

181

he could feel the disturbed grit and dirt falling onto his battered body. This final insult was the limit of what his tiny *female* frame was willing to take. Her eyes narrowed and Murray passed into unconsciousness.

Chapter Twenty One

"Doctor Reynolds," Nurse Miles called across the ward at the young doctor. He turned to face her and she glanced down at the patient in her care.

"He's got rapid eye movement, a lot of it!"

"That's a good sign. Any other indicators?"

"Blood pressure's up… and heart rate too, one ten, one eighteen, one thirty five, oh God, it's rocketing!"

The white-coated physician threw the chart he was perusing onto the foot of the bed he was standing by and quickly moved toward the patient being monitored by his colleague. As he did, the young man began to convulse. His body, totally devoid of movement up until that point, painfully arched upward. Rigid for a moment, it crashed back down on to the bed. Monitoring equipment surrounding his bed burst into a cacophony of alarms.

Nurse Mills slammed her hand on the crash button on the wall behind the bed and, in the corridor outside the ward's entrance, a rapid, high pitched beeping began to summon additional staff to their assistance. The patient continued to thrash about on the bed as a massive, violent seizure took hold of his every muscle. Reynolds, holding the man's arms in an effort to prevent him throwing himself off the bed altogether, turned his head to greet his colleagues rushing into the ward. Accompanied by the rattling crash-cart their entry was about as far as it could be from the polite 'quiet please' request made by the signs dotted about the ward.

"Help here," Reynolds calmly directed, but, as soon as he turned back to face the bed, the man fell motionless onto the mattress. The heart rate monitor instantly changed its tone from an uncontrollably rapid beeping to a single ominous note.

"Christ," Reynolds remarked. "He's crashing." He tore open the patient's pyjama shirt and began to rhythmically compress his chest while the arriving staff beside them started setting up the life-saving cart. Young Nurse Mills, already hand-pumping the bladder of the face-mask she was holding over the man's mouth and nose, looked anxiously at the doctor for instruction.

The staff busied themselves in a professionally rehearsed ballet of actions and, within seconds, a senior-looking female doctor called, "Ready."

Dr Reynolds ceased his efforts and quickly checked the monitor for signs of a pulse before tearing the sensors from the man's chest in preparation for the defibrillator.

"Charging," the female doctor narrated as she monitored the equipment's building shock status. The increasing pitch of the machine rose to an almost inaudible level as the doctor rubbed conductive jelly between the plates of the shock pads.

"Okay, stand clear," she instructed while simultaneously placing the device's pads on the chest of the motionless man.

A characteristic thud shook the bed as the man's body jerked in response to the current passing through his torso. Pads retracted, Reynolds moved in with his stethoscope to check for a response.

The female doctor was already preparing the life-saving machine to administer a second shock when Reynolds shook his head.

"Nothing," he confirmed, standing back again to allow his colleague to make another attempt. The machine's tone had already peaked.

"Stand clear," she repeated. Another shock, another jolt and Reynolds moved in again; still no response.

Across the ward Wazzer and Thomo stood silently watching the scene unfold. The guys back at the nick weren't going to believe this, not after the day they'd already had. They'd both been police officers long enough to have seen death dozens of times but it was quite the rarity to have it happen right in front of you.

The hospital staff's efforts continued but to no avail.

"I'll call it," Reynolds eventually offered to his colleague as she wiped the pads and tucked them back into the cart's storage compartments.

"Okay John. Sorry."

"No worries," the young doctor replied. "It was an unusually severe case. I'm surprised it hadn't happened already to be honest."

He turned to the two detectives he had been speaking to.

"Sorry guys, I'll get back to you as soon as I can. I've obviously got some things to tidy up here for a minute or two."

Wazzer raised his hand in a no-need-to-apologise manner.

"Take your time Doc. We're going nowhere." He added to the gesture.

"Nurse Mills. Would you check Mr Lewis's vitals once again please and let me know of any changes? I'll be in the office."

"Yes doctor," the young woman replied before walking around Wazzer and Thomo to where Lewis lay quietly sleeping, undisturbed by the furore which had just taken the life of the unfortunate soul in the opposite bed.

***

Looking for an easy target, he decelerated toward the entrance to the railway station car park. The police radio he had been listening to had been unusually quiet. He, of course, was unaware that the channel selected was that of Backhouse's small team and that the main, divisional channel, which was never quiet, was just two button-clicks away. No, it was quiet, and to him that could only be a good thing. No chatter, no cops, no search.

He turned the corner into the car park only to be faced with a marked, police estate car. A sudden panic rose in his chest and he braked harshly in a rash and obvious way. Fortunately for him, the police car was empty. The officers, sent there by DCI Callander to effectively close down the station as a potential escape route for Lewis, had simply parked in front of the station entrance and walked onto the platform to check for him waiting for a train out of town.

They'd not considered anyone might arrive while they were there and so had made no effort to conceal their brightly liveried vehicle out of sight. Besides, with the search for the captured Lewis now called off and new orders of areas to search for the still-missing DC Murray not yet received, these two fine officers had time to finish the cups of tea they'd bought while conscientiously preventing Lewis's escape.

Unaware of their current status, he considered searching out another, less policed location to change vehicles. Then it occurred to him that this was probably a better place than most. If the police were still searching for Murray's car they'd be stretched out all over town and he knew exactly where the officers allocated to this location were. He could see them on the far platform drinking tea at the news stand and chatting up the young girl serving there.

'Yeah,' he thought. 'This'll do nicely.'

He carefully drove the plain hatchback to the farthest point he could reach in the car park while staying out of a direct line of sight of the two idle officers. He slipped the car into an empty space, concealed from view by the other parked vehicles and, checking the brunette was still unconscious, stepped out into the car park to search out a potential replacement.

***

David awoke with a start. The bright light, shining through the large ward windows, flooded into his suddenly open eyes and he immediately squinted to counter the sharpness of the sensation. With the associated groan, he alerted the detective guarding him, recumbent in the high-backed armchair he had acquired from the adjacent bed area while he waited for Lewis to regain consciousness.

Wazzer lowered the newspaper he'd been reading for over an hour and looked at the seemingly helpless man laid out before him. The urge to shake him to full awareness was almost overwhelming. Wazzer wanted to find out what this insignificant individual had done with his colleague, Lizzie, as much as anyone.

It was Wednesday afternoon and she had been missing for over forty eight hours. She could easily have been dead already but, even if she wasn't, she must have been immobilised in some way; scared and alone, now that her captor was securely held in police custody. She hadn't been in the silver Lotus recovered at the scene of Lewis's arrest and she hadn't made any contact with them, as she would have otherwise done.

The search of the factory had shown that the blood found by John Evans' dog, Satan, had indeed matched Murray's DNA. However, despite a thorough search of the whole building she had not been found. Lewis had a lot of questions to answer, that was for sure, but Wazzer knew that his supervisor, DS Backhouse, was the man to be asking them.

Just at that moment the heavily built Thomo walked back into the ward from his excursion to the hospital canteen. He was carrying two cups of coffee in a recycled-card tray and a plate of stereotypically law-enforcement donuts. Before he reached the bed Wazzer rose from his armchair to address his colleague.

"He's awake," he said, gesturing flippantly at the prone patient.

Thomo hurriedly deposited the tray and plate onto the empty, adjacent bed, adding the donut already in his mouth back to the pile.

"Has he said anything yet?" he asked Wazzer, stepping closer to the bed and leaning over to gauge Lewis's reactions.

"No, nothing," Wazzer replied, taking a half-hearted grip on his friends arm and knowing that Thomo's feelings about their prisoner were as strong as his own.

"Let's get in touch with Backhouse. He'll be wanting to know about this."

"Yeah okay," the larger officer responded. He leaned over, close to the face of the groggy Lewis. "We'll speak later," he menacingly announced to the young man.

Lewis, still half dazed and not yet able to chain two words

together, recalled the adage of 'out of the frying pan...' His vision of Murray's experience at the river had left him exhausted. He had no idea how. He knew he hadn't physically been there but the details, so vivid on this last occasion, had left him drained.

His previous jaunts into the minds of those responsible for actions of violence, which he had been vicariously witnessing, were disjointed and confusing. However this time he had seen a full, chronological sequence of events. It was as if his *abilities* were improving. Some unknown force was tying the subconscious synapses of his mind neatly together to become a device for the recollection of others' memories, but for what reason? That answer was still beyond him.

For now he had to think of what answers he was going to give Backhouse. He knew the old officer wasn't exactly his biggest fan and, although he'd convinced himself that his ability made sense, he knew he was going to have to find some special way of proving to the overbearing detective that his story, which was little more than a theory vaguely fitting the circumstances, was in fact the truth.

***

"I'm on my way," Backhouse responded as he placed his third cup of coffee down on the office table and then hung up the phone.

"Lewis awake is he?" Barnes asked his superior.

"Yep. I'm gonna get down there with the DI."

Barnes was a little put out by the fact he wasn't included in the Sergeant's plans but considered that, after his earlier, silent protest, it was probably to be expected. Unbeknown to him though, Backhouse had other plans for the whiz-kid detective.

"Get started on an interview plan for the robbery series," he instructed.

"Times, dates, locations. I want it to show any descriptions given and potential crossovers. In addition, I want a correlative chart of Lewis's work rota for the past six months. You can get that from that Seymour woman at the Job Centre. Get on that first as it's past four already and I don't know how long she'll be there. If this little toe-rag is going to be fit for interview I want to be ready to go by eight at the latest. Oh, and get the VIPER team on standby. I'll want a capture doing tonight so that Mrs Nugent can take a looksy before her bedtime. Atticker, is there anything from the search of his apartment yet?"

"The search team is just on its way in, Sarge. Tracy's reported in that there's no trace of Lizzie and nothing that relates to any of the robberies but they've recovered a diary, an address book and correspondence relating to a... Lucy Short. I think that's going to be the ex that his manager mentioned to the boss."

"He mentioned her on the phone just before his arrest saying she was in danger. Phone number?"

"Think so, Sarge. They're only five minutes away, do you want me to call her up or wait till she gets here?"

"It'll wait. I'm not looking for her anymore. I think his story about her being in trouble was just a red herring. Besides, we've got lover-boy in custody now."

Backhouse walked out of the room to the nearby Detective Inspector's office. However, Priest was not in and the DS returned to the incident room. Holding the doorjamb, he leaned around the corner into the office and spoke to Atticker who had been silently tapping away at his computer for hours.

"Atticker, have you seen the boss? I want him to come to the hospital with me."

"Not since you spoke with him earlier, Sarge. After you went next door, I noticed him heading for the stairwell but I've not seen him come back yet."

"Damn it," Backhouse spat out. "His phone's on his desk. I'm going to make for the hospital on my own. As soon as you see him let him know about Lewis regaining consciousness and get him to call me straight away."

With that he withdrew from the room and started to make his way to the station's rear car park.

"Sarge," Atticker called after him. Backhouse halted but did not return to the office.

"Yeah?" he called from the corridor.

189

"You may want to see this, it's about Lewis and it's a bit odd."

'*Something else odd about Lewis,*' Backhouse thought. '*There's a surprise!*' He span on his heels and stepped back into the room.

"What now?" he asked.

"Well, you know Lewis has no record?" Atticker started.

"Not an exactly stunning revelation," Backhouse sarcastically retorted.

"No," Atticker agreed, "but I decided to do a little digging on the curious Mr Lewis. He rents his apartment. He has no passport, no vehicle, in fact no driving licence at all. He has no company records and a credit check shows no CCJ's, no loan activity before an application for a sofa just eighteen months ago and a single bank account, which appears to just receive his wages and has a clean credit history."

"So he's a cash-in-hand type of guy. Not particularly what I'd call *odd*."

"Maybe not, but get this. I did some checks with the National Statistics Office." Atticker pointed at a page he'd restored to his computer screen. "*David Edward Lewis, born March twentieth nineteen eighty six…..*"

"So?"

"*Died May twelfth nineteen eighty six*. That's less than, what, eight weeks old."

Backhouse raised an eyebrow. His interest was snared.

"Yeah but come on, David Lewis is a common enough name, surely? Besides, he looks at least five years older than nineteen eighty six would make him."

"Maybe so, but the date and place of birth match his employment record provided by his manager and there are no other 'David Lewis's' born that day anywhere in the country. In fact none that month."

Backhouse pondered the possibilities for a moment.

"There's more," Atticker proudly added.

"Go on."

"His National Insurance number…"

"Bogus?"

"You got it."

Backhouse was perplexed. No wonder this guy had no record. He didn't exist! 'David Lewis', 'David Edward Lewis', had been living with a false identity for at least eighteen months, but why? Even if he was wanted for a string of murders, a false ID wouldn't protect him from DNA testing. Why go to all that trouble to work in a Job Centre, and then as the police liaison of all things? Keeping your enemies closer than your friends was one thing, but this was taking the cliché a little far.

"Okay, I'll bear it in mind. Let the boss know about it when you see him."

Backhouse started out of the room again and then shouted back from the stairwell door."

"Oh, and Atticker."

"Yes Sarge?"

"Nice work."

Atticker grinned like the proverbial Cheshire Cat and lifted his legs to swing gleefully back around to his computer screen, which was about as much fun the techno-geek would permit himself.

Chapter Twenty Two

He searched the car park for his favoured model. The late year Ford Mondeo was well positioned for his purpose. Over on the far side of the irregular car park, it was out of sight, both of the tea-drinking coppers on platform three and of the security camera he had spotted covering the entrance to the car park.

Searching for the required tool, he quickly found a half-brick fallen from the rotten masonry of the perimeter wall. He checked around for onlookers. As usual, mid-afternoon, the area was devoid of the daily commuters who parked here before continuing to work by train.

He picked the sweet spot on the front bumper of the car, graciously parked nose in to the wall. With a harsh bang on the collision sensor, a muffled explosion sent a cloud of dust into the car's interior from the activation of its multiple airbags.

While potentially life-saving the safety measure also snapped open the vehicle's central locking system. After all, why save the occupants from a collision only to have them trapped inside when the emergency services arrived? Another quick look round, to check if his action had attracted any unwanted attention, and he surreptitiously slipped behind the smoking driver's wheel. Tearing the deflated bag from the hub, he reached under the cowling and tore the lower half away revealing the ignition barrel and the wiring beneath.

Within seconds, the well-practised thief had the engine running and he gingerly drove the car to the previously hidden hatchback to recover the unconscious body of the attractive brunette. Pulling alongside the rear of DC Murray's car, he tugged on the boot release button and slipped out of the stolen Mondeo.

Opening the rear passenger door of the metallic hatchback, he reached under the arms of the tracksuit-clad female and dragged her from the rear seat. Staying low, he gathered up her featherweight frame and bundled her into the boot of the larger saloon. Surprised that she was still unconscious from his single blow, he pressed his grubby fingers into her neck and, feeling a gentle pulse to satisfy himself that she wasn't actually dead, he closed the lid.

It was as simple as that. He returned to the driver's seat and gently accelerated away to exit the car park. On his way out, to add insult to injury, he wound down his window and reached out, wrenching the passenger wing mirror off the unattended police car. He laughed to himself.

'Wankers!' he thought.

***

"So, when do I get to speak to the bastard then?" an angry Backhouse barked at the young physician blocking the entrance to the neurological ward.

Trying to remain calm, the good Doctor Reynolds once again explained the situation.

"Mr Lewis is in a very delicate situation. He was in a lengthy coma less than a week ago and has been hospitalised twice now since then. I have grave concerns that his body will not bear up well under the stress of a police interrogation."

"My heart bleeds. Listen, this guy is a suspect in a number of serious offences including the abduction of an outstanding victim. I need to get into his head now and I suggest you get your schoolboy face out of mine, or else."

"Sergeant Backhouse, I'm not sure I appreciate your tone and I'll have to ask you to leave the hospital, or else I'll be forced to call security."

By this time, Backhouse was flanked by Wazzer and the enormous Thomo and was in no mood to be threatened.

"Listen, you little piss-ant. That outstanding victim is a colleague of ours and if you think you're going to stop me getting her location out of that twat in there you've got another thing coming. Call your security. We'll be happy to deal with them accordingly."

The young doctor glanced from Wazzer to Thomo, both of whom were staring intently at him. He was at a loss, not only as to what to say next but as to how this sort of brash police officer existed outside of a seventies television drama. Then, from behind him, a quiet voice interrupted his dilemma.

"Doc, it's okay. I'll speak with them. I need to speak with them."

The fully conscious David was sitting up on the bed, his feet already on the floor. Reynolds quickly left the ward entrance to intercept David's efforts to get to his feet prematurely and was closely followed in by Backhouse and his cohorts.

"Mr Lewis, you're in no fit state…"

David interrupted him. "It's important, as much to me as to them. Please?"

The outnumbered Reynolds was dumbfounded. Medically, he had never seen such a rollercoaster condition as that of David Lewis.

"Well, I can't condone it but I'm hardly in a position to argue with all four of you. Keep it brief," he said, addressing the solemn-faced Backhouse.

"Oh, don't worry. It'll be brief," Backhouse sternly replied as he approached the doctor's young charge.

Reynolds wasn't at all happy with the ominous tone of the Sergeant's reply but silently slipped by the trio and retreated to his side office.

***

"Incident room, DC Atticker."

"Hello, it's Phil Faint here from the Lab. I've got the result of the DNA test on the syringes recovered from the factory on…," the man paused checking his notes, *"…The Link Estate. I believe you wanted a call as soon as possible."*

"Yes, go ahead", Atticker beckoned.

"Yes. We have a hit against PNCID nine eight, slash three four seven six two x-ray, a David Anthony Caldwell born twentieth March

194

nineteen eighty six. Full profile; match confirmed on all three of the syringes and also against a mattress swab and also one from a burgundy purse. There are still a number of additional exhibits to check but I thought I'd let you know what we've already got as it's pretty conclusive this Caldwell character is going to be of some interest to you."

"He certainly is. Thanks."

Atticker hung up the phone and, immediately re-dialling Backhouse's mobile number, punched up the details of David Caldwell on the computer. Behind him Barnes, busy completing the interview plan as instructed by Backhouse, looked up in response to the renewed flurry of activity from his colleague.

"Something juicy?" he quizzed.

"You're not kidding. We've got a hit on the forensics from the factory."

"Nice one. Anyone we know?"

"Sure is," Atticker replied, scanning the latest page to appear before him. "Drugs, aggravated burglary, vehicle crime, you name it."

"Not Lewis then?" Barnes responded in a disappointed tone, knowing that Lewis had no previous convictions.

"Not by name, but the date of birth matches and, low and behold, David Caldwell has no arrest summons history for the last two years, which fits with Lewis having no record."

"You're thinking they're one and the same person?"

"Don't you? Too much of a coincidence to overlook I'd say, surely?"

"I guess so. And don't call me Shirley!"

The excited pair laughed at the awful but classic gag and Atticker realised it was the first sign of humour he had seen from the rather stiff Barnes since the team had been formed the previous week.

'Perhaps you're not such a tosser after all,' Atticker thought.

***

"Well, Mr Lewis, if that *is* your real name, where is DC Murray?"

David was confused by the insinuation regarding his identity but dismissed it as some sort of police tactic to put interviewees off guard.

"I don't know exactly but she was alive the last time I saw her. I can describe the place to you but you've got to believe me – *I* didn't take her there."

"Meaning what exactly?"

"Look, this is going to sound crazy but I need your help. Lucy, the friend I told you about, is in real danger."

"Okay, so she's in danger. Frankly, I don't give a shit. Tell me where Murray is and, maybe, I'll think about helping this *Lucy* character."

"Alright, here goes. Up until a week or so ago this never happened to me but since I helped an old lady onto a bus I've been seeing crimes in my head."

He paused for a reaction but the trio of officers, unconvinced by his opening line, stared, stony-faced, back at him. He would have to improve his story quickly if he was going to retain their attention.

"At first," he continued, "they were disjointed and pretty confusing but each one has become clearer until the last one, about Murray, was really clear. They happen after I touch anyone who is a victim of a violent crime. First, I feel the pain of the crime and then I have a seizure, during which I see how the offence will take place. First was the old lady, then Murray at the police station, then Lucy at the hospital. That's how I know about the muggings, the factory and Lucy. Only the crime with Lucy hasn't happened yet. Well, I hope not. The last one was after I touched the guy in the car that kidnapped Lucy. After that I saw him take DC Murray to a railway tunnel to kill her but she kicked him in the balls. That's what I felt after I touched him. She ran away from him but because she was tied and blindfolded she fell over a bridge nearby and into a river. But don't worry; she managed to get out and reach the bridge's support before passing out. That's when the vision finished, when she passed out. Oh yeah, I think her leg is broken as well, quite badly."

Suddenly, David realised he was rambling. He paused

again for a response. The seconds stretched out until the uncomfortable silence was broken by the weary Sergeant. Backhouse began to slowly clap, the action a physical precursor to the sarcasm about to leave his lips.

"Very nice, Mr Lewis. What a wonderful story. How convenient that it lets you know all about everything while giving you the perfect alibi. 'It was a vision your honour, I'm an innocent *medium* your honour.' What a crock of shit!"

"It's the truth. What else can I tell you?" Lewis pleaded.

"How about where is DC Murray? Make it good this time, you little prick."

"Okay, believe what you will but here goes. I don't know where it is but there's a railway tunnel, with two lines going through it, and about a quarter of a mile away there is a railway bridge that is about a hundred feet high above a river gorge, and it's a really wild river. The bridge is made of steel girders and is a dark primer-red colour, a bit like the Golden Gate Bridge in San Francisco. It has a concrete block at the bottom of the single support and the block has a set of rusted ladders on the side of it. Know it?"

"I do", Thomo intervened. "It's about twenty miles west of town out beyond the A1(M) motorway."

Wazzer and Backhouse turned to the giant of a man.

"You sure?" Backhouse asked.

"Yeah, my dad used to take us white-water kayaking out there when my brother and I were kids. I remember the bridge because I always used to get caught in an eddy near to the ladder he's on about."

Wazzer's expression of disbelief that his huge colleague could ever have fitted in a kayak was written all over his face. Thomo instantly saw through it.

"I was a late bloomer, okay?" he comically explained.

"Okay good," Backhouse accepted, ignoring the comedy between the two detectives. "Thomo, get the co-ordinates to the Air Support Unit straight away and get an ambulance and rescue unit en route. I don't want to waste a second if she's injured."

Turning his attention to Lewis he continued, "And don't

you think that us finding her is going to help you in any way. Knowing where you dumped her just adds to the case against you."

"But I didn't dump her there. She ..." David didn't bother continuing his plea for understanding. He had to accept that Backhouse was right. Everything pointed to him being responsible for Murray's disappearance and current condition. He just hoped they found her quickly. She would explain he wasn't her kidnapper. She would confirm his story, wouldn't she? Once she did they would believe him about Lucy and concentrate on finding her. However, until then Lucy was in immediate peril. He tried appealing to Backhouse's sense of duty again.

"What about Lucy. The guy that took Murray took her too. She's in real danger. I think she's going to be shot by one of your people, some sort of mix-up in a factory. Are you not going to do anything to help her?"

"I tell you what," the doubtful detective sarcastically offered, "if we find Murray at your Golden Gate Bridge we'll talk again and you can tell me *all* about it."

"Why don't I believe you?" David remarked.

"Perhaps it's because you're a lying son-of-a-bitch and it's rubbing off on me?" Backhouse said, continuing his sarcastic tone.

David despaired. He suddenly felt that putting his trust, and Lucy's fate, in the hands of this particular policeman was a bad decision.

Backhouse leaned in close to Lewis. "But believe this you little bastard." He spoke slowly, softly and deliberately. "If you're wasting our time on a wild goose-chase or if Lizzie is found dead then, whatever the ponsey courts decide to do with you, I will hunt you down and I *will* kill you."

David believed him.

Chapter Twenty Three

"Tower to Whisky Charlie Nine Nine, you are clear for take-off. Winds; ten knots south by south west; clear up to broken cloud at four thousand feet. You are traffic free up to eight thousand feet local, descending to four thousand as you approach the designated search area; beyond that watch for heavies entering the Tottenshall approach vector. Tottenshall control are aware of your planned search pattern but I recommend you monitor their frequency from five miles east of the search area as you're going to be right on the edge of their perimeter airspace and any emergency deviations are going to be right on top of you, over."

"Whisky Charlie Nine Nine, roger that Tower, ten knots south by south west and clear to four thousand; will monitor Tottenshall approach. We are wheels clear, departure two seven zero for a three thousand feet cruise to the search area; ETA, one zero minutes. Nine Nine out."

The black and orange helicopter's engine powered up and the recently purchased, and sleekly modern aircraft rose once again from the small, privately owned airfield. The gloss painted body, shimmering with vibration, paused momentarily a few feet from the ground before spiralling upwards and then dipping forward as the cyclic plate tipped the rotor head in the direction of the evening's search zone.

Despite the ASU Supervisor's concerns about the previous day's excessive flying hours, he was more than happy to despatch the vital tool once again in the search for DC Murray, particularly now that they had a specific location to look at. Thomo had phoned them less than half an hour before the machine had lifted off and, in that time, the Air Observer, a police officer trained in the use of the aircraft's multitude of electronic gadgets, had plotted a course to the co-ordinates while the pilot, a civilian aviator, had carried out the pre-flight checks on the latest addition to the Wrenshire Force's vehicle fleet.

Thomo's map reading skills had been on the nose. The co-ordinates gave the precise location where the railway, as described by Lewis, traversed the River Gant. A high level bridge crossed the gorged waterway several miles from the nearest main roadway. If Murray was there no-one would have been likely to find her without knowing exactly where to look.

Fortunately for her, they *did* know, and were en route to do just that. Simultaneously, Ambulance and Fire Rescue teams had been despatched from their respective stations and were rushing, sirens a blare, along the Midland Road by-pass out of Hopefield.

***

Slits of bright, evening sunlight roused Lizzie from her involuntary slumber. Unaware of how long she'd been there, she squinted up at the interlocking beams of steel that towered away from her, up toward the parapet she had so ungracefully stumbled over two nights before. As she responded to the encroaching light by opening her eyes wider, the grit and dirt from two days' worth of locomotive vibrations slipped between the lids and immediately sent them into a fit of blinking against the discomfort.

Reactively, she went to move her hands to her face to wipe away the offending intrusion but was quickly, and painfully, reminded of the fact her hands were still cruelly bound behind her. Instead, she rolled to one side to allow gravity to assist her now streaming eyes in washing away the particles of earth and rust. However, this manoeuvre served only to remind her of the second debilitation she had suffered after her encounter with the aggressive side of David Lewis.

She let out an agonising scream as the numbness, caused by forty eight hours of chilling river spray and night air, was overcome by the twisting of her lifeless, lower limb. Loud though it was past the gag, now almost completely dislodged by the efforts of her watery escape, the noise paled into insignificance against the solitude of her location and the roar of the angry waterway below. Only she was aware of the single echo that bounced from the nearest wall of the gorge in which she was trapped.

The pain of the shattered limb was intense; she felt light headed and likely to pass out again. Despite the pain, she wanted to stay awake. She *had* to stay awake. Bravely bearing the agony and reducing her screams to a controlled squeal, she folded at the waist to bend her now side-on body so that she could more closely examine the damage to her right leg.

The site of it only added to her queasiness. Instead of facing toward her, as it should have been, the toe of her right foot was twisted around a full one hundred and eighty degrees to be facing her left foot which, from her viewpoint, was dutifully oriented in the correct manner beyond it. Unwittingly, by rolling painfully on to her right side, she had reduced the unnatural twist by ninety degrees, her instep having stayed loosely flat to the stanchions surface as she had climbed from her immersion in the chilling river. However, the fact didn't detract from the horror of the sight.

Not aware of which way the trouser-covered limb had got into its current position, she pressed down on her right elbow and arched upward toward a sitting position. This, of course, was the wrong way for her lifeless limb and the torture of re-twisting it tore through her body as though someone was ripping out her spine. Unable to re-position the foot with her bound hands, she countered the pain by lying back down and continuing her previous rotation onto her face while simultaneously bringing her left leg over the trailing appendage to allow the right leg to unravel.

She continued the roll onto her left side and her right knee, drawn up and away from its foot by the raising of the associated thigh stretched the lifeless, lower limb in a vague simulation of traction. Agonising as the movement was, she felt a dull click inside the shattered portion of her leg followed by a spectacularly welcome drop in the level of pain. She allowed herself a short sigh of relief before again opening her eyes to check for any other damage to her battered body.

As she did, she immediately saw the dirty brown puddle where her left leg had been at rest. Although unmistakably blood, she took solace in the fact that it was at least a dry brown, a fair indicator that whatever had been bleeding had now stopped. She again brought her hands as far up her back as she comfortably could, spreading her elbows like the drawn arms of a car jack. Then, elevating her torso sufficiently for her to tip her body vertical with a throw of her head, she jerked herself up into a seated position.

Her now correctly positioned limb was more forgiving to the effort and she carefully withdrew her left foot from beneath the raised flex of her right knee in order to support her new viewpoint. Apart from the brown stain of her blood, her perch was dry. There was no sign of the water she must have brought up with her on her clothes from the river below. The bright sunlight, which had woken her just minutes before as it had breached the shadow limits of the deep ravine, was low in the sky.

Knowing that she had fallen from the bridge high above her at night she surmised she had been unconscious most of the day. That said, her clothes were more or less dry, as was that large stain of blood. It occurred to her that if she'd been gone for more than a day then she would have, surely by now, been missed. Hadn't anyone been searching for her? They must have been. So why was she still here?

She looked around again. Below her, the river, utterly impassable in its torrid state, was unlikely to host any passing visitors to the otherwise idyllic spot. The almost vertical walls of the gorge, sparsely strewn with small shrubs clinging precariously to the crevices, had no signs of pathways or indeed any access from the heavy tree-line above. As for the bridge, it soared heavenward above her, its unkempt condition evidence that it was rarely visited by the maintenance crews suggested by the rusty ladder which had, albeit viciously, saved her life.

No, she was very alone and if she was going to survive she was going to have to get out of this mess on her own. First things first, she had to release her hands from the unseen binds behind her. Checking around more deliberately for a potentially sharp edge, she painfully dragged her semi-crippled body rearward toward the rusted, steel uprights of the central bridge support.

***

A muffled cry lengthened into a panicked scream in the rear luggage compartment of the Mondeo saloon. No worries. She could scream for now. After clearing the town, he had driven back to the shopping centre and, despite the presence of another police patrol, had nonchalantly bought a roll of duct tape from the huge and impersonal do-it-yourself store. After that a deserted lay-by, set off the road as a seasonal picnic area, was the perfect place to administer the purchase to his then unconscious prey. No, she could scream for now. The brunette was well and truly bound and gagged. Feet as well, he wouldn't be making *that* mistake again.

Where to take her though? He'd been born in Hopefield, then known as Atherton, and had grown up in the aftermath of the '80's recession which had eventually led to its renaming. He'd never strayed far from its limited amenities; he'd never been able to afford to, until now that was. The Crabtree brothers' takings had topped six hundred pounds and he unimaginatively decided that, without the advantage of knowledge local to the other smaller towns of Wrenshire, he would head west to the larger city of Tottenshall in the next county.

Bound to be awash with drugs, as most cities were, he could easily find a new source for his addiction. In fact, with the dealing wrap he'd found in the Crabtrees' car, he might even be able to elevate himself the heady ranks of street-dealer. Such were the limits of his ambition.

On the pedestrian-free dual-carriageway Lucy's stifled cries for help went unheard and she squealed herself horse while her captor simply turned up the saloon's powerful radio to drown out the annoyance.

***

"Press the green button for room service," Backhouse said as he slammed the heavy steel door closed on David's police cell. The clattering noise echoed about the unfurnished room and David found himself yet again confirming the old detective's distain for him by finding, of course, there was no 'green button'.

Sitting at the hospital wasn't going to bring Lucy back to him so, despite Dr Reynolds protestations he had discharged himself into the custody of DS Backhouse. A police cell wasn't exactly what he had in mind as an improvement to his situation but at least he knew that as soon as they found DC Murray he would be in the right place to convince Backhouse of his innocence and, more importantly, of Lucy's plight.

Backhouse and Thomo returned to the custody suite's main desk. Although an old station, Hopefield boasted one of the larger facilities in the Wrenshire Force. It had two wings of sixteen cells, each spurring off the central reception area. This, in turn, included several holding cubicles for busy periods when there would be a queue of incoming prisoners. Tracy, Dave, Wazzer and Barnes were waiting round the desk like a Wild West posse waiting for a glimpse of a wanted poster and a direction in which to ride off.

"Did you sort out the VIPER team Barnes?" Backhouse asked his subordinate.

"Lyndsey is on her way in now, Sarge."

"Good. Get it rigged up and have her put the finished product onto a laptop so we can take it to the hospital for the Squadron Leader to take a looksy."

He turned to the custody Sergeant.

"No solicitor, no calls. He's incommunicado for now."

"Who's authorised that?" the surprised uniformed Sergeant asked.

"I just did," the older detective retorted. "I'll get the boss to write it up later."

The younger officer was perplexed at the digression from procedure and hoped that *later* would be soon enough to keep the tactic within the bounds of the Police and Criminal Evidence Act, part of which included the rules on prisoner care whilst in custody.

"Dave, Tracy, get Lewis, or whoever the hell he is, live-scanned*. I want to know if this joker is the match for the factory DNA hit. What was the name again?" the overtired officer asked Barnes.

"David Caldwell, Sarge," Barnes responded, glad once again to be asked for an input, however small.

"Right, Caldwell," he unnecessarily relayed back to the other two detectives still standing in easy earshot of Barnes. "Let me know as soon as you do. I'll be in my office."

"B twelve out please," Dave shouted down the alpha wing to the civilian gaoler who was busy serving the prisoner's evening meals.

"Yeah okay, okay, five minutes," the gaoler replied, not one to be diverted from the task in hand.

Dave was familiar enough with the miserable old sod to know that insisting would not get Lewis out of his cell any quicker and would only serve to slow the completion of any further requests later in the night. Five minutes was fine for now.

Backhouse led the remaining three officers out of the custody area, the buzzing doors releasing with a click as they passed, firstly into, and then out of the air-lock style corridor that led to the relative freedom of the police-station-proper beyond.

"Barnes, you're with me. That interview plan ready yet?"

"Yes Sarge," Barnes answered, fervently aware that he may be in on the interview of Lewis after all.

"Good; and it better be," Backhouse added, chopping the eagerness from under Barnes as if he were a variety act on stilts. "Wazzer, in the meantime I want you and Thomo to make for the search area in case *Pocahontas* here needs to help them out pinpointing his canoeing exploits."

"Will do Sarge," Wazzer dutifully replied. He and Thomo diverted off the main corridor toward the rear yard and their waiting crime car. The diminutive Wazzer, smirking at his supervisor's comparison, playfully elbowed his giant colleague in the ribs. "You'd look good in a black, plaited ponytail singing *'just around the river-bend'*!"

"Funny," the much larger officer said. "I'll bend your bloody river if you start that as a rumour around the nick," he added.

Wazzer didn't quite know what part of his anatomy Thomo might select as his *'river'* but, based purely on the size differential between them, decided the private chuckle they shared would remain the safer option.

Chapter Twenty Four

"Excuse me officer. Sorry to disturb your, err, *break* but my car seems to have been stolen from the station car park sometime today," the elderly gentleman said, lightly touching the elbow of the policeman. The officer, leaning on the stall of newspapers on platform three of Hopefield railway station, lowered the cup from his lips.

"Oh dear, Sir," the officer replied, changing his jovial chat-up-the-news-girl tone to a much deeper, more official one. "What sort of car was it?"

"It's a Ford, a blue one and it's quite new. I parked it here this morning so that my wife and I could catch the train to Tottenshall to go shopping. You know how parking in the city can be."

"Very good, Sir," the uniformed constable added, reaching for his note book; not so much commenting on the gentleman's misfortune but on the fact he was happy to take the report. "Can you tell me the registration number of the car please?"

"Err… oh dear. Ethel, do you know the registration of the car, dear?"

"The what?" Ethel asked, not fully able to hear the question.

"The registration number, you know, the number plate."

The officer held his pen clear of his note book, awaiting some confirmation of detail before committing to paper the fact he was looking for a *blue car* with anything up to an eight hour head start.

"Ooh, let me think. There was a zed in it. I remember that. Do you remember George? I said, ooh look there's a zed in it when you got it. You never had zeds on car numbers in my day," she pointed out to the officer as he folded the note-book closed and slipped it back into the pocket of his large, fluorescent jacket. "No," she continued, "you see they looked too much like twos, that's why. No, never had zeds. But we did, didn't we George?"

"Yes, that's right, a zed, oh, and a five. There was definitely a five in it."

"Okay, Sir. I tell you what. Here's the number of the station helpdesk. When you get home you need to find your v-five. That's your registration document." The man's face was blank. "The one that says you own the car." George's expression was still glazed. "The blue one," the officer finally added.

"Oh yes, the blue one," George replied unconvincingly.

"Yes, the blue one," the officer confirmed, glancing at his colleague who was standing behind the old couple, smirking and thinking he had definitely chosen the right end of the news stand to lean on.

"Call that number and the person at the other end will take all your details and we'll try to find your car."

"Oh thank you officer, you've been most helpful," the pleasant, old man answered as he looked at the card given to him by the officer before placing it into his pocket. He gestured to his smiling wife and the couple began to shuffle away toward the station's taxi rank.

"Sir, before you go. Where was your car parked?" the second officer interjected.

"In the car park, didn't I say?"

"Sorry, Sir, I mean whereabouts in the car park?"

"Oh yes, sorry. It was over by the back wall. I tried to get a disabled bay for Ethel but they were all taken so I had to drop her at the entrance and park right over on the other side. Do you think that's why it got stolen, because of where I parked it?" George said, almost apologising for *creating* a crime by his choice of location.

"Possibly, Sir, but you shouldn't blame yourself. You were not to know it would be stolen from there any more than it could have been stolen from a disabled bay," the officer offered, in a poor attempt to console the old man. He knew damn well it was chosen exactly because of where it was.

"Oh, okay. Thank you then," George replied. Content with

the explanation, he turned back to support his wife's elbow.

With that, he and Ethel left the officers to continue their *break* and, laden with the day's shopping, wandered off the platform and out of sight.

"Taking a butchers?" the second officer quizzed as the first grinned and shook his head at the ineptitude of the old man and wife.

"No rush. I've got my tea to finish first," the senior man retorted, raising the polystyrene beaker back toward his lips.

***

"Whisky Charlie Nine Nine, control. We are TA* at area one, commencing search of the Gant river gorge."

"Control, Nine Nine. TA, roger that."

Wazzer and Thomo hurtled at break neck speed along the duel carriageway toward the river crossing short of Tottenshall. Overhearing the radio conversation between the Hopefield control room and the Force helicopter they knew that, if Thomo had correctly interpreted Lewis's directions, their missing colleague would easily be found in the next few moments.

Thomo was explaining to Wazzer that Lewis's description of the bridge only having one central support was spot on. The ravine he knew was less than a couple of hundred metres wide and the sides were steep, like cliffs. Sure enough, the message they had been hoping for came back quickly.

"Whisky Charlie Nine Nine, control. We have a single female sighted as described at the base of the rail bridge crossing the River Gant. It's a concrete block about fifteen feet by thirty feet. The river is pretty wild so I think a launch rescue is going to be out of the question. The female is seated and waving at us. The pilot says we're unable to get anywhere near her but from the camera I can confirm it is DC Murray. She's alive but not getting up so I'm guessing she's possibly injured. Ooh yeah... nasty," the camera operator let slip over the air. *"Her right leg is badly broken and there appears to be quite a bit of blood nearby. You might want to check with the Air Force SAR* helicopters but our winch is definitely not going to be long enough to get to her. Next best thing looks like it's going to be a*

209

rope team down the bridge support. Either way it's going to be a tricky recovery."

"Control, Nine Nine, roger that. Will advise, stand by."

"Nine Nine, control. For information there's a gravel track leading toward the bridge area from.... the B5643 which can be accessed from the A765 about a quarter mile from its junction with the A1(M). There's a clearing at the railway end of the track. We're going to put down there and await the ground staff and rescue team."

"Control, Nine Nine. That's understood. Ambulance and Fire are en route ETA fifteen, one five, minutes. I believe some of DS Backhouse's team are also en route."

"Quebec India Five Three. DC Holliwell, interrupting. We've just past the ambulance and fire on the A1(M). We're five minutes away."

"DC Holliwell, roger that. Five minutes. Nine Nine copy."

"Nine Nine, roger, five minutes. We'll meet them there."

The helicopter hovered lower toward the bridge and PC Fisher, the air observer, flipped the switch on his equipment panel, activating the external loudspeaker.

"DC Murray, we have you sighted. We are going to land nearby but rest assured help is on the way. Please wave if you understand."

Murray leaned back onto her left arm and waved a large slow wave over her head with the other. The helicopter was around a hundred and fifty feet above her but the downwash, channelled toward her by the sheer sides of the river gorge, was still enough to limit the gesture to once-left-once-right motion before she had to return the free hand to her face to protect her eyes from the swirling dust and grit kicked up by the machine's rotors.

The helicopter gently sidled across the gorge's edge and out of Murray's sight. She listened as the reassuring whine of the twin turbine engines dwindled away and the roar of the river below once again became the prominent sound. Exhaling a long sigh of relief, she knew she was going to be alright. However, as the adrenalin which had been keeping her alive faded away in the light of her impending rescue, the nerve impulses from her shattered and bleeding body began to regain their full strength. The pain rose and she found herself laying back down in response to the agonising sensations. The tortuous feelings soon overwhelmed the young detective and, arms dropping to her sides, she passed out once again.

***

Back at the office Atticker, monitoring the radio, let out a loud "YES!" as the news of Murray's discovery was broadcast.

"Sarge," he shouted down the corridor to Backhouse's office. "They've found Lizzie and she's alive!"

"Great news," the relieved Sergeant exclaimed in a gruff and meaningful tone as he strode toward the main office once again. "Right, Barnes, bollocks to that for now," he said referring to the interview plan Barnes was reviewing. "The scumbag can wait for now. We've got Lizzie back safe so let's get down to the hospital to meet her coming in."

"Okay," Barnes simply replied, more than happy that the *scumbag* could indeed wait, now that Lizzie was safe.

***

"You sorted then?"

"Okay, okay," the older man replied as he thrust the last piece of a large, chocolate muffin into his face.

The two uniformed officers left the platform newsstand and its pretty young attendant and wandered across the link bridge to the station's main entrance and the car park beyond. They walked by their liveried estate and through the car park, passing amongst the three hundred or more vehicles between them and the yard's long, rear wall.

They scanned along the high, stone barrier and found an empty space in the area described by the old victim-of-crime. However, there was no tell-tale broken glass, just a half-brick, seemingly out of place, about three feet from the wall.

"Anything?" one asked the other as they searched for clues in separate areas around the empty space.

"No, nothing," came the reply. The younger officer scanned around and spotted the surveillance camera over toward the ticket office. "Better check the security recording."

"It's not even pointing over here."

"Yeah, maybe, but the exit's covered so we might at least get what time it left."

"Are you *really* going to check *eight hours* of tape just for the back of a stolen car leaving the car park? It'll be crap quality so you know you'll not be able to make out the reg'."

The younger officer pondered the question for a moment, aware that his senior colleague's motivation was not as keen as it once was.

"Yeah!" he eventually responded in a jovial tone, attempting to raise his partner's game from under the weight of the numerous muffins he had consumed at the station that day.

"I bloody well knew you were going to say that. Come on then Sherlock, let's go."

The pair left the empty space and started back toward the station buildings.

"Hang on a minute," the younger, keener officer said. "Isn't that …? Yeah, it is. Better call it in Chris. That's Lizzie Murray's missing car!"

***

"Okay David, let's go," Tracy said, beckoning the recumbent Lewis to get up from the thin, foam mattress of his police cell. "We're going to take your fingerprints and photograph now."

David rose from his rigid resting place and followed the attractive officer through the open steel door. Outside the cell Tracy's partner, Dave Walker, was waiting in the corridor. They set off back toward the central reception area and, from there, entered the open door to the adjoining documentation room.

Inside, David could see a camera on a hinged frame on the far wall with a large, dish-reflected, flashlight assembly fixed up above it. In the far corner, at the point he imagined the folded away camera would be pointing when in use, there was a grey panel screwed onto the wall with white bars either side marked with graduations of inches on the right and centimetres on the left. On the wall next to that another folded frame was flat against the wall. This one loosely held a laminated card, blank except for some lines separating it into several empty blocks. He presumed his name would be written on it shortly.

Across the room a desk with a chair either side supported a computer screen and keyboard. Behind that, in one corner, was a sink with a wall-mounted, hot water boiler. A number of large, grey, steel cupboards and an upright fridge-freezer made up the bulk of the remaining fittings. Finally the opposite wall sported a single, upright machine, not dissimilar in size to an arcade game.

It was this device that the female officer approached and, sliding a keyboard from an opening at waist height, she began a well-practised instruction of David.

"Okay David," she said. "I'm going to take your fingerprints with this device. It's called Livescan and it takes an electronic image of your fingerprints using laser light. It works best if your hands are moist but not sweaty. So, if you wash and dry your hands, over there please, we'll see how we get on. If you get them too dry we have some hand-cream here to get a better image. Okay?"

"Yeah, whatever," David glibly replied, having no reason to object to the procedure.

Tracy began tapping away at the keyboard, briefly making note of some lengthy number generated by the machine onto a clipboard of dated log-sheets on the table. Pushing the keyboard away into its housing she lifted a metal panel that uncovered two glass plinths, one large and one small. Beneath them a bright, red light was reflected upward by some sort of angled mirror arrangement.

From a rack on the side of the machine Tracy produced a small plastic canister and squirted what smelt to David like some sort of window cleaner on the two platens, wiping them dry again with a tissue. The upper half of the machine consisted of a large monitor and as she wiped the glass David could see black smears appearing and then disappearing across the screen.

"Okay, give me your right hand please. Relax; let me move your hand on the panel. Don't press down. I'll apply any pressure that's needed," she instructed.

David complied and the detective arranged the four fingers of his right hand into a flat, palm down position. She gently pressed the four fingers onto the larger of the two screens. The monitor, initially a clear, white screen with a simple, red box in its centre now displayed a large black-on-white image of his right fingerprints.

He was impressed by the clarity of the image, the separate peaks and troughs of his personal identification marks boldly contrasted in great detail. Tracy manoeuvred the fingers until all four images were within the red boxed area before depressing a foot-pedal on the floor which David hadn't even noticed until he heard it click under her shoe. The screen, previously fluid in its appearance, jolted to a captured halt and Tracy clicked the pedal once again to clear the monitor.

"Okay good. Left hand," she directed, letting go of his right.

The left set of fingerprints was similarly saved, along with separate images of his thumbs. Tracy depressed the foot pedal again and a larger red box appeared.

"Okay, now each in turn," she said. She took up his right thumb and rolled it, left to right, across the smaller platen. A large image of the single digit's tip appeared in a detailed oblong as she smoothly scrolled his thumb across the glass. Somehow retaining the extending imprint, the image grew until it filled the whole screen. The detail was amazing. David could even make out the individual pores between each groove and the swirls in the pattern which made it unmistakeably unique.

Tracy repeated the procedure for each finger and thumb and then finished by taking palm images. Next she brought up the full set of captured prints, checking each one until she was happy they were to a standard David could only guess at. Finally, she had him sign an electronic pad with a plastic pointer, his oversized signature appearing in yet another red box as he did so.

"Right David, that's sorted. Now, go and take a seat please while DC Walker asks you some questions."

David sat at the desk, opposite her colleague and began to answer questions regarding his description. As he did, the detective inputted the details into a computerised form. Everything was covered from head to toe: height, weight, tattoos, scars, eye colour, hair, birthmarks, even teeth peculiarities.

Meanwhile, Tracy had electronically dispatched the captured *tenprint*, as it was called, off to Hendon for comparison to the millions of fingerprints already held on file. By the time Tracy's colleague had finished his questions, taken a cotton-bud-like swab of David's DNA from the inside of his cheek and had stood him behind the name board for a photo the result was back.

"Well!" she exclaimed. "Looks like we have a hit."

David was perplexed. He'd never had his fingerprints taken before. Had he?

"So, Mr *Lewis,* are you going to let us know your real name?"

"Sorry?" David asked, puzzled at the request.

"David *Caldwell* ring any bells?" Tracy asked.

She could see in his eyes he was genuinely surprised at the semi-sarcastic remark but there was no denying the accuracy of the machine. It was showing a ninety nine point five percent probability that the man stood before her was, indeed, David Caldwell.

The name was no surprise to her. She knew it matched the DNA result from the factory and merely confirmed that the man in front of her was likely to be responsible for numerous robberies and the kidnap of her colleague, and friend, Liz Murray.

David, on the other hand, had no clue who she was talking about.

Chapter Twenty Five

He was getting close to the outskirts of Tottenshall and so quietened the car's radio to listen for whether his passenger was still screaming. She wasn't. Her efforts had been for nought and her cries for help had devolved into the low whimpering of a caged animal. Lucy was bound, gagged and scared to death. She had no idea what was going on. David had been there, she'd been so close to him but then... what on earth had happened? She couldn't even remember the man's face, just a fist hitting her square and hard in the nose.

"That's better," the awful man said, calling back from the cab of the car. She let out retaliatory scream from beneath her gag.

"Now come on, don't start again. I need you to be quiet now. Believe me, if you don't do as you're told you'll not be seeing your precious David again."

'David.' She was stunned into silence by the mention of his name. *'What did this man want with him?'* she thought.

She knew David was in trouble with the police. The missing female officer she had seen on the television back at work had not yet been accounted for and the suspect's face, albeit blurred, had indeed been David. Then again, this man couldn't be a policeman; the boot of a car was no place for anyone the police might have an interest in. Besides, David had been there. If the driver was in the police why take her and not him? She dismissed the question as ridiculous and returned to her first thought; this was definitely *not* a policeman.

So, who was he? The voice was familiar. It had the same depth and accent as David so he must have been local to the area. That said, the voice was somehow rougher, more troubled than David's. What did he want with her?

"We're nearly at the city," the voice continued, "so keep quiet and you'll see out the day. When it's safe I'll have you call David and get him to meet us. No messing with me though or I *will* kill you. And don't think I won't either. The last pair of bastards that thought I was a soft touch got what was coming to them. Don't think because you're a girl I won't do the same."

Lucy pondered what he meant, exactly, by *'got what was coming to them'* but decided that it probably wasn't pleasant. Why was he going to call David to meet them though? He had been right there when she had been knocked out. David must have even seen it happen. Yet now, this guy wanted him to come to them.

Then it dawned on her; she was a hostage. That said what had David done that had been so bad that this man was willing to take her captive over it? David may have started drinking before she had left him but, surely, that alone could have nothing to do with this? Did David owe him money? Perhaps it was about the policewoman. Was this guy her boyfriend maybe, unhappy with the progress being made by the police?

No, that didn't make sense. He would just have taken David instead of her. In fact, how did he even know who she was? She and David had only just arranged to talk about getting back together.

Her mind ached under the barrage of questions. She could taste the blood in her mouth from the split lip she'd received when punched in the face. Plus, her inability to breath properly through her nose was more from the swelling then the gag around her face. She knew it was broken as she'd suffered the same injury as a child and the sensation was identical.

Whatever the driver of her *cage* had in store for David, she knew he wasn't someone to be trifled with. He was willing to injure her and, from his threats, probably happy to do a lot worse. She decided that, for now at least, it would be best to capitulate and do as she was told. The tears of pain and confused fear continued to roll down her soft, white cheeks and she muffled her earlier whimpering to an almost silent murmur.

***

Trussed up like an Egyptian mummy in the safety cage of the rescue team's stretcher, Murray once again opened her eyes. The sudden shock of facing out into the open air of the ravine and the raging river some hundred feet or so below was quickly overcome by the reassuring smile of the mountain rescue officer guiding her vertically up the side of the railway bridge stanchion.

"Well hello there, little lady," the handsome rescuer softly said. She considered his equally precarious position, dangling from a single line to his teammates above them, and was amazed by the calmness of his voice

"She's awake," he called out looking upward toward the parapet.

"Excellent," the reply came, encouragingly close. "Just a few more feet now, steady, steady."

Murray could hear the conversation from above them and, as her cot twisted away from the climber's face and her feet rose to put her in a horizontal position alongside the bridge's edge, she could see the hands of the other team members reaching down to secure her and lift her to the safety of the crossing's surface.

Despite her head being secured by a supportive neck brace, Murray could still move her eyes around enough to see the sheer number of people involved in her rescue. Too many to count, the differing uniforms being evidence of the concerted effort made in coming to her aide. A paramedic knelt next to her, her reassuring voice as comforting as the helmeted climber now gingerly hopping down from the bridge parapet to join her on the ballast of the railway line.

"Hello Lizzie," the blonde medic said. "You're safe now. Let's just give you a quick check over and we'll get you to the helicopter, okay?"

Murray let out a croaky "Yes", her throat dried by two

218

days without liquid sustenance. Despite this though, she couldn't help but also let out a wincing cry as the paramedic's hands ran down her shattered right leg.

"Okay, sorry about that Lizzie. We're going to have to stabilise that. We'll just give you something for the pain and we'll have you on your way in a jiffy."

The woman's green coveralls were paired as her partner joined her at Murray's left side. Murray felt the tugging at her clothes as the male medic snipped back the sleeve to expose her arm. A cool chill was followed by the sharp prick of a needle entering the skin just above the elbow and a blurry headiness came over her as the painkilling medication flushed into her body.

A few minutes of awkward and uncomfortable tugging and a dazed Murray felt herself being lifted from the ground. The floating ride continued to the clearing beside the railway lines and the noise of crunching footfalls faded away as the group around her passed onto the grassy surface of the open space.

As her levitating repose passed the familiar orange and black of the police helicopter, silent and stationary in its original landing spot, Murray glimpsed the smiling faces of Wazzer and Thomo. Wazzer gave a reassuring, albeit childish, double thumbs up and Murray found herself breaking into a hazy smile.

Her carriage floated on and, passing beneath the tail boom of the bright red air ambulance, she slipped into the rear bay of the larger aircraft. The female paramedic said her goodbyes to return to her more earthly mode of transport and the bay doors closed behind her.

Inside the machine she was quickly joined by another medic, this one in bright red overalls, matching him to the helicopter which was now beginning to groan and whine as its transmission came to life. The man leaned over Murray, gently placing a pair of soft-cuffed ear defenders onto her head, and the machine's engines became louder and louder as the helicopter lumbered into the air.

***

Backhouse and Barnes pulled into the hospital car park and, with the sliding doors parting in response to their approach, passed through the entrance and into the reception area.

"Excuse me," Barnes introduced himself to the Accident & Emergency receptionist. "We're here about Elizabeth Murray, the police officer brought in from the river near Tottenshall."

"Are you family?" the receptionist quizzed.

"No we're police colleagues."

"I'm sorry but only family are allowed into A&E," the woman said officiously.

Backhouse stepped forward, casually pushing Barnes to one side with the back of his hand.

"Listen sweetheart," he began in an unforgiving tone. "We are *her* police colleagues. I am *her* police boss and this is a *police* matter. I'm not asking for your permission to enter A&E. I just want to know where she is so tap on your little computer and find out. Okay chuckles?"

"There's no need to be rude," the prudish woman replied. She checked her screen as directed and offered, "I've no record of her so she mustn't have arrived yet. I suggest you see the ward sister. She'll be aware of any incoming patients."

"Thank you," Backhouse answered sarcastically. "Now that didn't hurt much did it?" He didn't wait for a reply but instead span on his heels and made toward the doors leading through to the ward desk.

The ward was characteristically busy. The different coloured uniforms, differentiating the various ranks and positions within the department, flashed back and two like worker ants, each carrying out its tasks in accordance with some unseen directive from a higher authority.

Suddenly, that authority stepped out from behind a drawn curtain and snapped it to, behind her.

"Nurse Langrish," she called to a passing subordinate. "Put a call out to the on-call cardiologist please and get two units of 'O' Negative for Doctor Shelmerdine."

"Yes Sister," the nurse answered before scuttling away to comply with the fresh instruction.

Her response had identified Backhouse's target and he homed in like a guided missile.

"Hello, Sister?" he quickly introduced himself while catching her in an unspoken moment.

"Yes?" the navy clad woman answered, maintaining an eye on the ward about her.

"DS Backhouse, Hopefield Police."

The efficient ward Sister was already a step ahead of him. "You're here for Miss Murray I imagine. They're just about to touchdown on the roof which is why I'm trying to clear some space down here. If you'll excuse me..." With that she turned away and continued her tirade of instructions to her bustling staff.

Barnes found himself smirking at the manner in which she had so easily dismissed Backhouse. She'd left him, statue-like and dumbfounded, in the centre of the ward corridor, hospital staff parting about him like the water around a rock in a stream. If just for a few sweet seconds Barnes watched as his sexist supervisor was firmly outmatched, by a woman. The moment passed and Backhouse casually flipped his warrant card closed and slipped it back into his rear trouser pocket.

"We'll wait," he instructed the bemused Barnes, as if he hadn't already had the decision made for him.

They waited in silence, Barnes cherishing each passing second of the Sergeant's disgruntlement. Within minutes the doors from the elevator lobby were burst apart by the entrance of Murray's hospital gurney. Still packed into her supportive cradle of back-board and foam braces, Backhouse was shocked at her apparent condition. Appearances aside though, as she passed them, Murray raised an arm and reached out for the stunned detective's hand. Instinctively, he grabbed hers and walked along with the wheeling stretcher.

"It was Lewis," she mumbled through her swollen lips.

"We know," Backhouse replied. "Lizzie, you were right all along. It was Lewis and we have him. We have him in custody, Lizzie. You were right."

Lizzie let the weight of her arm signal the old man to release it and, with some small portion of responsibility lifted from her for allowing Lewis to entrap her so easily, let it drop back down onto the matting beside her.

Backhouse and Barnes watched as the recovered officer was wheeled into the booth emptied, only minutes before, by the ward Sister. With at least half a dozen staff bustling around her in the small enclosure, there was no place for the pair. Besides, they could offer her no help themselves at the moment. There would be plenty of time for questions and explanations later. For now, content in the fact she was safe and alive, Backhouse silently led his subordinate away to the hospital canteen, pausing only at the ward desk to pass over his card and request that he be called as soon as Lizzie asked for him.

***

"All patrols, all patrols, stand by for observations", the Tottenshall operator announced over the air. "All patrols, observations for a navy blue Ford Mondeo saloon registration Golf, Romeo, Five, Seven, Alpha, Charlie, Zulu; Vehicle stolen since zero eight hundred today from Hopefield railway station in Wrenshire. That's repeating observations for a navy blue Ford Mondeo saloon registration Golf, Romeo, Five, Seven, Alpha, Charlie, Zulu stolen since zero eight hundred today from Hopefield. Message ends nineteen forty." The operator typed in the open incident *'Observations passed out to all patrols'* and marked the out of Force log as *'closed'*.

The elderly couple from the railway station had followed the muffin-chomping officer's instructions to the letter. Old George had found his *blue form* and had called in the details of his stolen car to the Hopefield crime desk. They, in turn, had circulated the car as stolen on the police national computer and had also generated a surrounding forces dispatch so that neighbouring patrols, who may have potentially sighted the taken vehicle, would report it as located.

Fortunately, Atticker, who had kept himself busy monitoring all incoming incidents, radio transmissions and crime reports for the slightest chance of them being connected to the previous two days' events, had noticed the proximity between the location of the stolen report on the Ford Mondeo and the recovered SIU car. He had reached the conclusion that one had been stolen as a replacement for the other and had reported his suspicions to Backhouse. In full agreement with the computer specialist, he, in turn, had requested the Hopefield FIM to generate an additional marker to notify any patrols finding the car of its importance to his investigation.

The FIM, duty bound to disclose any potential safety issues connected with such a report, had insisted on adding the potential for a firearms connection. After all, Backhouse had agreed with his theory the previous day that Lewis could have been the person responsible for the double murder in the park and, as such, could have had access to a firearm. The links may have been tenuous but the implications for officer safety could not be ignored if the message on the vehicle's computer report was to go national.

In closing, the incident the log was automatically recycled, but, instead of leaving the Tottenshall operator's screen, it flashed up a newly received *'critical information'* warning. Briefly thrown by the surprising and rare event, he re-opened the incident and clicked on the information icon, now signalling the additional marker's existence by flashing in the centre of the log's summary page.

"All patrols, further to the last observations standby for additional information," the operator transmitted, instantly gaining the interest of the thirty or more officers currently out of the station on mobile patrol. Even those monitoring the airwaves whilst desk-bound with the day's paperwork paused to raise the volume of their radios in response to the rarity of the announcement.

"All patrols, further to the last observations for a navy blue Ford Mondeo stolen today from Hopefield. Information has been received that suggests the vehicle may be connected with the abduction of a police officer from Hopefield SIU. If sighted unoccupied it is to be preserved for a full forensic lift."

There was a short pause, as if the operator was reading the last portion of the message and then receiving instructions on its dissemination. "From the control room Inspector, if mobile, the vehicle is not, repeat, not to be stopped at this time as the occupants may have access to firearms which have not yet been recovered by Wrenshire police. Report any sightings to control and await further instruction. Message ends nineteen forty two."

Chapter Twenty Six

"Want another brew Sarge?" Barnes asked his supervisor.

"Err, yeah, cheers," the senior man responded, snatched from his thoughts by the offer. Just then his phone began to rumble in his pocket. "Hang on," he called the younger detective back to him as he reached in to retrieve it. "This might be Lizzie."

He tugged the silently vibrating phone from his pocket and, depressing the answer button, placed it to his ear.

"Backhouse," he acknowledged.

"Hello, its nurse Henderson from post op recovery. I'm told you wanted to be notified once Elizabeth Murray was ready to be seen?"

"Yes, that's right. Post op you say? I thought she was in A&E?"

"She was, but she had to be moved to surgical for her leg to be reset. She's still in the recovery bays at the moment but will back on c-fourteen in around half an hour. Do you know where that is?"

"Yes, I was there just last week," Backhouse confirmed, referring to their visit to the elderly Mrs Nugent. "That's good news. We'll be there in half an hour, thanks."

Backhouse ended the call and returned the slim phone to his pocket.

"Good news then?" Barnes beckoned.

"Well, yeah," the Sergeant said, surprised at the speed of Lizzie's treatment. "She's already been into surgery with her leg and will be on ward c-fourteen in half an hour."

"Nice one. That's where Mrs Nugent is, isn't it?"

"Yeah, it is. Talking of which, any news on the VIPER of Caldwell?"

"Tracy said on the phone that she was getting it jigged up after confirming the Livescan result. I imagine the capture will be done by now. It just needs the compilation completing and downloading to the laptop for Mrs Nugent to view in here."

"Good, at this rate we'll hardly need an interview. He'll be banged to rights once the old dear picks him out," Backhouse announced confidently.

"I'll get those brews for now then, yeah?"

"Yeah right, and get me a couple of those chocolate biscuits will you? I'm bloody starving."

The half hour passed quickly, Backhouse and Barnes sipping tea and munching biscuits. Discussing the incarcerated Lewis, they pondered the possible explanations he might try to conjure up to explain his change of identity. In addition there was that bogus National Insurance number. How had he managed to successfully pass that off for so long?

Looking at the low-level hoodlum's record Barnes found it peculiar, at the very least, that Caldwell would have had the wherewithal, or indeed the connections, to facilitate such a thorough identity fraud. Stealing the identity of a dead child wasn't easy but once the birth certificate of the deceased infant *David Lewis'* had been obtained Caldwell *could* have applied for a plethora of false, but otherwise legitimate documents to support his new identity; driving licence, passport, bank accounts.

He could have created a completely new life for himself, but had curiously not done so. Why had he returned to a life of street crime, mugging old ladies for petty cash? There was definitely something odd about this *David* character. Still, it was going to make for an interesting interview.

"Come on," Backhouse said, ending the increasingly circular discussion over the whys-and-wherefores of their prisoner's life. He sharply rose to his feet, skittering the metal canteen chair back from the table and across the linoleum floor.

Barnes slugged back the remaining mouthful of tea from his non-descript hospital mug and set it down on the table. The seemingly now better-matched pair left the refreshment area and made their way to the surgical ward.

As they entered the second floor room Barnes wondered if

the condescending consultant, Mr Chivers, was going to be on duty. After days without proper sleep he doubted his acerbic supervisor would be as polite to the pompous practitioner as he'd been when discussing the ex-RAF Officer's condition.

Behind the nursing station the same buxom nurse greeted the pair, well Barnes at least, with a wry smile. He returned the glance, nodding in recognition of her welcome. Barnes felt the elbow of his superior once again.

"Time for that later, you horny beggar," Backhouse said, chastising Barnes in a distinctly less lustful manner than he had used when pointing out the pretty nurse the week before.

Backhouse had already spotted the semi reclined figure of Lizzie in a bed half way down the ward and was by-passing the formality of an introduction at the nursing station in favour of a bee-line to his recovering colleague. Barnes allowed himself a boyish half-wave at the ward nurse, as an apology for not engaging her in conversation, and followed his Sergeant to meet Lizzie.

Although further down her lower limb, Murray's bedclothes suggested a familiarly cringe-worthy cage supporting the pinned bones of her right leg and, in memory of the sensation Barnes found himself looking around the ward for the still bed-bound Mrs Nugent. The old lady, so helpful to the detectives the week before, was more-or-less opposite Murray's bed and was quietly sleeping the evening away. Murray, on the other hand, was wide awake and smiled as broadly as her facial injuries would allow.

She reached beneath her hips and pushed herself up the bed into a more upright sitting position. The fact that the bedclothes, supported away from her reset leg, didn't move was a reassuring sign that, unlike the unfortunate septuagenarian on the other side of the ward, her cage wasn't as intrusive as the one supporting the old lady's hip and thigh. Without waiting for the pleasantry of any greeting, Murray was straight into it.

"You got him then? Lewis? What has he said?"

"We've not interviewed him yet," Backhouse offered the inquisitive detective, reluctant to tell her of their detainee's bizarre claims as to how he knew where to find her. "But there's something you'll be interested in; he's not called David Lewis."

Murray's expression, initially surprised by the revelation, soon dropped back into one of reflective realisation.

"That explains a few things. No record for one," she said.

"Well it does, and it doesn't," Barnes interjected. "His Livescan result identified him as a David Caldwell, a local low-life with a string of petty thefts and burglaries. And that name matches DNA found at the factory where we found your blood and car tyre tracks."

"So what's the problem? I'm ninety nine percent sure his voice was David Lewis, the same that I had heard in the station that day. He tried to disguise it at first but I'm sure it was him. And when I called him David he was surprised that I knew him. He wasn't expecting that I'd recognise him because he'd blindfolded me. It was definitely Lewis that abducted me."

Before Barnes had the chance to raise the curiosity of Caldwell's change of identity or the possibility, albeit slim, of the abductor being an accomplice of Caldwell, the mere mention of the offence brought Murray's brave façade crashing down and the young woman's eyes filled up with the painful memories. She burst into tears and blubbered out an unnecessary apology.

"Lizzie, it's okay. Your safe now," Backhouse reassured the junior detective, curling a comforting arm around her shoulders.

Barnes was shocked at the compassion shown by his wiry supervisor and found himself becoming even more attached to the otherwise abrasive old sod.

"You've confirmed what we expected you to say so rest assured he'll be getting what's coming to him. You have my word on that."

Backhouse held the young officer for a few moments before releasing her back against her pillows.

"We'll let you rest for now. We're going to be back later with the VIPER officer to see Mrs Nugent over there so we'll have another chat then. Okay?"

Murray nodded, unable to speak through her blubbering, and Backhouse gestured to Barnes that it was time to go. The pair left the emotional Murray to slip back down her bed into a tearful sleep.

***

In his cell David sat with his back against the side wall, his feet up on the raised, wooden bench which, for the lack of any other furniture, he imagined was to double as his bed for the night. His knees, raised toward his chest, supported his elbows and he held his head in his hands. Oblivious to the heavy smell of bleach, vainly trying to cover the equally acrid stench of the cell's previous drunken tenant, David's mind was racing over the events of the previous week and a half.

In discharging himself from hospital into the custody of police, he'd hoped to finally convince them that he needed their help, or rather Lucy needed it. The idea that he'd, technically, been *in custody* since his collapse in the street was lost on his naïve mind.

However, now they were calling him David Caldwell, but why? Caldwell. David Caldwell. David ran the name through his entire memory, straining to place any recollection.

Suddenly, he visualised a large pond on a sunny afternoon. A man stood over him, his relative size suggesting that David was seeing the scene as a child. The man was silently laughing and he was struggling with a large fish, thrashing about above a keep net until it finally flipped out of his grip and back into the water.

Then the images flashed forward to a graveside scene, then a fight, then a field, then a police car, then a smashing window, another police car, a court room, a prison cell, a factory. The images accelerated beyond comprehension until they suddenly crashed to a halt.

David was alone in a clinically sterile, circular room. Staring up at the bright, white ceiling, he realised he was strapped into a semi-reclined chair with his arms and legs immobilised.

Unable to fully move his head, he strained the flesh of his

face over to one side and, out of the very corner of his right eye, could see a bank of liquids in glass containers. Set in chrome clamps, the three tubes were atop an equally stark bank of lights on a brushed steel panel. Pipes emanating from the top of each tube rose and arched over to a junction box down toward the floor and a single ominous pipe led from that box to another chrome clamp, fixed horizontally out from the right arm of his chair.

Then he realised the pipe, continuing through the chair clamp, led to a needle strapped to his bare forearm which, piercing the skin, was swelling the underlying blood vessel. Whatever was in those glass tubes was about to be in him. A sensation of panic welled up inside him and, snapping his eyes over to his left, he saw a long, glass panel. Beyond it, a row of stony-faced strangers sat staring at him. Within seconds, a curtain, electronically drawn, slowly swept between them. David quickly returned his attention to the glass tubes and, in solemn succession, the lights on the panel, from left to right, lit up. Pistons began to slowly rise inside the tubes, forcing their contents along the pipes to the junction box below.

David watched in silent horror as the mixed liquids progressed along the pipe, through the chair clamp and into his arm. He screamed in panic but heard no sound. The warm sensation of urine filling his pants was followed by a steady fading of his vision into pinpoints of light. A sharp, bitter taste, an electrically sharp bolt of sudden pain and the vision ended.

David woke from his surreal stupor with a jolt. The sudden sharp pain pulsed once again in his head and his body violently jerked, throwing him the short distance to the hard, tiled floor. The yell he let out this time was loud and clear. He felt a warm glow pass down his body from the crown of his head to the very tip of his toes; its steady pace was almost mechanical.

Rolling onto his back David stared up at the dirty cream ceiling of the police cell and then, with a clarity of mind he had never experienced, he knew everything. He was there, in Hopefield, for a reason. The only problem now was that he was in the right time but the wrong place. He still had to get

Backhouse to believe him, only now he knew how to do it.

David quickly got to his feet and banged on the door of his cell.

"Hey, somebody! I need to speak to Backhouse. It's urgent. I need to speak to Backhouse NOW! HEY!"

***

"Director, we've got full acquisition."

"It's about bloody time. Okay what have we got?"

"Standby... Hang on a minute, that can't be right."

"What now?"

"It's the Consequential Paradox Reading. The signal stammer has gone altogether but the CPR... it's in the negative, seventy six percent and rising."

"So what are you trying to tell me, sending him back is actually making things worse?"

"Well, err, I'm not sure. But if this continues and it reaches a hundred percent it could be really.... well.... bad!"

"Bad? That's your technical appraisal is it; bad?" The Director turned to another man standing over a wall-mounted panel behind them. "Johnson, get me a techie up here, NOW!"

***

"Hi Lyndsey," Backhouse said, greeting the VIPER officer as she entered the incident room office.

Atticker silently raised a hand and smiled as she passed him. He had worked with PC Hall during the development of the VIPER software and they had remained friends since.

"Hi Sarge," the pleasant constable responded. "The Caldwell compilation is ready for viewing and, as requested, I've loaded it on this notepad for you." She lifted the laptop bag she was carrying and patted it as she lay it down on the table in front of the Detective Sergeant.

"Excellent. Listen, Lyndsey, thanks a bunch for staying on so late. I'll sign up your overtime form, no problem. Just send it up when you've done it."

"No worries Sarge. How is Lizzie anyway?"

"Surprisingly good, all things considered."

"Good. I was horrified to hear of her kidnap. I just hope this helps," she added, gesturing to the computer.

"Tell you what. Atticker was going to do the viewing but if you want to stay on to show the VIPER to the witness you can meet Lizzie there. She's in the same ward."

"I'd love to meet Lizzie Sarge but you know I can't show the video to the witness. It would leave us open to allegations of influencing her selection, if she makes one that is."

"Yeah, of course. I was thinking about Lizzie rather than the VIPER rules," Backhouse replied, admitting his error.

There was another first for the nearby Barnes, another chink in the senior detective's armour. Backhouse really *did* care about Lizzie, about her disappearance. Barnes had seen the detective appear to shoulder more responsibility than he would have expected before. Then again, she was safe now. Was Backhouse still making errors out of a continuing burden of responsibility? Was he worried about the internal investigation that was bound to follow the whole affair? Or... was he just tired?

Whatever the cause, Barnes had grown fond of the older man's quirks. Whatever his faults, he was someone who cared about those around him and was willing to do whatever was needed to keep them safe. No, Barnes had decided that if there was going to be a witch-hunt over this particular episode in Backhouse's career he wasn't going to be a *witness for the prosecution*.

"Okay Atticker," a freshly confident Backhouse announced, trying to wash away his previous error. "Cut your umbilical to that desk and get your coat. You're with us."

Atticker closed down the computer on the aforementioned desk and crossed the room to the nearby laptop, scooping it up like a child who had misplaced its favourite teddy only to find it just a few feet away.

"Give Lizzie my best won't you?"

"Of course we will. And thanks again Lyndsey. We'll see you tomorrow and let you know how we got on," Backhouse promised the young woman.

"Okay, good night," she finished, leaving the office door to slowly close behind her.

***

Re-entering the surgical recovery ward, Backhouse, Barnes and Atticker wandered down the wide central aisle toward DC Murray. She was lying fully prone, sleeping peacefully. Her relaxed face bore little reference to the ordeal of the previous two days and Backhouse gestured to his two detectives to remain quiet and let her untroubled state continue as long as it could.

It was nine in the evening of the eventful Wednesday. The team had caught their offender, rescued their victim and were about to close their case with the positive identification of the mugger they had originally been set up to capture. The nurse had already roused the sleepy Mrs Nugent and had helped her make herself presentable to the arriving trio.

"Hello again Mrs Nugent," Barnes re-introduced himself. "You remember DS Backhouse?"

"Of course dear," the old lady said, smiling at the older policeman. "Have you got those pictures for me to look at?" she added.

"We've got something better than that," Backhouse said. "This is DC Atticker," he continued, directing Mrs Nugent's attention to her third visitor, who, in turn, was searching behind the booth's high backed chair for a power socket.

"Hello," the officer said, acknowledging the introduction.

Backhouse continued his interruption, "Atticker here is going to show you a series of video clips of some men. Now the man who stole your bag may or may not be among them but we'd like you to see if he is. Okay?"

"Oh, certainly dear. Bring it on!" she comically added.

Atticker powered up the laptop and Backhouse ran through the VIPER procedure. After the last video had finished Mrs Nugent look perplexed. Backhouse was concerned at her apparent doubt. He was sure, from her previous description of the offender, that she would have easily selected Caldwell from the video line-up.

"Anything?" he asked the old witness.

"Oh, I recognise one of those men there. He was number five," she reassuringly confirmed.

Backhouse had him.

"But he's not the man who attacked me," she added. "He was the nice young man who helped me on the bus that morning."

'Helped her onto a bus? Caldwell had mentioned that at the hospital before they had taken him to the station,' he thought to himself. His short lived triumph fell, shattered, about him.

"Number five wasn't the mugger then?"

"No. He looks very much like that, almost identical in fact, but the man who attacked me was rougher looking. He was thin in the face and dirty. And he smelt too. The chap helping me that morning had a particularly pleasant odour, so I know it definitely wasn't number five. No my attacker isn't amongst those pictures, sorry."

"No, no, don't apologise," Barnes reassured the old lady.

Backhouse and Barnes threw each other a confused glance. If Lewis... if Caldwell wasn't the mugger then why was his DNA at the factory, with the handbags and Murray's blood; an accomplice perhaps? Identical twins would explain the DNA match but not the fingerprint discrepancy; or was that just a coincidence, an administrative mix-up at some point in the past that would mean the real Caldwell, the real mugger, was still at large and the man in custody, his twin, had just used his brother's details when previously arrested?

If not twins, then had Lewis merely been there before Murray had even arrived at the derelict building? Some amateurish sleuth wanting to admonish his own petty-criminal past by tracking an offender to the factory and handling the bags previously abandoned there by the real mugger, by Murray's real abductor? Still, sleuth or otherwise, why the change of identity? And why confess to the crimes in the first instance?

There had to be another option, another truth. Both hypotheses were complete colanders when it came to holding any water, but the possibility that they had the wrong man in

234

custody was not the result Backhouse had wanted to achieve from this visit to the hospital. On top of which, if it were true, it would mean the real offender was still out there.

He turned around and looked over at the sleeping Murray. Was he going to let her down? Was he going to break his promise to make Lewis pay? She'd been so sure it was Lewis, or at least Lewis's voice; but a memory of a voice wasn't evidence. The disappointment welled up inside him, twisting in his gut and transforming into growing anger. The slightest chance that that they were wrong, that *he* was wrong, meant the real kidnapper may still be free and Backhouse did not cherish the idea of explaining *that* sort of mistake to his bosses.

The falling house of cards, which was his earlier confidence in a quick conclusion to this fiasco, continued to shower revelations down upon him. Was Lewis, damn it, Caldwell, telling the truth about the abductor having another victim? Could his ridiculous story about having visions have any credence? He walked silently from the ward. Barnes made their excuses for the rapid departure and Atticker hurriedly packed away the laptop before they both scuttled after their fast disappearing Sergeant.

Chapter Twenty Seven

"*DS Backhouse?*"

"Yeah, go ahead."

"*This is Sergeant Twigg down in custody. It's your man, Caldwell.*"

"Yeah, what about him?"

"*He's going nuts in his cell. He says it's urgent that he speaks to you. He says he has a* code *that'll prove he's telling the truth about someone called Lucy. Personally I think he's crazy but he's adamant that only you will understand.*"

"Okay. Get Tracy from my office to calm him down. We're on our way in."

Backhouse hung up the phone and turned to Barnes who was driving the car away from the hospital.

"Caldwell says he has a *code* of some kind that'll prove he's telling the truth. What do you reckon?"

"It means nothing to me. Do you think he might be?"

"I don't want to, but the Squadron Leader's really put the cat amongst the pigeons. Without her confirmation that Caldwell was the mugger, the fact his DNA was on her handbag means diddly-squat. And until we get any forensics on Lizzie's car, *if* we get any, it also throws enough doubt on the situation to get him off any involvement in her abduction. Lizzie's recollection of a voice is useless."

Whatever errors he had been making before, Barnes knew that Backhouse's reasoning was squarely back on form. The frustration of the failed VIPER identification had re-focused the Detective Sergeant's mind. Unfortunately, just when the case seemed to be wrapping up, he was now faced with a new set of questions to figure out.

"What was that car stolen from where Lizzie's was found?"

Backhouse asked, diverting the enquiry along its only other current line.

"The Mondeo?"

"Yeah. Did it get circulated?"

"I think so, why?"

"Come on Barnes, keep up. If Caldwell isn't the kidnapper then who do you think is? Have *you* seen that Lucy girl since Tracy and Dave lost her en route to the town centre?"

"Come to think of it, no. But I thought you weren't bothered about her after we got Lewis, err, Caldwell."

"I wasn't, but think about it for a minute. We were after *her* to get to *him*. What if we weren't the only ones? What if someone from David *Lewis's* past has recognised him and is trying to get to him for some reason. Maybe that's why he changed his identity, to escape something he did as David *Caldwell*. Do you remember he called me just before we got to him?"

"Yeah," an intrigued Barnes replied.

"Well, he was surprised and relieved that Murray was only missing, not dead. He thought she was dead. If he'd killed her he would have known it without any doubt. He said he got the impression she was dead from somewhere else, from some*one* else. Shit, I can't remember. Maybe it was one of his crazy visions."

"You don't believe he has visions do you?" Barnes asked, surprised at Backhouse's sudden lateral train of thought.

"Not yet. But there's always been something odd about him. What's more is that when I tested him about his Lucy coming to see him he just said 'cheers' and hung up."

"So?"

"*He* called *me* remember. He wanted to know if we were still following her. Why go to that effort only to hang up just on the strength of that comment? No, she was there. She had reached him at that very moment. But when we got to him did you see her?"

"No."

"No. And neither did any of us. We were all so damn wrapped up in getting him in the bin, we all totally forgot who had led us there in the first place. And if she wasn't there then where the hell was she? I'm sure if I'd walked half way across town to meet someone I wouldn't leave them lying in the gutter."

"Perhaps we scared her off. It was a pretty noisy arrival."

"No, he was down before we got there. She would have been crouching over him. We'd have seen her leave even if she did run. He was there, she was there. Then he was unconscious and she was gone. Say anything to you?"

"Another abduction?"

"Damn right, and we let it happen right in front of us. Shit. Get onto the control room and get those observations passed out again. That Mondeo has our offender in it, and, no doubt, this Lucy girl too. Damn it, I'm getting sloppy in my old age, very sloppy."

Barnes turned up the volume on his radio to make the call.

"Control to DS Backhouse or any officer with DS Backhouse."

"Looks like they want to speak to us too," Atticker remarked from the back of the car. Barnes responded to the operator.

"This is DC Barnes with DS Backhouse. Go ahead."

"DS Backhouse, this is the FIM, Inspector Hopley. Steve, we've had Tottenshall City Police on the phone. They're going nuts over the report you asked me to put on that Mondeo we circulated earlier. They have the vehicle sighted in an old industrial area of the city but their FIM is refusing to make an approach on it until you clarify the strength of the firearms connection. Can you give me anything to tell her? She's really not happy about the vague nature of the report, or the time it's taken me to get hold of you for that matter! Your phone's been engaged."

"Shit," Backhouse commented to his two staff. "This is where it goes south real quick." A moment of thought was all that the hardened detective needed. "Bill, call me now. The phone's free. Before you do though get me the direct number for the Tottenshall FIM and their Firearms TAC* advisor. And get our chopper to meet me in Westgate Park. No wait, the hospital roof has a pad, get it to pick me up there." He twirled an upright finger at Barnes to indicate a U-turn was required.

"Get it quickly Bill, I've got a bad feeling about this."
"Christ Steve, what the hell have you got me into this time?"

***

"Come on sweetheart, don't fuck around," Caldwell swore at the defenceless girl as he pushed her through the newly smashed-open doorway.

Lucy, her feet freed but still bound about the knees, wobbled under the painfully tight grip he had on her just above her right elbow. Her hands were taped behind her and she was still blindfolded and gagged. He pushed and pulled at her, manoeuvring her forward into the darkness of the canal-side factory. She stumbled and fell but his grip on her arm remained tight, digging even further into her triceps' tendons.

"Come on," he ordered again. "Get up."

She winced as he pulled at her arm, the awkward angle of the opposite limb's shoulder joint accentuated by the movement. Frustrated at the impossibility of the request she squealed through the sticky gag and rolled over, breaking his grip and tumbling into some unseen liquid on the cold floor.

"For fucks sake," he angrily snapped. "Okay," he announced, "I'm going to free your legs. But if you fucking try anything…"

Lucy heard the familiar sound of a pistol barrel being slide-cocked. Of course, she had never handled a gun or even seen one in real life but she recognised the noise from the movies. The seriousness of the man's tone suddenly seemed ten times worse and, as she felt the tape straps around her knees silently give way, she concluded his arsenal included a sharp knife as well.

"Right, now get up."

She rolled on to her front, the oily puddle in which she had landed wetting her face and, by its odour, suggesting the industrial nature of her surroundings. Using her forehead as a third limb, she shuffled her knees up under her chest until they could support her weight. She lifted her head and the man immediately grabbed her arm again, forcing her to her feet.

"This way," he ordered, pushing her forward again into the darkness.

Thirty or so paces later, he sharply changed her direction. "Up here."

The toe of her now less-than-white trainer hit a full stop and she instinctively lifted it to find the top of what she assumed, from his command, would be a step. Sure enough the short upright gave way to the flat of the first stair in the concrete well and she was led, more quickly than she found comfortable in her visionless and balance-deprived state, up several flights of stairs.

***

"This is most irregular," the ward Sister protested.

"Listen sweetheart, this is a police emergency. Now where's the access to the roof helicopter pad?" Backhouse quizzed.

The senior nurse harrumphed at the sexist nature of the Detective Sergeant's demand but compliantly led the way through the Accident & Emergency ward to a foyer area and a lift, clearly marked 'STAFF ONLY'. Backhouse and Barnes, left at the hospital by Atticker, stepped inside the large, steel compartment.

"Press UP", the disgruntled woman sarcastically said, remaining in the ground floor foyer.

Looking across, Barnes noticed just two buttons on the elevators control panel, 'UP' and 'DOWN'. This was obviously *not* a public lift. He followed her instruction.

"Cheers darlin'," Backhouse offered, grinning at the hand-on-hip redhead through the already closing doors. She sighed and turned away, back to her duties, as the doors finally came together.

"Right," Backhouse started, as the lift's seldom-used machinery snatched at the metal container and jerked them both skyward. "The Tottenshall FIM says that, since the car was initially spotted, a patrol has seen a male leading a female into a factory in the south east industrial district of the city. He says the building is already surrounded but that their firearms unit is still en route. Their RV* point is in some park nearby. Did you get the co-ordinates from their TAC advisor?"

"Right here," Barnes confirmed.

"Good. Give them to the pilot as soon as we get on board. Caldwell said that his girlfriend was going to be shot in a police mix-up at some factory. I can see this all going to rat shit because I have no idea how to explain this to the Tottenshall TAC, but his prediction is unfolding too close to the quick to ignore. We've got to stop this turning into a siege. If that team confronts whoever they've got in that factory that girl is dead and I, for one, am not having that on my conscience."

The elevator doors trundled open onto a bright, white hallway with a wide ramp leading up to a set of double-doors. Barnes and Backhouse, aware from the noise beyond them that the police helicopter had already arrived, ran up the ramp and pulled open the doors. A sudden rush of air hit them both square in the face as the still-descending helicopter's downwash reached its peak against the steel mesh of the landing pad.

Backhouse turned to Barnes and shouted over the uproar. "Stay sharp, Jem. I don't want any of the Tottenshall SIU riding over us with any of their big-city-jack attitude."

Barnes nodded, his supervisor unaware that the tight-lipped smile on his face, over the fact he had used the young detective's first name, was anything more than a grimace against the down-blast from the nearby machine's rotor disc.

***

Caldwell harshly tore the tape from the lips of the kneeling Lucy.

"Ouch," she shouted out as the gag was released. "You... you bastard," she hesitatingly cursed at her captor.

"Oh, ho," the unseen man chuckled at her uneasy use of the profanity. "Just settle, petal. Let's just remember who's in charge here."

Lucy felt the cold tip of the pistol barrel lifted under her chin to hold her mouth shut.

"Now," he continued, Lucy silenced by the touch of the cocked weapon. "Who, the fuck, is David Lewis?" he asked slowly. "Is he your boyfriend?"

"Well, sort of," she meekly replied.

"Sort of..?" Caldwell recounted, unsatisfied with her response. "Okay then what does he know about me, anything? Did he send the police to find me back in Hopefield, back in the factory?"

"How can I answer that? I don't even know who you are."

Lucy felt a sharp tug forward as Caldwell snatched at her blindfold and then tore it upwards and away from her eyes. Closing her eyes in pain, as the strong tape ripped out great clumps of hair, she screamed again and then opened her eyes to look directly at the gun-toting offender.

"DAVID!" she loudly exclaimed.

***

Nearby, in Grizedale Park, a short twenty minute flight from Hopefield hospital, the Wrenshire police helicopter set down. As the rotors slowed and the engine's whine started to die away Backhouse and Barnes leapt from the rear passenger door.

The dark overall-clad figure of the Tottenshall TAC, unnecessarily hunched over and holding his dark baseball cap as he passed beneath the still turning rotors, reached out a greeting hand to the older man.

"Chief Inspector Wallace, firearms TAC. Are you Backhouse?"

"Yes," Backhouse responded as they both left the area of the slowing disc.

"So, what the hell is this all about? I've got two teams on standby to enter this building where your man is held up but I've been instructed to hold for your arrival. He is armed. A patrol spotted him entering the building with a pistol. Know something I don't?"

The moment Backhouse was dreading had arrived.

"Has he made any demands?"

"I doubt he even knows we're here yet."

242

"Good, it might be best to keep it that way."

"Why so? I've a negotiator en route but we're going to have to search room-by-room just to find out where he is. I doubt a ground level speaker is going to reach all six floors of the place and I'm not going to risk confusion over poor communications. I want to pin him down to a tight area of the building so we can talk to him more directly," the senior officer said, explaining his initial tactics.

"Let's just say I've information that says if you enter the room he's in the girl he has is going to be shot."

"Listen, there's risk attached to any operation of this type but how can you be so sure he'll shoot her immediately?"

Backhouse was reluctant to continue but found himself left with little option.

"I didn't say that *he* was going to shoot her. My information suggests she'll be caught up in a cross-fire."

"What?" the TAC advisor sharply replied, astounded by the insinuating nature of the suggestion. "What the hell are you on about man? Hopefield SIU recruited Mystic Meg have they? This is ridiculous."

The Chief Inspector turned away back toward the large, liveried truck which held his specialist unit's communications centre.

"Wait, please," Backhouse pleaded. "Shit," he mumbled to himself, setting off after the departing commander. "Sir," he pleaded, stalling the ranking officer as he climbed the steps to the open rear door of the command vehicle. "We have a guy in custody, a David Caldwell, the partner of this girl. He's been having visions of crime, of muggings and abductions. He's seen this one and it ends badly. I know it sounds ridiculous but you've got to believe me."

"This is outrageous. I've never heard anything so insane. Believe me, *Sergeant* Backhouse; I'll be talking to your Chief Officer Group about this. You've wasted precious minutes that could prove vital later on. Let me do my job. I suggest you return to Hopefield and do yours."

With that, he continued inside and slammed the door behind him.

"Bollocks," Backhouse exclaimed, firmly put in his place by the senior officer.

"You've got to admit," Barnes calmly announced from behind him, "it does sound pretty crazy."

"Thank you, Professor Freud!" he sarcastically replied.

"What now?" Barnes asked.

"God knows, I'm out...you?"

Barnes shrugged his shoulders. "Sorry. My deductive reasoning left when fantasy took over."

"You're a big help", his supervisor quipped.

Chapter Twenty Eight

Silently, the helmeted, respirator-clad officers moved up the dank stairwell to the sixth floor. Signalling to his eyes and then to an open door the team leader directed his subordinate to take a look around the corner into the entrance of the large, open-plan office. The junior woman nodded and, lowering her machine-rifle to her side, quietly glided her head sideways across the door jamb. Seconds later she returned to face her Sergeant.

Using an intricate chain of linked hand signals, she imparted the information of what she had seen. *Two seated people, one armed, one bound; thirty metres into the room at a two o'clock position to the doorway.* The supervisor indicated that they hold position before quietly sidling away, back down the stairs.

Within a minute he returned with the trained negotiator. Similarly dressed in body armour but without the masked helmet, the man made his way past the armed officers and crouched, against the wall, adjacent to the large room's entrance way.

"DAVID!" a startled woman's voice could be heard from within the room.

"This is the police," he announced in a loud, firm voice. "Stay calm; we just want to talk to you."

Inside the room Caldwell, still recoiling from his captive's surprised recognition of his face, jumped to his feet from the old, wooden chair he had been sitting on in front of the girl. It rattled to the floor behind him, its echo sending confusing reverberations around the empty, open-plan office.

"What the fuck!" he exclaimed. He reached down and snatched the diminutive Lucy up in his left arm. How did the police know where he was so quickly?

Dragging the now screaming Lucy into the darkness across the room, he shouted back at the unwelcome officer.

"Get the fuck back. Get the hell out of here. I'll kill her. Get back."

"It's okay. David is it? It's okay David. You're in charge. We just want to talk," the negotiator calmly replied.

However, with the increasing distance across the room, the conversation became warped by the growing echo and was made even more incomprehensible by the screams of the still-bound Lucy.

"Shut up," Caldwell commanded her, tightening the grip around her throat.

Still writhing against his grip, the frightened female could not help herself and continued to squeal as loudly as her involuntary asphyxiation would allow.

"I'm unarmed," the negotiator called out, holding his empty hands into the open doorway.

However, across the darkened room, dimly lit by the streetlights beaming from below, Caldwell only heard *'armed'* and saw a hand with something in it. The floor to ceiling window frames were throwing misleading shadows across the negotiator's empty palms and a panicked Caldwell, inexperienced in this sort of situation, fired off two shots in the direction of the door.

"SHOTS FIRED, SHOTS FIRED! GO, GO, GO!" the firearm's team leader shouted from beneath his face mask. The officers, poised directly behind the crouching negotiator, poured past him into the room and spread out in to a well rehearsed fan across the open floor space.

With the advantage of nigh-vision goggles, the officers were happy to operate in the dark. Caldwell on the other hand, confused by the flickering, red beams that now danced about the space before him began firing aimlessly across the room. The shots rang out, interrupted only by the thunderous clap of a flash-bang grenade. Ready for the tactical use of the device after the call of *'grenade'* had been shouted, the officers had all averted their eyes to save their vision but the untrained Caldwell was blinded by the intense light.

Plunged back into darkness and choking on the smoke from the grenade, which had gone off just feet in front of him, Caldwell released his hold on the equally disabled Lucy. Feeling her lurch forward, he blindly clutched at the neck of her tracksuit, swinging her back across in front of him. Unbalanced by the sudden change of direction, she began to fall at his feet.

Muzzle flashes from his weapon illuminated his exposure as a target and Caldwell felt a heavy blow to the chest followed by sharp pain in his head. Indiscriminately, he kept firing the semi-automatic pistol, now pointing downward at the collapsing Lucy. Releasing his failing grip on her collar, he staggered backward under the repeated blows from the machine-rifles. The glass shattered under the weight of his body and he crashed through the full-length window toward the canal below.

"MAN DOWN, MAN DOWN. CEASE FIRE," the firearms Sergeant ordered.

The room fell instantly silent, the lifeless girl motionless in front of the smashed window. The negotiator ran into the smoky room and, crossing to the gusty opening, looked down to the murky water below. There was no sign of David Caldwell.

***

"Ma'am," the smartly dressed officer announced herself while tapping on the doorframe of the Detective Inspector's glass walled office.

"Hi Josie, come in, come in, close the door," the supervisor beckoned.

The young, uniformed officer stepped inside. The door slowly reached its closure point, activating the privacy-glass to instantly change from transparent to opaque.

"What can I do for you?" Murray asked the younger woman.

"Do you recall a case with a guy called David Caldwell? It's before my time but I'm told it was about five years ago."

247

Murray felt her hand instinctively reach down to rub her right knee under the table. "Yeah, I certainly do, although its one I'd rather forget."

"Oh, why's that?" the inquisitive officer asked, freshly recruited and still questioning everything.

"Let's just say that everything that *could* have gone wrong *did*. Three people died; the third, according to the final report, after the killer assaulted a female detective and escaped custody right here. Somehow he got to a girl before the firearms team did. What made it worse was that we never actually got to prosecute the guy. The report finalised that he was killed by Tottenshall FSU* but that his body fell into a canal and was never found."

"Well, actually, that's what I'm here about."

"How so?" the intrigued Inspector enquired.

The young girl checked the note written on the piece of paper she was carrying to make sure she got the message correct. "DCI Barnes has asked me to tell you that he's just been notified by Interpol that a 'David Caldwell' has been arrested passing through one of the new customs fingerprint scanners at Madrid Airport. Apparently, he was boarding a plane for Manchester. DCI Barnes says it looks like he's been living out there for the past four years, totally off the radar."

Murray slumped back in her chair. "Holy shit!" she quietly exclaimed. "If only old Backhouse was still around to hear this."

"Who's Backhouse?" the constable asked.

"In short, Josie, he was a bloody legend," she contemplatively added. "He saved my life on that case but it ended his career. DCI Barnes and I were both DC's under Backhouse, but after the girl died in Tottenshall he was a changed man. Jem always upheld that Backhouse was somehow justified in a belief that the girl was killed by someone other than Caldwell, but the forensic evidence was undeniable. Backhouse was ridiculed by the inquest and medically retired from the police. I always thought something was very odd about his departure but we simply never heard from him again"

"I suppose something like that takes it out of a man," the young woman naively added.

Murray looked her in the eye. The comment was harmless enough. The girl was just making pleasant conversation.

"I suppose," Murray eventually concurred. "But I always had the impression that he would have done anything to have changed the way things had happened. Has Caldwell been shipped back here then?"

"When he phoned from HQ, Mr Barnes mentioned an incoming flight tomorrow but I'm not sure of the details. He wants you to pick him up from headquarters in the morning. He said you're to go with him to meet the plane and arrest the guy yourself."

"So, you haven't just come from his office upstairs then? If he phoned from HQ, why didn't he just phone me directly?"

"He said he wanted *someone* to see the look on your face and report back to him."

Murray laughed. Despite the promotion rocket up her old colleague's backside he'd always remained a joker since his brief tutorage under Steve Backhouse.

***

"Mr Caldwell, stand up please. David Anthony Caldwell, you have been found guilty by a jury of your peers. The evidence presented to this court by the Police Prosecution Authority has been overwhelming and so, under the Survivors Charter of twenty thirteen and the subsequently amended Police Act of twenty fifteen, I have only one course of action open to me. It is regrettable that your flight from custody back in twenty eleven has meant that your sentence falls under the remit of this re-instated legislation but under the circumstances I feel that the punishment does, indeed, fit the crime."

The Judge reached under the desk and lifted out the small, black square of his silk sentence-cap. He placed the ceremonial cloth upon his head.

"Have you anything to say before I pass sentence?" the Judge traditionally asked.

249

"Fuck you," Caldwell defiantly responded.

Unperturbed by the indignant reply, the Judge continued. "Very well. David Anthony Caldwell, without cause or authority for appeal, I hereby sentence you to death for the murders of James Crabtree, Jonathan Crabtree and Lucy Short. You are to be taken from this court to a place of execution where, at a time to be no greater than seventy two hours from now, you will be executed by means of lethal injection. Officers, take him down."

Lucy's family applauded from the public gallery as the prisoner was led away to his doom. As he passed through the exit from the dock, he jerked back into the courtroom. The two burly, court-security guards held him fast and continued to guide him out of the door but the aggressive offender, who had remained silent throughout the trial, shouted back at the assembled officials.

"Who, the fuck, is David Lewis? Who is he? Tell me you bastards?" The calls trailed away as he was dragged out of earshot.

Quietly, at the back of the court's upper gallery, an elderly man in a black suit and tie sat watching the finalisation of the proceedings. He knew who David Lewis was, or at least who is was going to be. He stood up from his chair and quietly left the room, unfolding his heavy coat from over his arm as he went.

Out in the court building's Grand Hall, DI Murray and DCI Barnes stood talking with the prosecuting Chief Superintendent. Her successful conclusion to the sorry affair, which had dogged them both over the previous five years, was a commendable example of the power of the police's new prosecution division. Since its collapse in 2012, during the period leading up to the inception of the Survivors Charter, the prosecution of all criminal cases had been handed back to the police from the Crown Prosecution Service. The CPS had been considerably downsized and left to deal with matters of traffic violations and other minor offences.

The public outcry over repeated mismanagement of violent offences in 2010 and 2011 had led to a public referendum on the future of the Justice System. The people had spoken, in their millions, and with the introduction of the Charter in 2013, sentencing was being decided by the surviving families of violent-crime victims. Inevitably, this had led to the reintroduction of the death penalty just two years later.

The black-suited man watched surreptitiously from across the concourse. Their smiles warmed his cold and bitter heart but he had bigger fish to fry. He donned his Trilby hat and walked from the court.

"Hey Jem," Murray interrupted the legal conversation, prodding Barnes in the arm and gesturing toward the exit.

"What?" the DCI replied, glancing round to follow the direction of her gaze.

"Did you see that guy? The one there in black, with the hat."

"No why?" Barnes quizzed, staring after the man, now just a silhouette in the backlit doorway.

"For a minute I could have sworn... Oh, never mind." She dismissed the sighting as mere reminiscence brought on by the day's events.

***

David Caldwell was left alone in the clinically sterile circular room. Staring up at the bright, white ceiling, he tested the straps of the semi-reclined chair in which he was now immobilised.

Unable to fully move his head, he rolled his eyes over to one side and out of the corner of his right eye checked on liquids in a bank of three glass containers. Set in chrome clamps, the tubes were atop an equally stark bank of lights on a brushed steel panel and he calmly watched them for the inevitable procedure to begin. Pipes emanating from the top of each tube rose and arched over to a junction box down toward the floor and a single pipe led from that box to another chrome clamp, fixed horizontally out from the right arm of his chair.

He glanced down at the pipe, continuing through the chair

clamp and leading to a needle piercing the skin of his bare forearm. It swelled the underlying blood vessel but it wasn't a sight that troubled him. He'd seen that particular malformation a thousand times before. Only this time, a more lethal cocktail was about to be injected into him. A sensation of release washed over him and, slowly rolling his eyes over to his left, he saw the long, glass, observation panel. Beyond it, a row of stony-faced witnesses sat staring at him. Within seconds, a curtain, electronically drawn, slowly swept between them. Caldwell heard a click and returned his attention to the terminal device as it commenced its task. In turn, the lights on the panel, from left to right, lit up and electronically-driven pistons began to slowly rise in the tubes, forcing their contents along the pipes to the junction box below.

Caldwell watched in accepting silence as the mixed liquids progressed along the pipe, through the chair clamp and into his arm. He released a long, last breath and, as a final indignity, lost control of his musculature and felt the warm sensation of urine filling his pants. As his life ebbed away with the immutable fading of his vision a sharp, bitter taste and a sudden bolt of pain ended the execution.

Chapter Twenty Nine

"Okay Einstein, talk to me. Eighty two percent negative. Look, negative!"

"Well, the technology is new. There was always a chance this might happen."

"What? A chance that *what* might happen?" the Director insisted.

"Okay, well. A negative CP Reading suggests that the subject's actions have, somehow, disrupted the flow of time away from the planned juncture. As you know the CPR is calibrated against the required outcome, as monitored by the Differentiator. Once the subject's transfer is complete the CP Diff effectively takes the present-day consequences, of the period between their arrival and the juncture, *offline* in order to prevent any paradoxes. Then it puts us on a synchronous clock with the subject for the planned period before the juncture. It's that synchronicity which allows the CP Reading to work up toward the one hundred percent target as the subject's mission closes in on the proposed realignment."

"Oh come on, English, please!"

"Well," the technician continued, trying to dumb down the technology for his administrative controller, "the juncture in this case was the death of Lucy Short, the required outcome was her survival and the synchronicity period was the two days before her death that Lewis was sent back to, in order to complete his intervention."

"So, why so negative? Has Lewis failed his mission?"

"Not necessarily. Although the fact it's over three quarters toward a complete, implosive paradox does raise certain concerns."

"Certain concerns..? And why haven't I heard the word *implosive* before? I don't like the sound of that."

"Well, it just means that if the subject creates an *implosive* paradox instead of an *explosive* one then, because we can't monitor the consequences, we can't predict the outcome. Look, we can monitor the consequential paradox reading up to ninety nine percent, right?"

"Yeah."

"Well, in the positive direction, once it reaches a hundred percent saturation the synchronous clock expires and the time flow realigns to the planned outcome. It's the explosive effect of a successful change in the past, in this case the girl's survival, that sends out the temporal eddies we work with to calibrate the CPR and plan the mission in the first place. Picture it like we're using a lifeboat to cruise alongside our own ship while someone patches a hole which we've found in it. Once it's fixed we simply get back on board."

"And a negative reading?"

"Well that's where things get a bit out of hand. The technology has never allowed for the planning of a negative outcome. If the mission simply fails then the CPR would never reach one hundred percent; our ship would never be patched, as it were. A negative reading, however, would suggest the inception of an additional anti-anomaly."

"Whoa there, Mr Sagan, I said English!"

"Well, putting it simply, an anti-anomaly is something so negative it causes a hole in time, a void we cannot see into. A death is the likeliest culprit as it's the cessation of an entity's existence that wipes its consequential eddies from the flow of time. We've basically got nothing to tag the CP Diff to."

"Let me get this right. Lewis's mission was to save Short. But instead he's going around the past knocking off strangers?"

"Not necessarily. It could be that his actions, or inactions, have caused the deaths to occur. For instance he could have been in a car crash or not been around to save someone when one happened."

"But we researched all this before the transfer. No unnecessary interactions, minimal disruption to the flow of time. He was supposed to arrive in the area of the factory just two days before the siege went south."

"Yeah, great, but you're forgetting, the transfer crashed. The loss of signal we experienced could have meant any number of problems for Lewis when he arrived, especially if he landed outside the synchronicity period. Loss of memory, loss of mission protocol or even implant failure; for all we know his nanites could have even defaulted to their original medical-based settings and started confusing their intended memory augmentation with physical manifestations."

"Okay, so what now? What if the CPR reaches a hundred percent in the negative?"

"Well, the time flow will realign, just as in the positive. The problem is we can't predict the outcome. Continuing the naval metaphor, a negative reading would be like having a lifeboat with no windows. When the clock expired and we opened the hatch the ship could be a totally different one or, worse still, not be there at all."

"So, what'll happen?"

"Maybe nothing, but just as easily we could all disappear. The Temporal Police Authority may never have come into existence. Hell, time travel itself might never have been discovered. We just can't tell. That's why we call it an implosion, everything's hidden."

"Okay. As we stand then, Caldwell killed Short. The courts kill *Caldwell*. We send him back as *Lewis* to correct his crime. Now, because of some failure the correction has not only *not* happened but the flow of time is actually about to change uncontrollably. How come I don't remember it changing?"

The technician shook his head, reluctant to start all over again.

"Director, your thinking is too linear. The CP Diff uses sixth dimension probability calculations and is based on *action* and *consequence*. Every breath Lewis takes back in twenty eleven alters things one way or the other. If the Diff didn't hold things together at this end, if it didn't act as our lifeboat, until a hundred percent saturation was reached, then things here would be jumping around like jelly beans for every second he was interacting back there. If the transfer error was worse than we hope it was, he could have been there years, had a hundred kids, grown old and be about to die; now *that* would trigger a *massive* implosion! He could be talking to your past self right now and you wouldn't remember it yet because the Diff is holding us out of that consequence until the saturation limiter flips and resynchronises us with whichever time flow Lewis has created. After that you'd remember everything, except for, that is, me explaining this all to you now."

"This is giving me a headache. Is there anything we can do to prevent this implosive CPR?"

"No."

"Why's it all so bloody confusing?"

"The clues in the name," the technician sarcastically said, wondering how the old man ever got the job as Director of the TPA. "It's a *paradox*," he added.

"Is there anything we can do to prepare for the worst?"

"You could always bend over backwards and kiss your ass goodbye!" the technician finally said.

The Director turned to the seated controller whom he had ridiculed earlier for a poor explanation of the facts.

"Bad, eh?"

The young man shrugged his shoulders and nodded acceptingly.

"Shit," the Director said.

***

"Welcome back, Mr Caldwell," the effeminate recovery technician greeted the still-dazed David as his eyes opened for the first time since his execution. "Welcome to the TPA. Enjoy the funeral? I don't suppose you remember it, do you? You were dead," he humorously added.

"What the fu... arrgh!"

"That'll be the aggression inhibitor you've been given. You'll want to curb your angry side or that little baby will be shocking you all night."

"Fu......arrgh! Basta.... arrrrrgh!"

"Temper, temper now, Mr Caldwell. You don't want to go damaging yourself now, do you?"

"What the he... arrrgh... is going on?" the slightly calmer Caldwell asked.

"The boss will be down in a minute. He'll explain everything. I'm sure you've got a thousand questions to ask. A word of advice though: don't swear as much as he does or you'll be smouldering before midnight."

The technician removed the blood pressure monitor from David's arm and left the room. David, still horizontal on his bed, lifted his head and looked around. The pure white room, brilliantly lit from unseen lights, was stark and clinical in appearance. The gloss walls looked like they were plastic coated and the furniture, a table, two chairs and the bed, were bland and featureless. There were no windows and, seemingly, only one door which itself, after the technician had left, appeared completely seamless on the opposite wall.

David quickly sat up and swung his legs down to the floor. A sudden dizziness came over him and he groaned holding his head in his hands.

"That'll be your death wearing off," a voice said from behind him.

"Huh?" He span round, off the bed's edge, and fell to his knees under his still unresponsive legs.

Clinging to the bed in a prayer like crouch, he looked across to see a grey haired man, probably late fifties, in a black suit and tie. The contrast between him and the room was sharp to the point of painful on David's recovering eyes.

"Hello David. Welcome to the Temporal Police Authority. I'm Director Backhouse. Do you remember me?"

"No," the confused David meekly replied, mindful of the technician's warning about the inhibitor hidden somewhere within his body.

"Good, then you're the right David and we can get started." Backhouse saw the confused look on his subject's face. "Don't worry about a full explanation just yet. Suffice to say, you are dead to everyone but us here at the TPA. Follow our instructions, help us correct your mistakes, and it will remain

257

that way. Your alternative option is clear." The Director leaned down onto the bed and his voice turned as abrasive as a low grade glass-paper. "Cross me and you'll be fucking dead to everyone... period. Understood?"

'*So this was hell?*' thought David.

***

"Morning David, big day at last," Backhouse greeted the now healthy and retrained David *Edward Lewis* as he met him in the TPA breakfast hall.

"Yeah, but there's just one more thing I wanted to ask you."

"Go ahead."

"After the juncture, after Lucy survives, what happens to me? Do I simply cease to exist?"

"Sounds like a question for the techies, but as I understand it you'll live out your new life from that point onward. Look David, you've been with us what, six months now. You're a changed man. You're healthy. You're socialised. You're an intelligent lad. You've got your whole life, well, *behind you* at the minute," Backhouse joked. "Seriously though, the techie's tell me that they can't say exactly what will happen."

Backhouse called over to a passing technician. "Tim, tell David here about that paradox stuff will you. I can never remember all the gobble-de-gook. He wants to know what happens to him after the temporal juncture."

The technician was more than happy to share his own theoretical opinions on the newly discovered technology. He placed his breakfast tray down next to the already seated duo and began to explain. Backhouse smiled but just switched off. He'd heard it all before but it still made no *real* sense to him.

"Once you leave this point in time there's no coming back to it. Your actions, when interacting with the past, set you on a course to a different time flow to this one. Of course, you'll *age* back to this hour and date but a *point* in time has additional dimensions to it. However far back we send you, the *point* you left to get there will always stay that same distance, in time, ahead of you. Consider it a gap between then and now. The future you leave moves on, erasing what's behind it and you chase to catch up, creating a new present in each passing moment, to fill the void. You can't even snuff yourself out by interacting with the old you. Even if you killed him, his demise can't leap across the gap you created in reaching him in order to affect you. His death wouldn't remove you from existence because existence itself is time-relevant."

David pondered the explanation for a moment but then it clicked.

"So, why bother at all. Surely Lucy will stay dead in the time flow I've left in order to save her and you lot will be none the wiser."

"Well, yes, but it's really down to a matter of perspective."

Backhouse was astonished, someone actually understood this crap.

"You see, that's the beauty of the CP Diff, the Consequential Paradox Differentiator," the technician gleefully continued. "It's calibrated to monitor your progress toward the predicted temporal juncture, the intended outcome of the mission. Once you complete it the Diff accommodates the transition by realigning us with the new time flow, the one you've effectively created by your actions."

"And who are *us* then; the chosen few; the family of the victim?"

"Oh no, not at all, *us* is everyone, our entire existence. The time flow you originally left will technically cease to be; its trailing edge erased as the old version of it continues on into its own future. The only person who will fully recall the *old* flow of time, the gap after the juncture, will be you as the traveller. The rest of us will simply become part of the predicted present, having lived in the new time flow from the point of the juncture. "

Reassuringly, for Backhouse, David looked confused again. However, rather than argue, as the techno-phobic Director would have done, he simply answered,

"Wow, cool."

"Yes, cool," the geeky man joyfully agreed. "In theory, at

least," he worryingly added as he got up from the table, collected up his tray and wandered back to work.

Lewis looked at Backhouse who could only manage a shrug and a smile to add to the explanation.

"Don't forget David, I was a stubborn and grumpy old bastard back then."

David raised a questioning eyebrow. After six months of physical and mental training to prepare him for the punishing ordeal of time transfer he had grown very fond of the TPA Director, but he was *still* a grumpy, stubborn old bastard. Backhouse acknowledged the unspoken comment.

"Yeah, okay, funny. But remember, your National Insurance number is the key. The number is a straight reverse of my daughter's date of birth and Ted, my first dog's name. Okay? If you forget anything else remember that; daughter's date of birth, dog's name. No-one else I knew back then knows those details. If you get into trouble contact me and tell me that code. I'll believe you flew from the moon in a paper boat."

"Got it, Steve, thanks."

"Come on, it's time."

Backhouse rose from the table and started toward the transfer laboratory. Lewis grabbed his forearm to halt his departure.

"And Steve, thanks. Thanks for another chance."

"Good luck," Backhouse said, his final words to the soon to be time traveller.

Chapter Thirty

"I should have brought Atticker. You're ruddy useless."

Barnes didn't really know what to say but decided to turn the Detective Sergeant's suggestion on its head.

"Should I call him for you?" he sarcastically replied.

"You know what? You might just have an idea there. Caldwell has got us into this. Let's use him to get out of it. Call Tracy and get Caldwell up to the office."

"The custody Sergeant isn't going to like that."

"Like I care? Get Caldwell on the phone. Let's have a proper prediction out of the little bastard, something I can work with."

A doubtful Barnes made the call and the pair made their way back to the Wrenshire helicopter.

***

"About bloody time," Lewis said, standing up from his bench as the cell door opened."

"Come with me please, Mr Caldwell," Tracy asked the rising prisoner.

"Okay, Caldwell will do but I prefer David Lewis. Where's DS Backhouse?"

"He's in Tottenshall, some sort of hostage situation."

"Oh Jesus, you've got to be joking. I need to get there. I have to *be* there."

"Okay, calm down. We're going to the office upstairs. He wants to speak to you."

"Okay, come on, let's go." He hurried past the officer toward the central custody area. "Come on," he beckoned back to her. "Which way is it? Come on woman, I'm out of time, literally."

261

"David, I'm at an industrial area in Tottenshall. Lucy is in a multi-story factory held by an unknown male. The firearms team here are not listening to me. I need something more, something tangible. Tell me you know something else."

"Backhouse, Steve, you're not going to want to believe this but you have to. I know everything now. I need you to believe me so tell me if this is true. Your first dog was a Labrador called Ted and your daughter's date of birth is the sixteenth of October nineteen eighty nine."

Backhouse was shocked into momentary silence.

"Okay, so how the hell did you know about my daughter. No-one in Hopefield even knows I have a daughter."

"Here's the bit you'll not want to believe. I know because you told me. You told me because you sent me here to save Lucy."

"You're talking in riddles again. I never met you before Murray interviewed you."

"Okay, here it is. The visions, the predictions; they weren't some magical foresight. They were memories. Memories I still recall six years from now. The man who has Lucy in the factory? It's me. You gave me the name Lewis to live out my life here after the rescue. I've been sent here from the future to change my own history, and yours, by saving Lucy and we have very little time left."

Backhouse was again silent. The premise was ridiculous; time travel? No way. Then again, was it crazier than *visions*? He was standing in a field, out of his own Force area, on the strength of David's visions. The outrageous logic of it hit more facts than it missed: the matching DNA, the identical fingerprints.

"Okay David," he finally agreed. "What happens next?" he tested the theory.

"It hasn't worked like that. Something went wrong. I should have been in the factory to stop Caldwell, stop myself, from killing Lucy. I was supposed to arrive near the factory only two days before the police siege, not two years ago. I should never have even met Lucy until then."

"David, let's say for a moment I believe you. I'm no genius, but that makes no sense at all. The very reason he abducted Lucy was to get to you. If you're Caldwell's future self then you coming back here was the cause of this whole shit-storm. Murray was abducted because she followed your leads to where he... where *you* were waiting for her. You're chasing your own tail."

David recoiled at the revelation. It was so obvious. The failure in the time transfer had created a paradox all of its own, a self-perpetuating loop. He racked his brain, desperately trying to recall as many of the conversations he had had with the TPA techies. That 'gap' that Tim had gone on about just before he'd left the future? He wasn't even reaching the start of it. The paradox he'd created was bridging it, but was repeatedly striking off the far end and looping back from future's trailing edge to his premature arrival here two years ago. He'd been trying to fill the wrong 'void'. There had to be way out; he had to destroy that bridge. Otherwise he'd be back again living the same two years over and over.

He wondered how many loops had already occurred. How many had failed before him so that Caldwell could go on to be executed, reanimated and trained to carry out his mission, and countless failed missions before it? There could have been a multitude of parallel flows created out of each futile attempt to change this one history, unable to divert the course of events to successfully reach the intended outcome of his assignment. Had he ever even come close, or was even this eleventh-hour realisation another cruel and futile reoccurrence?

Perhaps Nature herself had created this paradox, a trap to snare the unwelcome technology in a bubble of repetition while she and the rest of existence moved on along another, more naturally, linear path?

The cycle had to be broken. He further recalled Tim's explanation that, in theory at least, he could safely, albeit fatally, interact with himself. He had to risk snuffing himself from existence and kill his past self in order to transfer the entire future to a more successful time flow.

"You have to get me into that factory. If you don't this whole cycle will just keep repeating itself."

"Put Wazzer on the phone."

"Go ahead, Sarge."

"Wazzer, get Lewis to the Westgate Park pronto. We'll meet you there in the chopper."

"Sarge?"

"Just do it... and fast!"

***

"Shut up," Caldwell commanded her, tightening the grip around her throat.

Still writhing against his grip, the frightened female could not help herself and continued to squeal as loudly as her involuntary asphyxiation would allow.

"I'm unarmed," the negotiator called out, holding his empty hands into the open doorway.

However, across the darkened room, dimly lit by the streetlights beaming from below, Caldwell only heard *'armed'* and saw a hand with something in it. The floor to ceiling window frames were throwing misleading shadows across the negotiator's empty palms and a panicked Caldwell, inexperienced in this sort of situation, fired off two shots in the direction of the door.

"SHOTS FIRED, SHOTS FIRED! GO, GO, GO!" the firearm's team leader shouted from beneath his face mask. The officers, poised directly behind the crouching negotiator, poured past him into the room and spread out in to a well-rehearsed fan across the open floor space.

With the advantage of night-vision goggles, the officers were happy to operate in the dark. Caldwell on the other hand, confused by the flickering laser-light that now danced about the space between them, raised his weapon to once again begin firing aimlessly across the room.

The firearms team leader released the pin from the stun-grenade in his hand.

"GRENADE!" he shouted, warning his colleagues of the impending flash as he hurled the device toward the far side of the room. From beneath his respirator and night-vision goggles,

264

he was the last to see its arcing flight, sparks from its burning fuse spitting from the case as it approached the armed assailant. About to close his eyes, he noticed a previously unseen, third figure step from the shadows behind his intended target. Entranced by the unexplained appearance, he continued to watch the unknown shape as it took hold of the gunman in a bear hug stance.

"What the ....?"

The flash-bang exploded and the Sergeant's view, accentuated by the low-light goggles flared into an agonising brilliance.

The explosion echoed around the large, empty factory floor. The ear-splitting noise died away and the officers, re-opening their eyes in perfect time with diminishing flash of the grenade, took aim at the space in front of the window. However, except for the horizontal Lucy, leaning prone on one elbow in front of the now smashed window frame, there was no sign of the gunman.

The negotiator ran into the smoky room and, crossing to the gusty opening, looked down to the murky water. There, far below, the body of David Caldwell lay, face down, floating motionless in the canal.

"Where's the other one?" the tactical team's Sergeant asked the negotiator as he joined him at the opening, rubbing his still stinging eyes.

"What other one?" the negotiator asked.

***

Director Backhouse intently watched the rising CPR gauge.

"Ninety seven, ninety eight, ninety nine, thank fu..."

Deep within the bowels of the Temporal Police Authority the CP Diff roared up into a brilliant, glowing ball of white then, within seconds, fell silent. Down in one corner of the control panel an insignificant looking counter clicked over to "7", the only reference, in the new flow of time, to the fact anything had occurred at all.

***

The young brunette tapped lightly on the open door to the office of the Temporal Justice Directorate's senior officer.

"Fancy a brew, Director Lewis?"

"Oh cheers, Lucy. Milk, two sugars please."

Only David knew of the somewhat less than subtle changes around him. As the sole traveller, and ultimate instigator of the paradox correction and realignment, only he was privy to the existence of the gap in time obliterated by his actions back in 2011.

With the rescue of Lucy from the grips of his former self, David had decided, long ago, to not become emotionally involved in her new life. He had a deep-seated feeling that that course of action was inherently perilous. As far as she was aware, he had never existed prior to the rather unexpected invitation she had received to join the highly secretive directorate from her position as a post-graduate technician at Tottenshall University.

In this time flow she had never met him back in 2009 because he had never been mistakenly sent there with the intended task of saving her in the previously tragic 2011. She had never been at the factory to be accidentally shot. Detective Sergeant Backhouse hadn't left the force over his mentally crippling reaction to the girl's death and had never gone on to become the Director of an organisation established to counter such travesties of fate.

No, in this existence it had fallen to time's orphan, David Lewis, abandoned after escaping the paradoxical clutches of his own repetitious past, to inspire a group of young scientists with the secrets of time travel. Armed only with what he had gleaned from his previous encounter with the belligerent old man and his long-suffering technicians, he had brought about the current existence of this parallel organisation.

The fact Lucy was an employee here at all was, he felt, a somewhat selfish need to keep a *tag* on his own disjointed history. Besides which, he retained a degree of responsibility for her safety and had decided that bringing her into the directorate would be the best way to keep an eye on her.

The mechanics of the consequential paradox differentiator

and the even more incomprehensible reasoning and theories surrounding time travel were still often beyond him. He had a basic understanding, but the more cyclic arguments of thread-theory, split-dimensions and causality paradoxes gave him a headache. As such, despite the techie's efforts to explain it to him, he shied away from the decision to use the device in all but the most extreme of cases. He knew enough to realise that the best intended of missions had far reaching effects on the present and that the farther each mission was sent back the greater those effects, however well planned, could be.

As for Backhouse, the need for a robbery squad had been deemed unnecessary after the curious cessation of offences almost immediately after its creation back in 2011. No further evidence, forensic or otherwise, had been uncovered to point to an offender and it appeared, to all intents and purposes, that the mugger had simply disappeared from the face of the earth.

Not that the remainder of his career was uneventful. *History*, Lewis had concluded, was as malleable as modelling clay and, unbeknown to them both, time had a few tricks yet to play on the unlikely duo.

Glossary of Terms

ANPR	Automatic Number Plate Recognition
CSI	Crime Scene Investigator
DSU	Dedicated Surveillance Unit
FIM	Force Incident Manager
FSU	Firearms Support Unit
E-fit	Computer based identification compilation system
Livescan	Electronic device for fingerprint recognition
NPU	Neighbour Policing Unit
O.P's	Observations Points
Pinged	Method of remotely triangulating the location of mobile phones
R -v- Johnson	Stated case-law relating to the use of covert O.P.'s
RV Point	Rendezvous point
SAR	RAF Search and Rescue Helicopter
SIO	Senior Investigating Officer
SIU	Special Investigations Unit
TA	Traffic Accident or Time of Arrival
TAC Advisor	Tactical Advisor
TK	Telephone Kiosk – Public payphone
TPT	Targeted Patrol Team
TSU	Technical Support Unit
Viper	Video Identification Parade